Preeti Shenoy, among the highest selling authors in India, is also on the Forbes longlist of the most influential celebrities in India.

She is the recipient of several awards, including 'Indian of the Year' award for 2017 by Brands Academy and Academia award for Business Excellence by the New Delhi Institute of Management. She has been interviewed on BBC World, which was telecast 14 times, reaching over 200 counties worldwide. She is a motivational speaker, having given talks in many premier educational institutions and corporate organisations like KPMG, ISRO, Infosys and Accenture, etc. An avid fitness enthusiast, she is also an artist specialising in portraiture and illustrated journals. Her other interests are travel, photography and yoga.

Her short stories and poetry have been published in magazines such as *Conde Nast* and *Verve*. She has represented India in International literature festivals at Birmingham, Sharjah, Abu Dhabi, among others. She has been featured by all major media, including BBC World, *Cosmopolitan*, *The Hindu*, *Verve*, *The Times of India*.

Her blog is among the top 50 blogs in India. She wrote a weekly column in *The Financial Chronicle* for many years. Her work has been translated into many Indian languages, and also into Turkish.

Connect with Preeti. She always responds.

: *www.preetishenoy.com*   : *ps@preetishenoy.com*

: *@Preetishenoy*   : *Blog.preetishenoy.com*

: *http://preeti.io/fb*   : *Preeti.Shenoy*

: *Preeti.Shenoy and Preetishenoyart*

Praise for the author and her works

One of India's most popular authors.

— Cosmopolitan

India's top-selling female author.

– BBC World

Feel-good air, crisp and easy-to-grasp writing.

– New Woman

Quick-paced read.

– DNA

Positive and full of life.

– Financial World

Woven intelligently with simple language... leaves a profound impact.

– Exotica

Amazing how deftly she weaves her stories.

– Eve's Times

Keeps the reader hooked from the first page to last.

–Afternoon Voice

Magnetic, engrossing and unputdownable.

– One India One People

Intense fiction that plays with your emotions.

– The New India Express

Preeti Shenoy makes it work.

– The Hindu

Has something for everyone.

– The Hindu

Heart-warming love story.

– Bangalore Mirror

Show-stealer.

– Deccan Chronicle

Keenly observant mind.

– DNA

Wonderful, passionate, common story.

– The Sentinel

When Love Came Calling

PREETI SHENOY

Srishti
PUBLISHERS & DISTRIBUTORS

SRISHTI PUBLISHERS & DISTRIBUTORS
A unit of AJR Publishing LLP
212A, Peacock Lane
Shahpur Jat, New Delhi – 110 049
editorial@srishtipublishers.com

First published by
Srishti Publishers & Distributors in 2020

Printed and bound in India

For Purvi, and all her social experiments!

From a notebook on a girl's desk

"A ship in harbour is safe, but that is not what ships are built for."

– John A. Shedd

Travel is great education. It pulls you out of your comfort zone, teaches you things, expands your mind, makes you grow as a person. It also gets you a ton of followers on Instagram.

But it is not so easy to travel. You need money, and you need time. Chances are, if you have one of them, you would most certainly lack the other. And without either, travel becomes impossible.

The other thing is, you have to be okay with discomfort. Travel makes you take a break from your normal routine. You have to choose your destination, carefully select your accommodation and plan how you will get around in a new country. You have to be aware of currencies, customs, culture, a new language and a million other things. All this trouble, for an experience which hopefully shall not be an epic fail. Travel is not a simple thing at all.

If you have motion sickness, fear of planes, or sea sickness, then it is an added torture . While the idea of travel is noble, liberating and even exhilarating when you scroll through magnificent locales posted by perfectly-poised Instagram influencers, the actual work involved is humongous.

Why should you subject yourself to great hardship to discover the world? It is easier to travel through Snapchat stories and Instagram videos.

You get the same experience.

Well, almost.

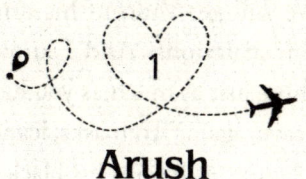

Arush

8.30 am: Wake up
Turn the basking light on
Change water in the bowl
Turn humidifier on
9.30 am: Feed banana/kiwi/watermelon/cantaloupe
11.30 am: Feed freshly-chopped green squash and add rocket or spinach.
Add calcium supplements
3.00 pm: Take Vincent to the garden to sunbathe
8.00 pm: Remove food plate
10.30 pm: Switch off the basking light

Iguanas are not hard to take care of, but you have to be meticulous. So, I write down the instructions and make three photocopies – one each for my three housemates. I stick the one I wrote on the wall in the yard, right above Vincent's home. It is a thirty-gallon aquarium tank fitted with a reptile humidifier, basking heat lamp, plants, branches for Vincent to climb on, a fresh water bowl and everything to make his home an ultra-luxury pad. The duties have been divided between the three of them. Given that all three are fond of Vincent, I think he should be fine. But a part of me is still worried.

'Don't worry. We will get Vincent his sunshine,' Josh assures me as he reads the instructions. 'And I know all of this. I have been taking care of him, just as much as you have,' he says.

'When do you leave, again?' Tom asks, leaning back on the bed, peering up from his laptop, as he sips his black coffee from Kofra.

'Tonight, I leave for my parents' home in Derby, and in three days, I fly to India.'

'Excited?' asks Jenna as she carefully pins my instructions on the peg board above her desk.

'Terrified,' I reply honestly.

'Isn't India home?' Tom frowns.

'That's racist. Derby is home. I haven't even been to India. Not even once. I was born here, raised here. I am as British as any of you. How can it be home?' I say, my voice deadpan.

'Of course. I'm sorry. That isn't what I meant. What I meant is, it isn't like you are visiting China or Ho Chi Minh City,' he hastens to add, digging himself into an even deeper hole.

'I am just messing with you,' I chuckle now, seeing Tom's intense discomfort. He has turned red at being called a racist.

'I fell for it. I thought I had offended you,' he says and throws a cushion at me. I duck. It hits Jenna on her head.

'Clowns!' she says, shaking her head.

I wasn't offended at all. There's nothing Indian about me except my looks and my name. When you grow up in a country where you look different from everyone else, you adapt. My father wanted to name me Andy or Aaron. My mother said that though she agreed on raising me as a Brit and not as an Indian, she wasn't willing to westernise my name. She insisted on Arush, which means 'first ray of the sun'.

My name is a compromise.

Like everything else in my life.

My father tries to be British, but deep down he is Indian enough to think that the only careers that count are Medicine or Engineering. Perhaps even Law or Finance. Everything else is lesser.

When I won a full scholarship for my art college here at Norwich, the full ride, which meant I don't have to pay any tuition fee, my father wasn't impressed. He thought he could make me back out by refusing to pay for my living expenses. But you cannot give up your dream of a lifetime for minor obstacles, can you? It wasn't hard to find part-time work at the charity shop, every other day for three hours. The best thing about it? I only have to sit behind a counter and it allows me to draw.

'Look at this! You are going here and you say you are terrified?' Tom raises his eyebrows as he turns his laptop towards me.

'Welcome to God's Own Country' reads the caption. The photos of boats in calm placid backwaters surrounded by miles of coconut trees, magnificent hill stations, unspoilt verdant tea estates and many such flash attractively across the screen as we watch.

I have looked at these pictures a hundred times.

'It is a slice of heaven!' exclaims Jenna. She is right, of course.

'You're a lucky bastard,' says Josh.

'He worked hard for it. He deserves this. His work is exemplary,' Jenna is a sport. She isn't sour that I got chosen and she didn't. We had both applied for the international programme where the selected recipient spends three months in a foreign country doing a bit of volunteer work and learning a new skill.

At the selection interview, when they asked me why I wanted to travel to India, I said I wanted to see the land of my origin and discover my roots. I wanted to see for myself where my forefathers came from, so I could understand my heritage and culture better. They were impressed by my answer.

The real reason was that my parents refuse to take me to India, and this was a chance for an all-expenses paid trip. I want to see for myself what it is about India that my father hates.

Though I had spoken with bravado and enthusiasm at my selection interview, I am a nervous wreck now. The tightness in the pit of my stomach refuses to go away. Three months in a foreign country is a long time. I wish I could back out. But the tickets have been booked, all arrangements have been made.

It's too late.

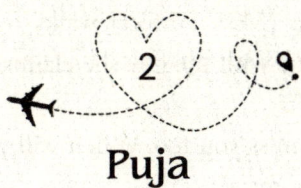

2

Puja

Every person who is successful (that includes my father, mother and sister) says the same things – 'Find your passion', 'Work hard', 'You have to love what you do', and the worst one – 'Everything happens for a reason'. They don't tell you how to find your passion. They don't tell you *what* the reason is. (For instance, what is the reason I am being forced to study in a course I have no interest or aptitude for?) I don't love what I do (or rather, what I am being forced to do).

Which brings me to the question: What do I *want* to do? I have no clue. Where do people like me go? All of this is just a load of feel-good new-age bullshit spouted by people who have already figured out what to do with their lives. They say it to make others feel worse about an already crappy situation.

Okay, I admit. I do feel good about *some things* for sure. One of them is what I am doing right now – sitting in my favourite spot on the wicker sofa at the far end of the expansive wooden-tiled balcony, overlooking the ocean with my cup of tea and onion pakodas (made by Shanti chechi just the way I like them), scrolling through Instagram. I click a picture and post it as a story. Then I check out my friends' feeds. One of them has posted pictures of her vacation in Koh Samui. Another has posted pictures of his trip to Egypt. They are travelling with their parents, but the pictures they post make it seem like they are on their own.

My sister Divya (Miss Perfect) walks out just then. She is chatting on the phone with the guy she claims to be her 'true love', her fiancé Karthik.

'Oh, my baby. I miss you too. When will you come here next?' she asks, not spotting me.

True love, my foot. I doubt if my sister would have agreed to marry the guy had he not been:

1. Wealthy
2. Dad's best friend's son (hence the built-in parental seal of approval)
3. Good-looking

I roll my eyes and focus on the ships sailing on the horizon. It is beginning to drizzle lightly now and the rain makes a foggy mist form on the horizon of the ocean.

The balcony is large with lots of greenery, a private lawn and a fibre-glass dome that keeps the sunshine in but the rain out. Papa believes in the finest things money can buy. He hired a top-notch interior designer from France when he bought all the four flats on the twenty-second floor, turning our home into an extra-spacious ten thousand square feet penthouse, with tastefully done interiors that channel in the great ocean. Its design allows us to have expansive sea views from all the rooms in the house. He has even named our home 'Life is Paradise'. My father is corny that way.

As though it is not enough that my sister is here to ruin my little soirée with onion pakodas, my mother has now walked out as well – a rare sight. Being a leading cardiac surgeon in one the best hospitals in Kochi means she ignores her family as she pleases.

Divya hangs up as soon as she spots my mother. But not before making those sickening kissing noises into the phone. People in love act as though no one else exists. They think they have invented love and are the first people on earth to feel this way. Annoying twerps. My mother smiles indulgently at her though. Divya can do no wrong in her eyes.

I try sinking deeper into the cushions, hoping to hide. But they spot me.

'Ah, there you are!' says my mother, as they both walk towards me.

Oh, hell.

'Have you thought about what you want to do for your summer holidays, Puja?' asks my mother as she settles down on the sofa opposite me, blocking my sea-view.

My mother and sister are the kind of people who do internships during college holidays so that it looks good on their CVs.

'Oh, nothing. I don't think I will do anything,' I reply coolly, as I sip my tea, watching my sister's eyes widen in horror.

'I don't think it is a good idea for you to sit at home,' says my mother.

'I agree,' Miss Perfect chimes in.

'I want you to enrol in a community development programme,' my mother tells me, placing a brochure on the table in front of me.

Divya helps herself to the onion pakodas and I glare at her.

'What?' asks Divya. 'I am sure Shanti chechi has made more. Don't tell me you were going to hog this all by yourself.'

'I don't want to do any community service,' I reply.

'It is a good programme,' my mother insists.

I idly flip through the brochure. Pictures of lush green forests, groups of happy young people posing with kids from underprivileged backgrounds, a picture of an older lady squatting on the ground, planting a sapling with a group of kids surrounding her – none of it interests me.

The NGO at Wayanad works with tribals, Dalit women and economically disadvantaged children. They require volunteers for teaching, gardening, marketing and an art project. They provide three traditional home-cooked organic meals. The minimum period one has to sign up for is eight weeks.

Eight weeks! That is the *entire* duration of my summer vacation, which means I won't get any free time at all. How can this programme be good?

'I don't want to go,' I say again.

'Look Puja,' my mother sighs, 'Do you have an alternate plan? Is there anything you would like to do instead?'

I shrug. Other than watching Netflix and sleeping, I have no plans, but I don't think that's what my mother wants to hear.

'Pack your clothes. I don't want you wasting your vacation. I will get Anthony to drop you, and you can carry your meds for travel sickness,' my mother says.

She pushes back her chair and stands up, handing me the forms.

It is clear there will be no more discussion on this. My mother isn't someone who will take a no for an answer.

She leaves the balcony and Divya follows her.

I stare in sullen silence at the ocean.

The ships have vanished from sight.

Arush

Ma has packed two cartons of stuff for me to take to India. She has been packing for the last three days, ever since I arrived from my college in Norwich. Had I known I was to carry all this, I would have left from Norwich, without coming to Derby first.

'Ma! Is this absolutely essential?' I ask, pacing up and down our living room.

'Yes. It is. Don't worry. Chandru mama will meet you at Delhi airport. You only have to hand both over to him,' she says, her brows forming little mountains as she seals them with packers' tape. She always furrows her brows when she is stressed. She has even made handles from the packers' tape, so I can carry the cartons like suitcases. They look exactly like the ones she brings her sarees in, on her trips back from India, and I hate them. They make me look like a saree salesman.

My mother runs an Indian garment shop in a small section of my father's grocery store in Derby which sells Indian groceries and other products. It's not too far from my home. Her brother and his wife run an Indian restaurant next door. It's a life I cannot imagine for myself.

'Will you call me and tell me about India?' asks my little sister Rhea, as she darts out of the house and out through the gate, right up to the waiting cab, on her big bouncy ball. There's a nip in the air and her cheeks have turned red from all the bouncing. She looks like a cherub.

'Of course, I will,' I assure her, as I ruffle her hair.

At six, everything is an adventure for her.

'Maybe I can visit you,' she says as she hands me a card.

'Rhea, this is lovely. Thank you!' I say. She has drawn a lady, a stick figure in a salwar kameez with criss-crosses on the wrists.

'What are these?' I ask as I study her drawing and point to the criss-crosses.

'They are bangles. Like the ones Ma has in her shop,' answers Rhea.

'Ah! You have captured all the details, haven't you?' I say. I recognise the colours she has chosen. She has tried to copy the mannequin in Ma's store.

'Yes, I want to be an artist like you,' she nods, pleased with my observation.

I smile at her. I tell her I have to leave.

I hug my family and I set out to Heathrow. I can't believe I am travelling to India.

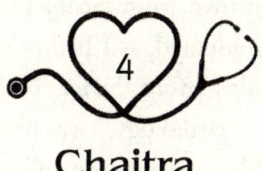

Chaitra

The problem with the Instagram and Snapchat generation is that they want things on a platter. They want all the finer things in life, but they aren't willing to put in the work for it. They are incapable of making a plan and sticking to it. They lack focus. They don't know how to set goals.

If all your time is spent on social media, mindlessly scrolling through other people's lives, how will you ever discover what you yourself want? Other people's thoughts will invade your mind and take over your life. I have told this countless times to Puja, and yet, it falls on deaf ears. I do not want to resort to taking away her phone like I did when she was in class 12. And even that didn't really help. 54% in the board exams is nothing to write home about. Had I not pulled some strings, she wouldn't have got into this college. She has no iota of gratitude or shame. She doesn't regret being suspended from school twice: once in class 11 for bunking classes, and again in class 12 for being among the group that played a stupid practical joke on the substitute teacher.

When I was growing up, I knew if I had to escape my claustrophobic one-bedroom home in Belapur, I had to work hard. I studied in that bedroom, which I shared with my two older brothers. And yet, I cleared all the medical entrance tests and got admission into all the medical colleges I had applied to. Even the fees for my education, I paid on my own, from the loan I took in my name. I had to work as soon as I graduated, as I had to clear the loan. I had no choice. My father couldn't afford the fees on his clerk's salary. When I studied for the MD in cardiology, I was pregnant with Divya. And I cleared that as well. Where there is a will, there is a way.

Now this is precisely the problem with Puja. She doesn't know what hardship or applying oneself is. She doesn't know what poverty means. She has been pampered by the opulent lifestyle we lead now. I too am partly to blame, as I am busy with my work. But my work is the only thing that gives me joy. Parenting these girls is a thankless job. (Actually, Divya is not too bad. But Puja? She is the reason I have grey hair now.)

I must say though, that Krishnan spoils both girls. He does not listen to me. He too has risen from a very humble, lower middle-class background just like I did, so he should know the value of money. But no. He keeps insisting that he wants to give the best the world has to offer to the three of us – me, Puja and Divya.

But sometimes, the best thing that you can do for others is to give them an opportunity to utilise their true potential. That is what I am doing for Puja. I know this programme will be good for her. I had enrolled Divya in something similar when she was in college. She never grumbled.

I suspect Puja hates me for doing this. But as a mother, I am doing what is right. In the absence of an initiative of any sort from her, I have to step in. At least if she gave me a plan or some indication as to what she would like to do, I could guide her. But she doesn't.

I just don't get that girl.

Adventure

Adventure is worthwhile.
— *Aesop*

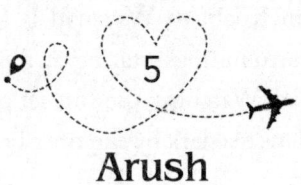

Arush

India is nothing like I expected it to be. The guidebooks and sites say it is crowded, noisy, dirty, dusty and that people will jostle you, trying to get you to go with them. I expect a small, nondescript airport, but this is world class. It is massive and I take at least seven walkways to get to immigration. It is just like Heathrow, except that all the people I see here look just like me! I feel instantly at home to see more black-haired, brown-skinned people rather than the blonde-haired white folks, which I am accustomed to.

I am too excited to be tired. Having slept in the flight, anticipation keeps me bright-eyed. It is 8.30 am local time. My flight from the UK being delayed has reduced my layover time in Delhi for my next flight to Kerala. After a short wait in the queue, the immigration officer asks me to look into the camera as he clicks my picture. A quick stamp on my passport and he waves me through.

India, India, India! This is exhilarating. I am still inside the airport, but the very air is different. I can tell. After I collect my baggage, I spot a counter for international tourists to get an Indian sim card. It is a simple process and in no time, I have my own India number. The data plans in India are extremely cheap compared to the UK. I try to contact Chandru mama several times, but I am unable to get through. I send a quick message to my parents that I have landed safely and am proceeding to Kerala. No point waking them up (it's the middle of the night in UK).

The journey from Kochi to Wayanad is long. But I love the drive. I take in the surroundings, staring at the greenery, staring at everything on the road. Watching the sun set on the drive through the ghats is spectacular. It is dark by the time I reach, the sun having set on the way.

The driveway leading up to Ashwaty Bhawan is brightly lit. The rustic building with a low, sloping, tiled roof and large steep steps leading to a reception area overlooking an indoor courtyard open to the skies, look like a painting waiting to be made. Red and pink hibiscus bobbing in a shallow, large brass vessel filled with water at the entrance makes for a visually stunning sight. Beside it stands a gleaming, polished five-feet brass lamp with oil and wicks, its top fashioned like a peacock. The lamp is lit and the flames dance brightly, celebrating my arrival. Millions of stars glitter and wink at me through the courtyard skies. I take in a sharp breath, mesmerised. The skies should be the same everywhere, but they are not. The night sky in the UK is not this beautiful.

Mrs Omana Umman greets me with a big smile when I arrive. She wears a deep maroon cotton saree, and her hair is slicked back into a tight plait. She is short, plump and matronly.

'Welcome, welcome to Ashwaty Bhawan, Arush. How was your drive?' she smiles, revealing a gap between her front teeth. She wears a small red bindi. She pronounces my name exactly like my parents do. In the UK, no one gets it and I am used to being called A—roosh.

'Fantastic! Kerala is so…' I am out of words to describe what I have seen.

'Beautiful?' she asks, laughing.

'Verdant, green, breath-taking, striking. It *is* truly God's own country.'

'Oh, wait till it is daytime. It is very beautiful. I will show you to your room. Come!' she says. She speaks in pauses.

She calls out to a young boy to take my suitcase and I am aghast.

'Oh, no! Thanks. I will take it myself,' I say.

'No, he will take it. In India, a guest is like a god,' she says, as she tells the boy something (I am guessing she is speaking Malayalam.). The young boy grabs the suitcase and the cartons, gesturing to me to follow.

As soon as I am alone, the tiredness kicks in. I unpack my suitcase, put away my clothes and make my bed. The adrenaline rush of being in a new country has subsided. Now I want to sleep. I text my parents that I have reached Ashwaty Bhawan safely, am exhausted by the travel and that Kerala is very beautiful.

Bright sunlight streaming in through the glass panels in the tiled roof act as a natural alarm the next morning. I squint my eyes. Even the sun in India shines brighter. It is harsher than what it is in the UK, but I don't mind it at all.

The bathrooms located away from the guest house seem ancient. There is no washbasin, and Mrs Omana tells me I can spit out the toothpaste at the foot of the coconut tree and cover it with mud when I am done, or I can use the bathroom floor and then pour some water to wash it away. It is the strangest thing I have ever done in my life – brushing my teeth outdoors, to the chirping of crickets and a million bird cries.

Once I am done, Mrs Omana hands me a cup of tea in a transparent glass. The tea is strong and sweet, and I like it.

'You can relax and rest for today. You can go around and see the place. Ashwaty Bhawan has more than ten acres of land. We grow many fruits and spices. We have more volunteers coming in. Tomorrow, we have the orientation. After that you can start,' she says.

'What will I be doing?' I ask.

'Asha will explain everything. She will conduct the orientation.'

She adds, 'You can come for Kerala breakfast at 8.30 am. Till then you can explore.'

'Thank you, that would be wonderful.'

I explore the property. Being located atop a hill, I can see winding roads stretching far below – the road we had taken last night. There is nothing but miles and miles of greenery. Tall trees form canopies. I walk around staring in fascination at tonnes of ripe jackfruits and mangoes that I have only seen in the fresh fruit aisles at Sainsbury's. The creepers with dark green leaves climbing up the palm trees seem like lovers entwined in an embrace.

Further on, groups of children walk into a large tiled shed. I notice the colourful mats spread on the floor and a blackboard. They are all neatly dressed, hair combed back, their clothes clean.

'Good morning, *chetta*… Good morning, *chetta*!' they greet me as they pass me. I am surprised.

I greet them back. They seem to be of different age groups, roughly between three and twelve.

After I get back to my room, I remember Chandru mama's cartons. I open them and stare at the tonnes of McVitie's, Jaffa cakes, Jammie Dodgers, Scottish shortbreads, Oreos, ginger biscuits and flapjacks that my mother has packed. Suddenly I know what to do with them. I take the cartons to Mrs Omana and tell her I have something for the children.

'You are generous, Arush. Very generous. The children will be very happy. We will distribute these,' she says.

In the evening, I wander around the property again. I watch the birds, the butterflies and the countless little creatures. Being in this green space does feel like paradise. Then I get even more lucky – I spot something that enthrals me. I move in closer to observe. This is incredible!

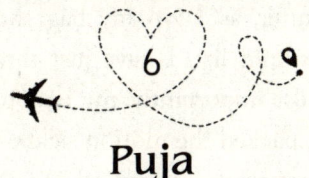

Puja

Essential packing list for Ashwaty Bhawan, Wayanad

1. Bedsheets – 1 no
2. Blanket –1 no
3. Pillow cases – 2 nos
4. Torch (must)
5. Small backpack – 1 no
6. 1 pair sandals with straps
7. Shoes (quick drying)
8. 5 pairs of socks
9. Hand towels – 2 nos
10. Big towel – 2 nos (preferably quick dry)
11. 2 big plastic bags (in case you need to carry wet clothes)
12. Personal toiletries
13. 3-4 vomit bags (travel is through ghat section)
14. Any specific personal medicines (we do have a first aid kit and a local health centre)

The list itself makes me want to throw up. Who in the world asks the volunteers to carry all of this? Getting unpaid work out of us is dreadful enough. My friends are vacationing in exotic places and I am being sent off to a bloody rural town.

'Grrrrrrr,' I mutter, as I zip my bag shut. I haven't packed according to their stupid list. I have just thrown in some shorts and t-shirts, and most importantly, my laptop, the phone and the chargers. I have also packed the motion sickness pills.

Shanti chechi is there to see me off. As always. It is never my mother; it has always been Shanti chechi. My mother is too busy at her hospital saving lives, performing critical surgeries.

She hands me watermelon juice that she has packed in a recyclable glass bottle.

'Bye Shanti chechi,' I say, as I hug her.

Despite having taken the motion sickness medication, I throw up thrice. It begins about three hours after I leave Kochi. Each time I signal to Anthony and he pulls over. I am sweating as I vomit. Anthony stands a little away, helplessly; offers me water and tissues when I am done. My throat burns. My mouth feels dirty. It feels like my intestines will spill out. The watermelon juice was a bad idea in hindsight. I clean my face with the wet wipes.

I am in a bad state. Embarrassed, tired, exhausted. The nightmare has started all over again. The horrendous car ride has transported me back to the time when I was seven.

Ma has taken twenty days off from the hospital. She has been planning this for two years. It is rare for her to take time off from work. Everybody is excited because papa has organised a trip to USA. It is a grand trip – the trip of a lifetime. We will cover Los Angeles, Las Vegas, San Francisco, Niagara Falls, Washington DC, New York, and will end with the grand Bahamas cruise. My father has just sold his first company and this trip is a celebration too. My sister and I dance about excitedly as we choose the clothes we will be taking on the trip. I can't be parted from my favourite stuffed toy – Mickey Mouse.

'You know USA is his home country? He will not want to come back with you,' my sister says.

'No! He loves me and he will come back with me,' I reply.

'Oh, no no! He will see America and he will forget India and stay there,' Divya teases me.

'Nooo,' I wail.

'Divya, that is enough,' my father stops her. I clutch my Mickey a little tighter as we drive to the airport.

We are flying to Mumbai and then to LA. It is on that ride to the airport that the nightmare starts. I throw up all over the back of the front seats which are covered in pristine white cloth. I also throw up on a part of my mother's clothes. Divya, who is riding in the front, screams 'Yuck' as drops of vomit splash on her.

I die of shame as we pull over and the driver cleans up, removing the front seat covers and throwing them in the boot. 'Oh, the smell!' he says, as he crinkles his nose. My mother splashes some water over her salwar kameez, not saying a word. She hands me the medicine she is carrying in her bag. I cry. I apologise. My father asks me not to worry about it. My mother is angry. 'You could have told us to stop the car. You are old enough for that,' she remarks.

The worst is far from over. I have an upset stomach. I feel my insides churning. I am terrified. I don't want to throw up again. No. I will not throw up at any cost. I somehow manage to hold it in. In the flight, I very badly want to go to the toilet; but I am too scared and too embarrassed to ask. I end up passing motion in my pants.

The other passengers wonder what the smell is. My mother takes one look at me and knows. She has to take a fresh change of clothes from the cabin bag that is kept in the overhead shelf. 'Thank god I brought a change of clothes,' is all she says as she holds me by the elbow and marches me to the toilet. I burn with shame. The airline seat is soiled. I *am sure every passenger can see my soiled behind. I sob, but I refuse to let go of Mickey.*

'Now enough, there is no need to cry for this,' my mother says. The toilet is occupied and we have to wait. This further lengthens my ordeal.

When I come back with clean underwear and a new pant, the seat has been cleaned, and now smells of disinfectant.

'Next time you have to go, tell,' my mother says.

I am very sick the entire duration of the trip. I have ruined it not only for my mother, but also for my family. 'I am sorry. I am sorry,' I keep saying throughout the trip. 'What are you sorry for? You aren't doing this deliberately,' my mother says. But her tone makes it sound like it is my fault.

I lose my Mickey somewhere in an airport toilet in between our transits. I find this out on the flight, but I am too frightened, too sad, too broken to speak. Divya notices it on the flight back to India.

' I was right. Mickey wanted to stay back in USA,' she declares.

I have never travelled again.

After what seems like an eternity through the nightmarish winding roads that climb up, on and on, we arrive. I quickly whip out my phone and look at my reflection in the selfie camera.

God. I. Look. A. Mess.

My hair is plastered to my head like I have worn a helmet that is too tight. The front of my t-shirt is drenched in sweat and perhaps water that must have spilled when I washed my mouth after throwing up. I look pale and I feel sick. I want to jump off the hill on top of which Ashwaty Fucking Bhawan is perched. If my mother had to send me for something like this, couldn't she have a chosen a slightly more accessible place? I curse my mother in my head, when a lady arrives, greeting me with a big smile.

'Welcome, welcome, Puja. I am Mrs Omana. How was the journey?' she asks in a pleasant sing-song voice.

It was the ride of death and I have thrown up my insides.

'Thank you, it was fine.'

'Good, good. I am happy to hear that. Come, let me show you to your room,' she says. The building looks old, almost ramshackled. It is constructed in the old Kerala style, with steep steps.

A boy appears and lifts my duffle bag. I gratefully let him take it and totter up the steps. I am in no state to even stand. All I want to do is crawl into bed and sleep for a few hours.

'Would you like something to eat? Tea perhaps? We serve it in the adjacent building where we have the dining room,' says Mrs Omana.

'No, thank you. I want to rest,' I croak and manage a half smile.

'Okay then, tomorrow is the orientation. Today you are free. Dinner is at 7.30 pm. You can explore the property if you like. We have ten acres,' she says proudly, as she throws open the door to my room.

'Oh, no bedsheets?' I ask, as I notice the two bare beds. Even the pillows do not have covers. All that the room contains are the beds, two desks and wardrobes. There is water in a copper jug and there's nothing else. I hadn't really given a thought to this, but I think a part of me expected it to be like a hotel with a kettle for making coffee and tea. Okay, I could even do without the kettle – but this? This is terrible. I expected something more. There are no attached bathrooms either.

'Er… we gave a packing list to all volunteers. We have clearly mentioned bedsheets in that,' says Mrs Omana.

How do I tell her I haven't packed according to the list and I never expected it to be this minimal?

'Sorry, I forgot. Is there somewhere I can buy sheets? I can send my driver to get it,' I say.

'Umm… no. The nearest shop is thirty-five kilometres away. And today it is closed,' she says, as she thinks. I wish she would hurry up. I just want to lie down.

'I can do one thing,' she says slowly. 'I can lend you a sheet, blanket and pillow covers from my house. That is the only way. You can use it till you stay here.'

'Thank you,' I say. But I don't mean it at all.

At this point I am ready to lie down even without any bedsheets. Any horizontal surface – even the floor would do. I just need to rest.

I decide that I am not going to tell my mother that I have reached. Let her worry, that is if she remembers to check where I am. She can check with Anthony if she is so concerned. I put my phone on flight mode. I don't want to talk to anyone. I just want to disappear from the world.

The boy appears in a few minutes with a bedsheet which has clearly seen better days. But it is clean, freshly washed and ironed. Beggars can't be choosers, I mutter to myself as I make the bed. I crawl into it gratefully and shut my eyes.

An hour later, I am wide awake and I feel surprisingly refreshed. Now that I am not in a moving vehicle, I am so much better. My brain has adjusted quickly and the rest has done me good. I glug down some water, brush my hair and tie it loosely in a pony tail. I pick up another t-shirt and change out of the sweat-soaked one. I wonder if I would be able to get that cup of tea which Mrs Omana had offered earlier. There's only one way to find out. I step out of the room and head towards the reception area.

As I go down the steps, I scream and nearly jump out of my skin in fright.

Right in the middle of the steps sits a large, ugly, grotesque chameleon with mottled deep green stripes and a long tail. It blinks its eye as it stares at me.

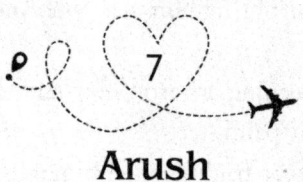

Arush

I am startled by the ear-shattering scream. I look up to see a girl who has stopped midway down the steps. She seems frightened, actually terrified, of my new friend Zelan, who I have spent the last hour with. She has turned pale and stands rooted to the spot. The sun shines directly on her, lighting up her face. It glows. Her eyes are enormous and her pale pink lips form a perfect 'O'. She has thick, really thick, black hair, swept up into a short, high pony tail. She is wearing denim shorts, open-toed sandals and a white t-shirt that says 'Not Your Type' in capitals. She seems strangely familiar.

I catch myself staring and then blush. I am too old for this kind of high school nonsense. Fortunately for me, she is too frightened to notice. Then mercifully, I remember Zelan.

I half expect Zelan to have bounded off, startled by her scream. But he poses serenely and blinks. He doesn't seem to be affected. Chameleons don't hear well as they don't have ears or developed hearing organs like the other mammals. Yet they can pick up sounds in the range of 200-600 Hz. I am glad her scream did not fall in the frequency range that would scare him away. I hold out my hand and he climbs onto my palm.

'Oh *fuck*!' says the girl. 'Aren't you scared?'

She now looks even more petrified than she did when she was on the stairs.

'Meet Zelan.' I grin.

'Eeks. Please don't bring him near me. And what the hell – he even has a name?!'

Her cheeks are turning crimson now and she stands stiffly, not taking her eyes off my palm.

'You don't have to be frightened of him. He is non-venomous,' I assure her. 'I have spent the last forty minutes taming him.'

She looks dubious.

'Are you for real? What are you? The Lizard Whisperer?' she asks, as she slowly backs off, climbing the stairs backwards.

I chuckle. 'Lizard whisperer! I like it,' I say, and I do.

I feel very important as Zelan is now climbing up my elbow. Out of the corner of my eye I can see that the girl is transfixed. I extend the other hand in front of Zelan and he climbs on to it. He is now getting restless and I can sense it instinctively. His movements are exactly like Vincent's.

I gently place him on the branch that protrudes from the large bush right next to the steps. Zelan makes his way up the branch, rotating his eyes as he moves. Chameleons can rotate their eyes independently of each other. One of his eyes watches for a predator, while the other scans the immediate environment for a prey. In a flash of a second his tongue shoots out and reaches for an insect which he chomps.

'Come back tomorrow,' I call out and gaze at him fondly, as he makes his way into the bushes in search of more food.

'Oh. My. God... that's insane! Did you see how long the tongue was?' says the girl, her pupils enlarging in wonder and surprise.

Now that Zelan is gone, I have no choice but to make polite conversation with her. I wish I wasn't horrible at small talk. But I am and I get self-conscious. She looks directly at me, waiting for me to answer.

'Yes, I did. The tongue of the chameleon is usually twice the size of their body,' I reply.

And then to cover up my nervousness, I blurt out, 'I have never seen this species before. It's *Chameleo Zeylanicus* – a species found only in India. I was hoping to spot one in India, but I didn't think I would get so lucky. *Zeylanicus*, so Zelan – get it?'

But she is not smiling back at me. She is staring at me now. Like I am from another planet.

That is when I know I have let my nervousness (and perhaps nerdiness) get the better of me. I have overdone it. How geeky and weird I must sound! I won't be surprised if she never wants to see me again.

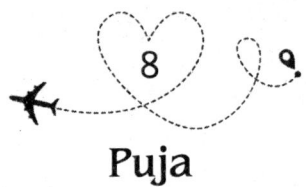

8

Puja

What a crazy thing I have just witnessed. How in the world can anyone *touch* lizards or chameleons or whatever that thing is? *Ew.* The Lizard Whisperer looks like he was almost in love with the damn thing. He has even named it. For a minute I wondered if I imagined the whole scene. How in the world does he know the species name? And what is with the British accent? He sounds posh and sophisticated.

I think he is awaiting a response because he is looking at me, waiting for me to speak.

'Ah, Zelan. Yes. Clever,' I say.

'Thanks,' he says. He looks almost pleased. Then he looks away. He is tall. Probably around six feet. He is dressed in a half-sleeved, deep reddish-brown checked shirt, khaki cotton pants and red sneakers with white laces. It is obvious that he has taken some thought to put together a co-ordinated smart casual outfit – unlike most guys who wear shorts, t-shirt and sloppy hawai chappals. His jet-black, straight hair is cut smartly: short at the sides, and slightly longish, messy and wind-blown on the top. I have never seen that kind of a hairstyle on any guy. His complexion, although clear, is very different. Pale. Like he hasn't ever been in the sun. He doesn't seem to fit in here. He is very different.

'So where are you from?' I ask, as I make my way down the stairs. He seems nervous, his eyes dart about anxiously.

28

'Norwich College of Arts, UK,' he answers.

Ah, no wonder. He didn't *seem* Indian.

'Is this a part of your college course?' I ask, stopping when I reach the step he is standing on.

'I should hope so,' he laughs.

'Eh?'

'Considering that I am spending twelve weeks on it, I reckon it would contribute to my college credits. What about you? Does it add to your credits too? What do you study?' he asks. He speaks fast, and I have to concentrate really hard to understand what he is saying.

'I am doing my BBM. And no, this doesn't add up to my 'credits'. We don't have credit system in Indian colleges.'

'Oh, really? How do they assess you then? And what does BBM stand for?'

'Bachelor of Business Management. We have exams at the end of the year. The final exams are conducted by the university. All that counts is how you perform then.'

'I see,' he says as he mulls over this information. 'I have to ask you – does it mean that any course work you do throughout the year doesn't really matter? It is only that one examination that counts. Am I correct?' he asks.

'Yep.'

'Oh, I see. It is more like our A levels then. We have that in school. But in college, we are assessed throughout the year.'

'What a pain! It means you can't goof off.'

He laughs. 'Goof off? Good lord, no! We can't fool around. We are very serious students,' he says. He laughs again. I can't tell if he is joking or not. So I smile.

'If volunteering here is not a part of your curriculum, do you get time off from college?' he asks.

'No. I have two months of vacation. After that I go back to complete my final year of degree.'

'I think that is very selfless and generous of you to spend your vacation here, helping out,' he rubs his chin as he speaks.

'Oh, no. I only came as my mother forced me to. I am no Mother Teresa,' I am quick to clarify.

'Umm… you are refreshingly honest,' he laughs as he speaks.

I didn't mean it as a joke at all, and I don't know why he is laughing. But he looks kind of cute when he does. His eyes crinkle and turn into slits. I notice that he has nice straight teeth. I am curious about him now.

'When did you move to UK? Where did you go to school?' I ask.

'Have always been there. Went to a school in Derby. Was born and raised there.'

It is taking me time to get used to his accent. I am familiar with American accents because some of my friends are from USA and Canada. But I do not know anyone from the UK and have to concentrate to understand what he says.

'First time in Kerala?' I ask.

'First time in India! And India is magnificent.'

'I don't see anything magnificent about it,' I reply and he frowns as though he is trying to understand whether I mean it as a joke or not. Then he laughs again.

I seem to be making him laugh a lot. It is completely unintentional on my part, but of course, he doesn't know that.

'I guess I would say the same if anyone told me good old England was magnificent. Hence, I see what you are saying,' he replies.

I have no idea if England is magnificent or not. I have never really thought about the UK.

'Is it?' I ask.

'What?'

'Is the UK magnificent? I mean, if you were not born and raised there, would you still find it beautiful?'

He furrows his eyebrows as he thinks. 'I think so. There is a lot of scenic beauty. Turner, Constable, Joseph Wright have all been inspired enough to elevate the British landscape art, putting it on the international scene way back in the mid-18th century. I reckon I would vote for yes.'

It is evident he expects me to have heard of the artists he has just mentioned. I have no idea what he is talking about and I quickly make a mental note and memorise the names. *Turner, Constable, Wright. Turner, Constable, Wright. Turner, Constable Wright*, I repeat in my head. I *have* to look them up and see what he meant. I don't want to appear stupid. I want to talk about an Indian landscape artist, but not a single name comes to mind. I am not even able to think of anything remotely related to art. This is terrible. I don't know what to say. Then I think of the perfect cop out. Tea, which was what I wanted before Mr Lizard Whisperer intercepted me. That is when it occurs to me that I don't even know his name.

'We haven't introduced ourselves. I am Puja.' I don't hold out my hand. He has just touched that lizard and I don't want to shake his hand till he has washed it. He doesn't seem to be bothered by that.

'Hello Puja. Pleased to meet you. I am Arush,' he smiles.

'Umm... I need a cup of tea. I am going to—'

'The dining area is this way. I love the tea here. Come, let me show you,' he cuts in before I can complete my sentence, and leads the way.

I have no choice but to follow him.

Arush

I think I have made a complete ass of myself with this strangely familiar-looking girl I have just met. When I am nervous, I laugh unnecessarily and I can't stop talking. As though the load of information on the Indian chameleon breed wasn't enough, I have overdosed on English landscape painters as well. I wish I had come up with a better answer when she asked me if UK was magnificent. I could have easily described it like the tourist brochures do, or I could have described Scotland or York or any other place. Unfortunately, I geeked out. In my defence, I was only trying to cover up my nervousness.

She follows me as we walk towards the dining area. When we get there, Mrs Omana greets us.

'Oh, hello Puja, hello Arush. Welcome. Welcome. Tea time is almost getting over. Come, have hot vadas and tea,' she says.

'You can wash your hands there,' she tells Puja. She points to a well outdoors, right next to the dining area, where a large plastic orange bucket stands. A pale pink plastic mug bobs in it. I am already familiar with it, as I have been dining here. I have even drawn water from the well. I have seen this kind of well only in illustrated children's books. It has a pulley system and a rope with an iron bucket attached at the end of it. Puja looks at the well and her nose crinkles up for just a second. Then her expression goes back to normal and she nods. She is completely unaware that I have caught that look.

We both wash our hands. (It seems to be another Indian thing – washing hands before each meal. I am learning to eat everything with my hands. Back home, we eat only rotis and parathas with our hands. Otherwise I always use a fork and knife.) There's diluted liquid soap kept next to the bucket in a recycled plastic bottle, which Puja handles like it is contaminated. There are no towels.

'You just have to shake your hands like this. Like how wet dogs shake themselves,' I say, as I shake them vigorously behind me.

She laughs and copies me. I am happy to have made her laugh.

When we go back to the dining area, we are joined by three other people, two boys and a girl. Mrs Omana introduces us to each other.

'It is nice that everyone is here,' Mrs Omana says. 'You will all be working together for the next two months. We have a total of five volunteers this time.' She points to me first. 'This is Arush from UK,' she says and everyone greets me. Puja just smiles.

We seem to be a motley bunch. There is Oshan who is from Sri Lanka but lives in the US; Leah, his girlfriend (I assume this as he has his arm around her waist and they can't seem to get enough of each other) is from the same college; and then there's Sujit from Kerala (I don't catch the name of his college or the place he is from).

Sujit is now staring at Puja. Puja is not paying any attention to him and is gazing at the greenery.

Suddenly he says, 'Puja! Puja Krishnan from Kochi? Do you remember me?'

Startled, Puja looks at him. A slow look of recognition flits across her face. Then she smiles a big warm smile that lights up her eyes. 'Oh! Sujit Nair! Whoever thought!' she exclaims.

'Oh, you two know each other?' Mrs Omana asks.

'Yes! We went to the same school,' says Sujit.

'Oh, that's wonderful. Carry on, I am going to supervise dinner preparations.' Mrs Omana bustles away.

The group breaks up. Leah and Oshan head off to a table by themselves.

Sujit is talking animatedly to Puja now. Puja throws back her head and laughs at whatever Sujit is telling her. I slip away and sit at a table by myself.

The boy who helps around the property places a banana leaf in front of me and serves the hot vadas and chutney on the leaf.

I look at Puja and the new entrant. They are still talking.

Now I miss the UK, my life there and my friends.

So, I take out my phone and start texting them.

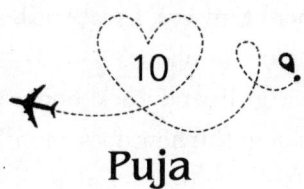

10

Puja

The last person I expect to see here is Sujit Nair. Sujit looks exactly as he did in school, except that he has put on some weight. He sports the same overgrown curly mop-top hair, an oversized shabby t-shirt, loose shorts which reach down to his knees and hawai chappals. He has the same old devil-may-care attitude. Everyone in school knew Sujit and his knack of getting into trouble. He had one hell of a reputation. His home was very close to school (just a few metres away) and therefore it wasn't unusual for teachers to ring his doorbell to complain to his parents about yet another thing Sujit had done. He was particularly famous in our school for riding into school on a motorcycle one morning when we were in class 11. Even the 12th grade boys couldn't do this as no one was old enough to get a driving licence. But that was the kind of thing that never bothered Sujit. Everyone stared at him in awe. Until his father turned up at school in a *mundu*, brandishing a sickle in the air, shouting that he would kill Sujit. Sujit ran around the school with his father chasing him. To escape, Sujit climbed up a tree and threw the key of the motorcycle down at his father. The whole school, including the principal and teachers, came out to watch this.

The first thing we talk about is this and we laugh.

'Boy, was I a nightmare! If I had a son like me, I would have definitely killed him that day. I don't even know what I was thinking.'

Out of the corner of my eye, I see Arush sitting all by himself. He is intently texting on his phone.

Maybe he has a girlfriend back home in the UK, I think. Suddenly I need to know. But how does one ask something like that directly?

'Come, let's join Arush,' I tell Sujit and I walk towards Arush.

Sujit follows me.

'Hey bro! Mind if we join you?' asks Sujit, as he pulls out the chair next to Arush. He sits down without waiting for a reply.

'Uh, of course, please sit,' says Arush.

Sujit looks at him and asks, 'Is the accent for real?'

'No. I was trained at a call centre here in India for speaking primarily to British customers,' says Arush, his expression and voice solemn.

'Oh, okay,' says Sujit.

I laugh out loud.

'What?' asks Sujit.

'Nothing,' I say but I am smiling at Arush, and Arush smiles back. His eyes seem to change colour when he smiles. It is almost like they are dancing.

'Sujit here was famous in school,' I tell Arush.

'Really? Were you on a sports team or something?' asks Arush.

'No bro, I don't play any sport,' says Sujit. He puts his head in his hands as I narrate the motorcycle incident. Arush is laughing now. His laughter is deep and rumbling. Warm and hearty. It sounds different from the time he laughed before. I now know why. Earlier it was a quick nervous laughter. But now it is genuine.

I am beginning to like the sound of his laugh.

Arush

After dinner, I go back to my room and video call my family. Ma is not too pleased to hear that the goodies for Chandru mama were distributed among the underprivileged kids in Wayanad.

'Come on, Ma. They are sweet kids and they deserve it,' I say.

My father just guffaws when he hears the story. Rhea is busy with her homework and isn't interested in talking to me. The internet is choppy, which makes the video freeze from time to time. I switch to audio.

When I finish the call, I take out my travel lamp, my art supplies and arrange them neatly on the desk. I connect my phone via Bluetooth to my mini-travel speaker and stream Steve Hackett's *Sketches of Satie*. I have clicked ample reference images of Zelan and these are going into the daily observation quick studies journal which I have to submit for assessment. I make a few quick sketches in it and write down facts about Indian chameleons. In my A3 journal, I make a large detailed painting of Zelan which takes me a while. Making art in a strange foreign land, with crickets and all kinds of creatures chirping outside, familiar music playing softly in the background, feels like a dream. Once I finish my painting, I carefully wash my brushes and dry them. I put away my art supplies, and while I wait for the painting to dry, I open my laptop to browse and see what I can do in Wayanad. A travel site I stumble upon highly recommends the Edakkal caves. The photos grab my attention.

I am startled when there's a knock on my door.

I frown as I glance at my watch – 11.20 pm. When I open the door, I am as surprised as the person standing in front of me. Puja.

'Oh, so sorry. I thought this was Sujit's room,' she says.

'I am sorry. You have the wrong room,' I say, unnecessarily. She can already see that.

She recovers faster than me. She holds out the toothbrush in her hand and says, 'But it's fine! I just wanted to borrow some toothpaste.'

'In that case you have the right room. Come on in,' I say.

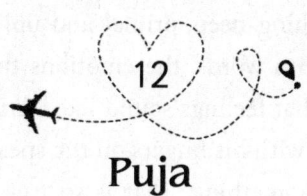

12

Puja

Oh, no! How could I have knocked on his door this late at night! I hope he doesn't think this is just an excuse. I don't want him thinking I am into him. This is a genuine mistake. But if I beat a hasty retreat now, it is going to look worse, so I walk in.

His room is neat and organised compared to mine. I haven't bothered with the unpacking; my clothes are strewn around. In contrast, his suitcase is unpacked and put away. There's not a single thing here that is out of place.

Soft enchanting music streams through a Bluetooth speaker. It is mesmerising and I have never heard this kind of music before. I stand there listening intently.

Arush looks at me and grins. 'It is something, isn't it? I love this music.'

'It is almost magical,' I say softly, as I listen.

For a second, almost involuntarily, I close my eyes as the music washes over me. Then I remember where I am and I quickly open my eyes. I find Arush looking at me with an indecipherable expression on his face. Like he is studying me. I cringe.

'You really do love this music, don't you? It's haunting. That's why I love it too,' Arush says and I nod.

'I wouldn't use the word haunting. But yes, there is something about this,' I reply.

'There is something deep, primal and uplifting in music that it is hard to pour into words, the emotions they evoke. Someone has said, music is what feelings sound like,' Arush says it all in one breath, as he drums with his fingers on the speaker.

'Wow! That is something. That is so true,' I reply, as I think about what he has said. It is profound. I am getting used to his accent now and I can easily understand what he says.

'Indeed,' he says. He has stopped drumming now and is smiling at me.

There is something warm and welcoming about his room. I wonder how that is possible. We have identical rooms. But he has managed to make his feel like a 'home'.

He has a focus lamp over his desk which gives the whole room a warm glow.

'My room doesn't have that lamp,' I say.

'Oh, that is my travel lamp, which I carry for my work along with my travel speaker. I came prepared,' he says, as he sweeps his hair off his forehead.

I notice his drawing book then, lying open on the desk. I can't help peeping. I gasp at his drawing. The chameleon he was holding earlier has stunningly come to life in his art.

'Your drawing – it is brilliant!'

'Oh, thank you,' he looks positively pleased now. His face is earnest, like a little boy's.

'Mind if I look at the other drawings in your book?'

'Not at all. Go ahead,' he says. 'Some of them are just quick studies.'

I am blown away by his sketch book. There are many scenes from the UK which he has drawn.

'Oh, my! Look at this!' I exclaim, as I turn the pages. I stop at a particularly striking colourful sketch of colourful tents – festive, happy and busy.

'That is one of my favourite places, the Norwich marketplace. I love sketching there,' he says.

'It is so beautiful! The place I mean, and of course, the sketch too.'

'It is. Norwich is a wonderful place. When I first joined college there, I was fascinated. It is different from Derby where I grew up.'

'Where do you live in Norwich? Does your college have a hostel?' I ask.

'No, three of my mates and I share a place,' he says.

'Are they all in your college?'

'Yes, but only Jenna is in my course, which is illustration. Josh is majoring in photography and Tom is into acting.'

I wonder if Jenna is his girlfriend. What is his relationship with her? What does she look like? I want to know this, but I think it would be churlish of me to ask. So, I make a comment about his college.

'How lucky you are able to go there. All we have in my college is Arts, Science and Commerce. And when I say Arts, in India it means Literature and Sociology. It doesn't mean Fine Arts,' I clarify.

'I take it you do not like what you are studying then?'

'I hate it!'

'Then why don't you switch? Why continue something you do not like? It is four years of your life, or is it three in India?'

'Three years for a degree. I don't have a choice. My mother wants me to do this. And then attend coaching classes for CAT. That's an important exam in India, which allows you to apply for a management degree into the finest Indian institutions like the IIMs, the Indian Institute of Management,' I explain.

I note that Arush has no clue how 'revered' IIMs are in India and I find that refreshing. He doesn't care about it. Whereas for my mother and for many people in India, an IIT or an IIM tag is the Holy Grail of Education.

'What's the point of doing something you don't like just because your parents force you? My father too, doesn't understand why I would want to do illustration. He expected me to be a lawyer or choose what he sees as a 'respectable' profession. But I knew what I wanted to do. I applied to the Arts college of my choice and I got a scholarship. I am also working and paying my way through college.'

I can see how proud he is of paying his own college fees.

'It is very different in India. I would only get a part time job at a pizza chain or something,'

'So? That's what I do too! I work at a charity shop.'

'You don't get it, Arush. India is different. Do you know there are thousands who do not have a job? If I take up that work, I would be stealing from someone who actually *needs* it. Also, my mother would never ever let me work. It is… just not done,' I finish, not knowing how to explain.

'Hmm, yes, I see now what you are saying. I did not look at it that way,' he says.

'An MBA degree for you then?' he asks.

'I guess I have no choice. My mother would be very upset if I do not get into IIM. My sister did her MBA from IIM and she got a job via campus recruitment. Now she works in a foreign bank. The bar is quite high.' I sigh.

Arush nods as he digests all this.

Then his eyes twinkle. 'Unless maybe, if you bend the bar,' he says and I laugh.

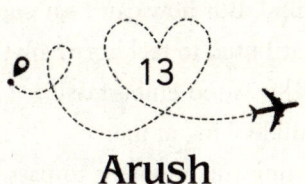

Arush

She tilts her head sideways when she laughs. The light from the lamp illuminates her face. She looks so familiar. Those eyes, that chin. Why does she look so familiar? Then it strikes me. A frisson of excitement runs through me as I observe her face with new eyes. She looks a lot like Selena Gomez who I had a massive crush on for two summers when I was in high school. I have secretly watched her *Heart wants what it wants* a thousand times and I can sing the lyrics by heart. I thought I had relegated that embarrassing phase of my life to the never-to-be-admitted-never-to-be-discussed corner of my brain; but now, out of the blue, it has suddenly popped up. God help me I am staring at her. I can't be doing this. I am too old for this kind of high school claptrap! Yet my heart thuds in excitement.

'Have you ever heard of Selena Gomez? The American actress? *Wizards of Waverly Place? Another Cinderella Story?*'

'I know Selena Gomez; you don't have to name all her shows,' she laughs.

'You look like her!' I blurt out.

'Do you like her? On a scale of 1 to 10, how much do you like her?' She smiles as she twirls her hair.

How do I answer that? On a scale of 1 to 10, it would be a thousand. Or perhaps I should make that a million? Several responses come to mind. But how can I say something that doesn't give away the fact that I used to feel horny anytime I saw her image or heard her voice? This is too embarrassing. I don't know what to answer. And she is still looking at me.

I look away, wanting this moment to pass. I wish I could take back the statement I just made. I can *feel* my cheeks turning red. This is a nightmare.

She laughs again as I hesitate. 'I just asked! You don't have to answer that,' she says.

I love it when she laughs.

'Errr… I think many guys have a crush on her. I used to. No big deal. I was in high school,' I admit.

But I think she knows that it *was* a big deal. I am so embarrassed now that I do not want to be talking about this anymore. Then I spot my laptop lying on my bed. The perfect distraction. The exit-this-topic card.

'Hey, you know, I found something remarkable,' I tell her.

Her eyes light up with curiosity.

'Really? What?'

'See? There are some caves to explore here,' I say gesturing to the laptop.

She goes over and sits down on my bed without my inviting her to.

My heartbeats are almost in my ear.

Thud-thud-thud-thud-thud-thud.

'Oh, is it?' she asks.

'Yes. I was going through it when you knocked. The descriptions and pictures are stunning,' I reply.

Calm down heart.

'Come, sit,' she pats the bed, 'Show me.'

I sit beside her, my heart now going into an overdrive, like drumbeats on an amplifier.

I open my laptop to the site I was browsing.

'What is this? Secret tips?' Puja asks as we both peer into the laptop.

The secret tips for Edakkal Caves
Don't take the usual route (the tarred road). Trek through the woods (take the road into the forest from the foot of the hills) to reach the ticket counter.

To find the trekking route, look for a tree with a white arrow painted, pointing to the left.

It is steep, but *very* scenic. Wear sensible shoes.

Carry food and water.

Pause and soak in the silence and greenery.

The secret trek route ultimately leads to the ticket counter, from where it is a steep climb up. *Highly* recommend it.

The caves have petroglyphs which are 7,000 years old!

Both of us read the list, spellbound by the descriptions, pictures and instructions. At the end of it is a picture of the guy who has written it.

'Eeeks, look at him. He looks like a dork,' Puja says.

'Come on, don't be rude. I think some girls will find him cute,' I tell Puja.

'I am not one of those then,' she shrugs.

'What is your idea of cute then?' I ask her.

'You are cute,' she says frankly, looking into my eyes. She smiles. She doesn't break her gaze even for a moment.

I feel the colour rising in my cheeks again, spreading slowly across my face.

I don't know what to do, so I say brightly, 'Let's see what else is there about Edakkal caves.'

I click on the various links furiously. But the internet is going slow now.

And when I look up from the laptop, she is still looking at me. Her eyes are soft, pensive, accepting. Like she knows me and understands.

I hardly know this girl. But why does it feel like she is looking into my soul?

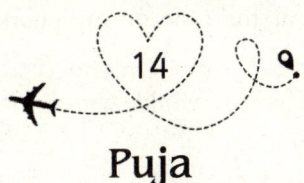

Puja

Is this a moment we have had? I think it is. I think our eyes have spoken in the secret language that only eyes have. I didn't mean to do this. It just happened. Also, I think he knew too, because he blushed. None of the guys I have known have blushed. I have no idea what made me openly proclaim his cuteness. Maybe it is the music, maybe it is this room, this cosy intimate atmosphere. Maybe it is his accent. I don't know. But I know I need to change the topic.

And I need to do it *now*. I *have* to make this moment pass.

'I think these secret tips are not so secret now, eh?' I say.

'Yeah, we could… err… maybe do the caves together?' he asks, his eyes hopeful.

I want to reach out and squeeze his hand and tell him to not be so shy, so hesitant. But telling him he is cute is scary enough for a day. I like that he has said: '*We* can do it together'. It feels nice. Like he has asked me out on a date.

'Yes, it will be so good,' I say, my voice taking a dreamy tone of its own accord, as I struggle to reign in my logical brain. Horrified at how wistful I sound, I give myself a mental rap and sit up straighter.

'I think we will have to put in some work first. Before asking Mrs Omana if we can take a day off,' he rubs his chin.

'We could skip the work and saunter off on day one,' I quip and he laughs.

When I glance at the time on my phone Arush is quick to notice.

'Past bedtime?' His eyes twinkle with mirth.

'Nah! I am a night bird.'

'What bird are you? An owl?'

'Owls are ugly!' I crinkle my nose. 'In India, owls are stupid. But the English think they are wise.'

'My mother uses '*Uloo ka patha*' when she is annoyed with a vendor,' he says.

The Hindi phrase he pronounces with an English accent makes me chuckle.

'You are so British!' I say and he bows.

'Guilty as charged, ma'am.'

Mustering up the courage, I ask him what I've been dying to know – whether Jenna is his girlfriend. But I am clever enough to not be direct.

'Tell me about your home in Norwich and your housemates,' I feign nonchalance.

His eyes light up as he opens his phone, showing me their pictures. He goes into detail about each one. I am relieved when I know that Josh and Jenna are in a relationship.

'What about Tom and you?' I ask. 'Do either of you have anyone special?'

There, I have casually thrown it in.

'Tom broke up a few months back. He is single. And my relationships – well, I have never been in one.'

'What!? Why?'

'I mean, I have never been in a serious relationship. They last a few months. Then I get bored,' he shrugs. 'What about you?'

'I know what you mean. Relationships are a lot of work. I had a boyfriend back in class 12. Then we went to different colleges; he moved to Pune. We tried to maintain a long-distance relationship. But after a while, the phone calls and messages just dwindled. And it died a natural death.'

He is still scrolling through his phone and he nods while listening to me. 'Meet Vincent, my iguana,' he says, his eyes shining. I look at what he's showing me.

'You have a pet iguana! No wonder you are so comfortable with lizards.'

I tell him I can't stand them and he chuckles.

'You just have to get to know them. They can be good. Really good.' His voice drops an octave when he says this.

Is he flirting with me? Maybe he is. I am having such a good time that I can't tell.

The conversation turns to favourite music, TV shows and films, and flows smoothly. When it comes to TV shows, we have a lot in common. But when it comes to books, I am ashamed. I am not much of a reader. Clearly, he is.

When he wants to know what my favourite books are, to cover up my inadequacy, I name a book which I have had as 'essential reading' in school, a translation of a work by a Hindi author and he hasn't heard of it.

I put the ball in his court by asking him about *his* favourite books, and he talks animatedly. He goes into great detail about why he likes each of them. He pauses and says, 'I am not giving you any spoilers, do not worry. I hate it when people do that.'

'Yeah, me too,' I say.

Mentally, I am taking furious notes of the titles he has just mentioned. I am so going to read those books. The way he has described them makes them sound very interesting. After this conversation with him, I want to be the kind of girl who can talk about books effortlessly.

When we look at our phones again, it is 4 am.

'Orientation is at 9 am. Goodbye sleep,' he says.

'Yeah. I think we will both need toothpaste now,' I say and he laughs.

Arush

Have we just talked the whole night? I can't believe this. She is so different from any of the girls I have been with before. I am not sure if it is her inherent Indianness or her refreshing honesty that is drawing me to her. There is something attractive about her curiosity. She hangs on to every single word I say. She asks questions. She listens intently as if what I am saying is of utmost importance.

She is dazzlingly unique.

I run into her again in the dining area, where breakfast is being served. She is with Sujit and she waves and smiles widely, calling out for me to join them.

The steaming hot idlis and chutney are served on banana leaves by a couple of ladies who also double up as cooks.

'Chechi, thank you, this is delicious,' Sujit says.

I nod as I bite into the idlis. I can feel Puja's gaze on me as I eat. A warm, happy feeling washes over me.

'Slept well?' she asks when I look up. Her eyes meet mine and they are laughing.

'Very well,' I reply, suppressing my smile.

Sujit is oblivious to our sly, little secret exchange and he continues eating.

Puja and I are developing our own secret code.

Orientation turns out to be an informal affair conducted under a large shady tree. We sit on colourful dhurries spread out on the ground. I am pleased when Puja chooses to sit next to me. Asha, a bubbly, jovial, enthusiastic, thin lady in a saree, who is doing her post-doctoral research, bounces around as she talks. She works with an organisation that has adopted Ashwaty Bhawan as a part of their Corporate Social Responsibility programme. She asks us to introduce ourselves and specifically tells us to speak on why we chose this particular project.

Leah and Oshan say that their college has a tie-up with the same organisation that Asha works for and this is a part of their final year project. I tell her that I wanted to travel to India, and I was chosen after an extensive round of interviews and work-evaluation.

'Oh, yes. They had told me about you, Arush. I have gone through your file. Your work is outstanding,' she says and I thank her.

Sujit says that he liked the concept of volunteer work-vacations and wanted to spend his holidays meaningfully.

When it is Puja's turn she sighs, 'I didn't choose Ashwaty Bhawan. It chose me. You can't escape some things.'

Everyone laughs. But I sense a resigned acceptance in her tone. I am becoming very good at deciphering her tone and her expressions.

Asha thanks us all for volunteering and tells us how important our contributions are, emphasising how the work we do helps towards community upliftment.

'I want it to be fun for you. Only then will you be able to give your best. You can tell us what you are good at, and we will assign you duties accordingly. Don't worry, we will find suitable work for everyone,' she says with a smile.

'Let's start with Arush. Would you enjoy making a large wall art for the classrooms?' she asks.

She explains that the classroom is a basic open shed and hence they want to turn it into a 'happy, cheerful space' for the kids. I am excited as she hands over the complete creative control to me.

Leah and Oshan opt to work with the local Dalit women who manufacture various items by hand, like soaps and embroidered cushion covers. Both being marketing students, want to work on branding. They are hoping to empower the women by making them financially independent.

Sujit wants to do organic agriculture. He loves plants and nature.

That leaves Puja. I am curious to see what she will choose. But she merely shrugs when Asha asks her.

'I am not really good at anything,' she says. I have spent enough time with her to know that her voice is wobbly. She hides it well though. She pretends to not care, but I know that something has unsettled her.

'Oh, everyone is good at something. Is there anything in specific that you dislike?' Asha asks.

Puja shrugs again.

'In that case, you can work with the children and assist in teaching. We have a local teacher, but since the number of children is large, we always need resources,' Asha says.

Puja nods. I can't decipher the expression on her face.

Maybe I am not as much of a Puja-expert after all.

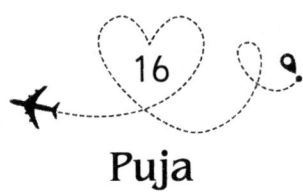

Puja

The orientation has thrown me off-guard. All these people here are so sure of themselves and why they are doing this. They are all good at *something*. But me? I am just here because my mother insisted. I feel hopelessly inadequate. I don't even *want* to teach kids.

But Asha has already taken Leah and Oshan to meet the local women and Sujit has left with Mrs Omana to the agricultural area.

That leaves me alone with Arush. I feel crappy now.

Arush picks up on it. 'Hey, what happened?'

'Nothing.'

'Are you looking forward to working with the children? I can't wait to start painting the classrooms.'

'I was assigned this. I guess I have to do it,' I reply.

'Come on, kids can be such fun. I have a six-year-old sister. She makes me laugh so much. They say it like it is and their energy is infectious,' he says.

'What's her name? What is she like?'

'Rhea. She is playful, observant and sharp. You can't fool her.' He looks happy when he talks about his sister.

'Like you?' I ask.

'Am I playful like a six-year-old? Nah! I don't think so,' he looks surprised at my unexpected comment.

'So, you agree you are observant and sharp?'

'*You* said it! I didn't,' he is quick to retort.

'I think you are. You figured that something was off and asked me about it too.'

'Yes, I did. I knew you were not okay.' He bites his lower lip when he ponders.

'How did you know? Do you have a hotline to inside my head? Or are you a psychic?' I tease him.

'Are you going to tell me what it is or should I use my psychic abilities to draw it out of you?' he is smiling now.

The smile takes off the anxiety in his eyes. They seem to be forever darting about nervously. His whole demeanour transforms when he smiles. Funny how a small thing can make a huge difference.

Before I can reply, Asha appears.

'Ready for classroom? Follow me,' she says.

As we walk to the classroom, Asha tells Arush that the wall at the far end of the shed has to be painted with a colourful, cheery mural that will brighten up the place. She says he can use a theme of exploration and discovery to ignite curiosity in the minds of the kids. Arush replies that he needs time to conceptualise so he can come up with design options.

'You can use the table and chair at the back of the room as your workstation. Once you are ready with the designs, you can show them to us, and we can all collectively vote on the chosen one. You can begin to paint after that. Sounds good?' she asks.

'Yes, perfect,' Arush nods.

Then she addresses me.

'Puja, I shall introduce you to Rukmini. Everyone calls her Rukmini teacher. You can assist her. She will tell you what she needs help with,' she says, as we follow her.

'It looks like we will be working in the same room,' Arush says in a low voice to me. Asha hears it and confirms, 'Yes. We have only one classroom here.'

My mood changes instantly when I hear that. For the first time since the orientation, I smile.

Arush

At the start of the class, Rukmini teacher introduces Puja and me to the kids. She says that Puja is the new teacher, and that I am an artist from the UK. She asks the kids, 'Do you know where UK is?'

'Yes,' chime two voices. She points to one of them and asks him to tell us where it is.

'It is in America,' he says.

I chuckle but quickly suppress it as no one is laughing. Rukmini teacher then opens a world map. She points out UK and she points to America explaining how the two are different countries in different continents.

'Are you from UK too?' one of the kids asks Puja.

'No, no! I am from Kerala, just like you,' she says in Malayalam.

There are surprised whispers and then there are smiles all around. With that single statement in Malayalam, she has won the kids over.

Rukmini teacher says that if they are good and behave well, they will get a fabulous painting for their classroom painted by Arush chetta.

Chetta! I love the term. I have never had a suffix to my name and it is strange, but nice, to hear the kids call me 'Arush chetta'.

The kids immediately declare that they will be good. I take my place at the 'workstation' at the far end of the classroom. It is a metal table with a plastic chair. I study the wall. It is about 20 feet by 10 feet. I would need a rectangular design. I sit down and start making some rough exploratory sketches, trying to think of something vibrant which would also fit with the theme.

Rukmini teacher is explaining the digestive system with the help of a chart displayed on a makeshift easel. The kids sit on mats, giving me an unobscured view of Puja from where I am sitting. Seated at a table identical to mine in the front of the classroom, she has been given some papers to grade. The first hour, the kids keep turning back to throw curious glances my way. I smile at a few. Rukmini teacher asks them not to disturb me. The kids are cute, a curious lot, have umpteen questions to ask. They remind me of Rhea.

Puja is so focussed on her work that she doesn't look up even once. She bites the middle of her thumb as she concentrates. She is engrossed as she meticulously reads the papers. I see her making marks on the papers, perhaps correcting spelling errors. She smiles at times – not a full smile, but the corners of her mouth turn upwards when she is amused. After a while she unties her hair and removes the scrunchie that keeps it in a ponytail. It falls around her face, framing it. She looks incredibly attractive as she scoops up her hair and makes a bun on top of her head in a swift knot, securing it with the scrunchie. She goes back to grading the papers with unbroken concentration. I watch her, almost in a hypnotic trance.

Stop staring.

But I can't. I have to force myself to look away. I don't want her to catch me looking at her this way and I don't want her to think I am a creep.

My eyes, however, move on their own. They keep returning to her. She is the personification of focus and concentration. Suddenly she looks up and for a moment we are looking directly at each other. She looks at me and narrows her eyes a bit. A big, bright glow lights up her face. Like sunshine. For that moment, nothing exists but us, looking at each other. I grin back.

Then I feel the blush creeping up on me and I look down and begin drawing furiously in my book. I don't even know what I am drawing. But when I am done, it *is* an unmistakable likeness of Puja. And I haven't even looked at her once while I have been sketching. It is all a subconscious process for me.

I stare at my sketch, shocked.

Oh, good lord! Help me. This is the last thing I expect to happen in India. I want to vanish off the face of the earth.

I think I am falling for this girl.

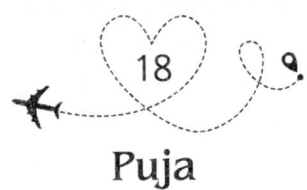

Puja

He is blushing furiously. I *know* that look. I know it. I know it! It is unmistakable. My heart leaps up inside me. *He likes me.* I don't know what to do, so I focus on grading the papers. They are science papers and are easy to grade. Rukmini teacher has given me a guide sheet to compare their answers with, which also has a marking scheme. I never expected to enjoy it this much. The spellings of many of the words are atrocious. The answers that some of the kids have written are so funny. One kid has written 'Sri Ram Sri Ram Sri Ram' about fifty times for a question! He has answered the other questions precisely.

I look up and Arush looks at me again. If he keeps this up, I won't be able to focus on my work. I force myself not to look up anymore.

By lunch time, the class gets over. The children thank me and Rukmini teacher. I have finished grading all the papers. Rukmini teacher is pleased.

'You finished all? That is nice! We break for lunch and then in the afternoon, we have crafts, dance and extra-curricular activities. Morning time is mainly for academics,' she says, speaking Malayalam.

'I enjoyed it,' I say, in the same language, adding, 'Are you joining us for lunch?'

'No. We all live nearby. The kids do as well. They go home for lunch. Many of them have to help with chores at home. Classes begin again only at 3.30 pm, and we have an hour of activity. After that we are done for the day.'

'Why is this not like a regular school? Sorry if I am sounding ignorant. I just don't know how these things work,' I query, apologetically.

'No, that's okay. This is one of the poorest areas in this district and we have the lowest density of population. We do not have the resources for a regular school, nor do we have teachers. If we did not run this programme, none of the children here would be educated. Therefore, a big thanks to all the volunteers who help us,' she says.

The enormity of the work that I am doing sinks in only then. I hadn't thought of it that way. That the work we are doing here, matters enough to make a difference in someone's life.

Rukmini teacher switches back to English when Arush joins us.

'Arush, got any good ideas? Can we see?' she asks.

Arush looks down. Is that a blush I spot creeping up again?

This boy blushes a lot and he looks cute too, when he does that.

'Er… Not yet. I am not ready to share the sketches,' he says.

'No problem! I just asked,' Rukmini teacher says. 'Let's meet at 3.30.' She waves and walks downhill on a rough-cut path which leads to a mud road. This place has many shortcuts, which I have not noticed before.

Arush walks with me and I am extremely conscious of his nearness. I love the fragrance he is wearing. I can feel the warmth of his body. This magnetic energy between us, envelops us, binding us tightly. I *know* he feels it too. I can tell by how silent we both are.

I have a crazy urge to reach out for his hand, but the very thought sounds weird inside my head, making me squish it.

At the dining area, we sit across from each other and we speak at the same time.

'How was—?' he asks.

'Did you—?' I say.

We both pause. And smile.

That smile. It's a killer. He looks so good; he brushes his hair off his forehead. He is wearing a plain white shirt today, and olive-green cotton pants. My eyes travel down his throat, his Adam's apple, and pause at the top of his shirt where the first button is undone. I catch a glimpse of his chest.

I think I have made him conscious now and he quickly buttons up. I find that endearing. Most guys would have thrust out their manly chest proudly. But Arush? He is so *different*. So shy. So quiet. So peculiar. So *sweet*.

'You first,' he says.

'No, you,' I reply.

'I don't remember what I was going to ask you.'

'Liar!'

'I never lie.'

'Never? Are you telling me you have never ever lied, Mr Arush from UK?' I ask.

'In the UK, we have to swear by the Queen to speak the truth, nothing but the truth, the whole truth, the absolute truth and not the relative truth. Not doing so will result in denouement, banishment and we cease to be subjects of Her Royal Majesty,' he says very seriously.

We look at each other for a second and then laugh together. I love hearing his laughter.

My phone rings. My father. Why is he calling me now?

'Excuse me,' I say, as I walk away from Arush to take the call. My father asks me how I am doing and if I am enjoying the stay.

'It is really nice, accha. Initially when I arrived, I didn't like it much. But the work I am doing is really useful to the school and the students. Do you know, they don't have access to proper schools? The things we teach them... that is the only education that they are getting.'

'That's a big responsibility!' says my father.

'It is.'

'I am happy to hear this, Puja. Your mother will be happy.'

Then he asks me if I want anything from home. He is sending Anthony over with some bank forms which he wants me to sign. My grandmother wants to transfer money in my name and she has called him up insisting it is urgent.

'You know how Ammuma is. When she wants something done, she wants it done. She says she won't live for long and that really irritates me.'

I laugh. Ammuma does have a penchant for drama.

'Send the forms, I will sign them.'

'Alright. They will send the welcome kit and the card here. You will be notified on your phone when they send it,' my father says.

'Does that mean I will have my own card and own money?' I ask.

My father laughs. 'Yes, you will. Do you want me to send anything from here?' he asks.

'I do,' I say. I name all the books that Arush had mentioned.

Arush

We are having breakfast together: Sujit, Puja and me. While one part of me is glad that Sujit is a 'buffer' between us, the other part of me wishes I was alone with her. But the thought of being alone with her – even if it is just for breakfast – makes the butterflies in my stomach flutter at dizzying speeds. The more I am with her, the more I like her. She hasn't bothered to tie up her hair today. It's messy and it flies freely around her face. Dressed in loose-fitting deep blue pants, white t-shirt and a checked cotton shirt rolled up at the sleeves with all the buttons open, she looks like a stylish well-dressed hippie, if there exists such a thing. Her earrings – long, circular and dangly, catch the sunlight. The motif – a fairy perched on a crescent moon, is unusual and beautiful. Just like her.

She catches me studying her.

'Hey, pretty earrings,' I compliment her and look away awkwardly.

'Oh, thanks! I stole them from my sister,' she says with a satisfied grin.

'Do you steal her clothes too?' Sujit asks. 'My brother steals all my shirts and it makes me mad.'

'Ha ha! My sister has so many clothes that she doesn't even know when I steal her stuff. I do it all the time,' Puja says.

Mrs Omana walks up to us and announces that Puja has a visitor, Anthony, waiting at the reception.

Puja hurriedly finishes her breakfast and excuses herself. I watch her as she cheerfully scurries off. She has an impatient walk. It is like she can't wait to get to wherever she is headed to.

'What was she like in school?' I ask Sujit.

'You like her, don't you?' he grins.

'Nah, I was just curious,' I say, horrified.

Is it that obvious? Is my face that transparent?

'She was a real time-bomb,' Sujit says.

'Excuse me?' I reply. I don't know what Sujit is implying. That she is hot? An irrational surge of jealousy shoots through me. It is unreasonable and completely uncalled for. I barely know her. It is ridiculous, I admonish myself and yet I find myself waiting for Sujit to clarify.

'She had a volatile temper and everyone was slightly terrified of her. She was also a kind of a rebel – bunked classes, got into trouble for failing tests, etc. She was always being pulled up by the teachers. She seems to have changed now,' he says. 'And hey, I am no one to speak. Back in school, I was an idiot too. You have heard my stories from her.'

'Yeah, we all have our fair share of crazy high school stuff,' I tell him.

Puja comes back and asks us what we were talking about.

'Arush is very interested in getting to know the *real* you,' Sujit declares.

I don't know where to look. I just want the earth to open up and swallow me whole.

But Puja laughs. 'I want to get to know the real Arush too,' she says.

'There's nothing to know. I am an open book. What you see is what you get,' I say.

'People with the most secrets say that. That's what my Ammuma says. There's a proverb in Malayalam *'Minda poocha kalam odikum'*. It means 'the quiet cat breaks the pot',' Puja teases me.

Sujit laughs heartily. 'Yeah this one here is a *minda poocha* for sure.'

'I know you are making fun of me in Malayalam and lying to me about the meaning. I think I should break into Spanish, except that I don't know Spanish,' I reply and they both laugh.

In class once again, Puja and I talk with our eyes. If this keeps going on, I will have no designs for the wall at all. This girl makes me forget everything. I look at what I have drawn and my design is all moon and stars and fairies. Her earrings. It is not a bad design for the classroom wall, but it isn't great either.

I will have to do better. I have the whole of this week to come up with designs, but the distraction is too much. I keep looking at her and she looks up from time to time, and she smiles. Each time she smiles, my heart leaps.

Every. Single. Time.

I want these ridiculous, juvenile reactions to stop, but the heart wants what it wants (Selena Gomez, 2014. I even know all the lyrics to that one). My heart darts in her direction every chance it gets. I am wasting my time and yet enjoying every second that I am wasting. This is foolish, but it is bliss.

When the morning session ends, I approach Rukmini teacher.

'I can help in the classes for the afternoon, if you need help. Till such time I begin painting the wall, I am ideating and I can do that later too,' I offer. (Anything to stop staring at Puja from across the room.)

'Really? That will be very nice. For the afternoon session, we are always looking for extra hands. We want some fun activities,' Rukmini teacher says.

'Leave it to us,' I say and look at Puja.

Puja nods. 'Yes, Arush and I will come up with something fabulous.'

Big mistake. Over lunch she tells me that she has a dance in mind for the kids for the afternoon session. I can't dance to save my life!

'No way,' I tell her.

'Yes way,' she nods assertively.

'How can you do this to me?'

'You offered,' she shrugs.

She knows I can't refuse, yet I protest. 'I never expected you to come up with dancing! Dancing, of all things.'

'You make it sound like I am asking you to murder someone,' she is not willing to give up.

'It's worse! Murdering someone would be easier.'

'Come on, Arush! Stop fussing. These are kids and it is a small dance. You will have fun. You just have to follow my moves,' she declares.

That is how I find myself standing with my fingers joined together and my hands on the top of my head, in front of sixty kids, singing: 'Oh my chi-chi.'

It is a silly song and Puja makes us repeat the words after her. Rukmini teacher joins in too. We have to move our legs back and forth, swivelling on our heels as we sing the song, and that makes us sway from side to side. This is so ridiculous that all of us are laughing.

After the top of the head, the hands move to the shoulder and the same bizarre steps continue. Then they move to the hip, the knee, and finally end (mercifully) at the toes. We are supposed to sing the song at each step and shake our shoulders and butts. The kids are having so much fun with this one.

I have never seen them this delighted. Puja is thoroughly enjoying herself. Her cheeks are flushed and she is radiating happiness.

After the whole ridiculous thing gets over, all the kids scream, '*Yayyyyy!*' and clap their hands. The session is a big success.

'See, I told you, you would enjoy it,' she says, her eyes glowing, a triumphant look on her face.

She has no idea that I enjoyed looking at her moving with carefree abandon, more than I enjoyed the silly dance. She is so in her elements when she works with children. I wonder if she knows it.

After dinner, I lie on my bed and think of my first day of work at Ashwaty Bhawan. All I have done is steal glances at Puja and dance with the kids. Now I *have to* come up with some good ideas. While the brief I have been given is very clear, no ideas come immediately to my head. Since the theme is exploration and discovery, all I can think of are quotes on travel, handwritten in large letters or a huge world map. But the quotes will not work. The kids' level of English isn't advanced enough for them to be able to appreciate the quotes. It has to be something which inspires the kids, is personal and at the same time fits in with the theme.

I have nothing much to show for today's work. For my daily sketches which I have to submit to my college, I open my phone and look at the pictures for inspiration. Puja is in the background in most of the snaps that I have clicked. I zoom into one of the photos and study her face. There's definitely something going on between us here. Something I am unable to give a name to. Calling it 'love' seems so corny. What is love anyway? I barely know her. Yet what I feel for her is nothing like what I have felt for any of the girls before her.

I want to go talk to her, get to know her better, listen to her laugh. I want to spend time with her. I am desperately thinking up any excuse to knock on her door. I wonder what I could come up with to do this. Perhaps I could ask her something about India? But why would this question occur to me at 10 in the night, and why can't I google it? Maybe I could ask to borrow something like she did? But I can't think of a single thing to borrow.

While my brain is busy trashing all the ridiculous excuses that I am coming up with, there's a knock on the door.

And just like that, my wish has come true. Puja stands there, looking incredibly cute in her matching polka-dotted nightwear.

She has a book in her hand. 'Hey. Can I come in? Just wanted to talk about this book.'

She walks in before I say anything.

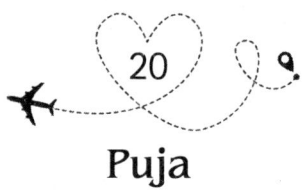

Puja

Arush greets me with a wide grin.

I know he is too shy to knock on my door and so I knock on his. Having just finished *The Time Traveller's Wife*, one of the books he spoke about, I am eager to discuss it. The last four hours that I have spent reading this magnificent story of love, have been enthralling, engrossing, exciting. This one has made me *want* to read. Who would have imagined!

I walk in without waiting for him to invite me in.

'Welcome, Miss *Minda Poocha*,' says Arush as I walk past. He pronounces it with such a heavy British accent that it takes me a few seconds to figure out what he just said. Then the penny drops and I laugh.

'What? Haven't I got it right? Have I called you something else by mistake?' he asks.

'Yes, you just abused my mother in Malayalam,' I gravely remark.

'Come on! I am not falling for that one. While you were gone, I made Sujit teach me the phrase. I practised.'

'Full marks for the bright boy. You did get it right.' I smile as I settle down on his bed.

It is strange how comfortable I feel now, around him.

'I *loved* this book,' I say, holding out the book.

'Oh! Have you finished it already? Is that what you were doing the whole evening? I wondered where you had disappeared.'

He noticed that I had vanished. For some reason, I am very pleased about this.

The long discussion that follows – of what love truly is, and whether age matters in love, whether love can last forever – is heady and refreshing.

Surprisingly, Arush's views are *not* idealistic. He says that love lasts forever only in novels and books.

'Like Nicholas Sparks' *Notebook*,' he remarks.

'I am yet to read that one, but I have it and will get to it soon.'

'What? How do you have all those books? Is there a library close by?' He is baffled.

'Ha, no! I got my parents to send all the ones you recommended.'

'You have an outstanding memory!'

The admiration in his voice makes me glow.

'My mother is pleased that I am reading. She has been after me to read. It maddens her when I tell her that I have watched the movies.' I grin.

'Ha ha! My mother doesn't bother with anything I do. But both my parents can't get why I chose art over any other 'respectable' professions,' he says. 'They think one can't make money with art.'

'What are the career options you have?' I am curious now.

He says that he can be an illustrator at an ad agency, or he can work in publishing, or he can work for a greeting card company. He says he has many options. He seems to have carefully thought about it.

'I may not make as much as a banker or a lawyer, but that is the price you pay for following your dream,' he says.

'Come on. You can't decide that following your dream can't bring money,' I say. Then I tell him about my father. I narrate the story I have heard many times – about how my father ran away from home at the age of thirteen to Madras (it was Madras back then) and how he apprenticed at a garage, doing whatever they told him to do. He started his own automobile service centre at the age of twenty-three. It was different from anything that was in the market. He standardised a lot of stuff and for the first time, there was transparency in this business. Cars got repaired while customers waited. He introduced waiting lounges with coffee and refreshments, and reading material. Business expanded. He established his brand name and then sold the chain for a very large sum to a big automobile company looking to diversify.

He started another business after that – exporting shrimps, sourcing them directly from fishermen. That was successful as well and he sold that business too. I tell Arush how he now wants to help small farmers grow organic stuff and is starting a company so that they are able to get very good prices for their produce.

'You see, following your dream and making money are not two mutually exclusive things. It is not an either-or. You can have both,' I explain. Arush listens intently.

'Wow! That is incredibly inspiring. Your father is a business tycoon. You must be wealthy then?' Arush asks.

I know that I have a trust fund which will come to me at the age of twenty-five. I had once overheard my father tell this to my mother. But I don't tell Arush this.

'I think it is my father who is wealthy, not me,' I say. 'While my father always says that it is only money that brings you respect, he also emphasises on good education. For him, it was a huge personal victory when my mother – a highly educated doctor – agreed to marry him. He jokes that his father-in-law was so impressed by his business acumen that he didn't look at anything else. But he always feels that though he is successful, he lacks education. Therefore, he is very keen for both his daughters to be very well educated. I have extra pressure on the academic front,' I say.

These are things that I have never told my friends. Yet, here I am, telling Arush all of this. There's something about him that makes me open up like never before.

Arush nods.

'I understand,' he says.

And I know he does.

Like no one else.

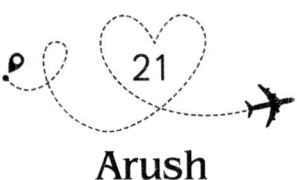

Arush

It has become a routine now. Every night after dinner, I wait for Puja to knock on my door. We talk late into the night. We're constantly sleep deprived. We never run out of things to talk about. We have been doing this for weeks, yet we can't get enough.

It is flattering that she has been diligent about reading all the books I recommended. The insights she offers are very different from the way I see it. She promptly disappears after class ends and turns up for dinner. In two hours, she knocks on my door. I finish my drawings for the day before she arrives.

I have also started washing my face, brushing my hair lightly and splashing on a bit of aftershave just before she comes.

If Puja notices these efforts, she doesn't comment on them at all. We go into detail about the characters. About love. About life. About the dreams of the characters and their actions. Then the conversation meanders to our dreams, our hopes, our lives.

'You are lucky that you have figured out what you are passionate about. I don't know what I want to do,' she says during one of these discussions.

'I have seen how much you enjoy working with kids. Maybe something on those lines?' I suggest.

'That's a thought. But with my current degree? A BBM? It's a completely different line,' she muses.

We talk about marriage.

'Marriage isn't everything, and having babies isn't everything,' Puja has a fierce look as she says it. I want to reach out and hug her.

But I don't have the courage. I don't want her to think of me as weird, or worse, desperate. I do nothing even though every cell in my body is aching to touch her, hold her, hug her.

'You know I love our talks,' she says, as she leans back on the bed, propping my pillow against the wall.

'Me too,' I confess.

Puja's eyes dance when she speaks. She moves her hands, makes sweeping gestures as she emphasises what she feels strongly about. When she doesn't like something, she turns up her nose.

'I haven't had this kind of connection with anyone. I mean *anyone*. Isn't that something?' she admits frankly.

I am slowly getting used to her candidness and the way her eyes bore into mine. This girl doesn't hesitate to speak her mind.

'It definitely is,' I admit.

The last few weeks have flown by at a frantic pace. Puja and I are spiralling into a tightly-knit closeness. Like we're a couple. We haven't talked about it at all. But I know there's something. She knows there is something. She leaves my room by about 1 am or sometimes 2 am. We wake up by 8 am and rush to breakfast. After that the day starts.

At breakfast one morning, Sujit brings up the idea of a trek.

'It's an off tomorrow because there's a local festival. I was just thinking that there are these fabulous caves nearby, called Edakkal caves. I think we should explore them. What do you guys say?'

Arush and I exchange a look. But neither of us mention to Sujit that we had discussed it and we wanted to go.

'I would love to,' says Arush and I nod in agreement.

Leah and Oshan want to join in too. Mrs Omana tells us that we have all been working hard, we have earned the break and she also recommends a local travel service.

In no time, Sujit has organised a five-seater vehicle, made an itinerary and announced that we will leave at 7.30 am.

That night, once Puja comes over and we have talked for a bit, I tell her, 'Look, we'd better sleep early as we have an early start tomorrow.'

But Puja is in no mood to end the conversation or leave.

'Come on, Arush! You don't have to be an old man. I am sure we will wake up on time.'

We sit next to each other, our shoulders touching. I don't know what comes over me, but I tap her nose. 'You always have to get your way, don't you?' I ask.

She is speechless – but only for a moment. She quickly recovers.

And then she taps my nose right back!

'Yes!' she grins. 'Any problems?'

'None, none at all,' I reply and we grin at each other.

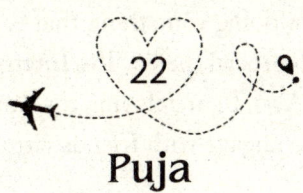

22

Puja

The trek is magnificent! I silently thank the dorky blogger for the secret tips.

'I came across an India travel forum and they mentioned a fabulous trekking route to get to the ticket counter before we climb up to the caves. Anyone game?' Arush asks. What a clever way to tell the others about 'our' trekking route!

Oshan and Leah prefer to take the straight route. But Sujit is gung-ho for our idea.

We begin our trek exactly at the spot that the blogger has suggested. The climb is steep and my backpack isn't making it any easier. Arush offers to carry it, but I refuse. He is already carrying a bag with heavy water bottles.

I have a rolled-up foldable mat and some sandwiches in my backpack which Mrs Omana got the staff to pack for us. I am panting and can barely speak.

'Bro, these mountains are something else!' Sujit exclaims as we trudge on and reach a plateau from where we have a bird's eye view of the miles and miles of greenery. The bright blue skies, the deep blue-green of the mountains stretching endlessly before us makes me gasp in delight. The climb is worth the view. This is totally Instagram worthy. But the strangest thing is I have lost interest in social media, ever since I started volunteering here. For the first time in my life, I feel I am doing something that is satisfying and I find no need to share it on social media. The Internet being choppy has contributed to this. Also, I am enjoying my time here so much that I can't be bothered to engage with friends virtually.

'It looks like someone has unrolled a celestial carpet of green on these hills,' I say in awe, as I plop down on the ground.

'Puja, you look exhausted. Let's take a break,' Arush suggests and I am relieved.

We unroll the mat from the backpack and polish off the cucumber and tomato sandwiches. We wash it down with tetra packs of orange juice.

Arush carefully gathers all the paper plates, the empty juice cartons, and packs them neatly in the brown paper bags in which the sandwiches were wrapped. He then tucks them into the backpack.

'The plastic ban is terrible. We can't even carry garbage covers,' Sujit comments watching Arush.

'Come on, Sujit! The plastic ban is surely a good thing. A country like India generates 1.5 lakh metric tonnes of garbage daily and that is awful. Eighty percent of it is just dumped in landfill sites,' I tell him. I had done a project on waste management last year at college and was shocked at the discovery. Now I have a chance to show off my knowledge. Arush looks impressed.

'Wow. That much?' he asks.

I nod.

'Whatever!' shrugs Sujit.

'It's not *whatever*. It is because people like us, who have the resources and education, are indifferent, that this problem still exists,' I reply. I am not willing to let it go and Sujit's casual attitude irks me.

Sujit sees I am getting annoyed and offers a truce.

'Alright, I take it back. It is an important issue,' he says. 'Let me carry the backpack now. You have carried it for a while now and it is my turn.'

My back is hurting with all the weight I have been lugging up. I am also sweating and panting as the trek is getting harder. Gladly, I give it to Sujit.

We climb on. The mountainous paths are narrow and tricky. The boys are much ahead of me. I struggle to keep up. But I love how Arush keeps glancing back to see if I am okay. Arush stops from time to time till I catch up, but Sujit doesn't even glance back. He treks on. On a particularly steep climb, Arush holds out his hand.

'Come on!' he says.

I look at him and I take his hand. He grips mine and *boom*! I feel a mini-explosion inside me. The air sizzles with electricity between us. His grip is strong, yet gentle. Firm, yet soft.

And now my hands smell of his aftershave, a spicy masculine fragrance. It drives me insane. It makes me want to reach out and grab his hands again. My insides are twisting up with desire for him.

Sujit is far ahead of us now and I can't see him. We trek in silence.

At the next climb, Arush once again holds out his hand to pull me up. And this time he doesn't let go. He gently pulls me towards him. I am facing him now. We don't need any words. The energy between us is charged. Everything I feel is heightened, magnified in that moment, and my life feels perfect. My heartbeats are frantic. I lean in towards his face and bury my head in his neck. His arms go around me. He holds me tenderly and we stand still for a while. Is it a minute? Or a few seconds? I don't know. All I know is that this feels like the safest place in the world. I don't want this hug to stop. I know at that moment that I am in love with him. This isn't just desire.

He pulls away to look into my eyes.

His eyes seek permission. Whether it is okay. Whether I am okay. His eyes are aflame. Yet anxious.

I lean in towards him and my lips brush against his.

Nothing matters in this moment except his lips on mine. His kisses are soft at first. Gentle. Like butterflies touching my lips. He tastes sweet. So sweet. He barely grazes my lips. And then he kisses me again, barely touching. Like I am a china doll and he is afraid of hurting me. I have been kissed before, but never like this. With so much tenderness.

In response, I pull him towards me and kiss him. Strongly, fiercely.

He is a little surprised. Then his arms go around my waist.

We can't stop kissing and if we don't stop, I don't know where it will lead.

I am burning for him.

This guy makes me want to throw caution to the winds. He makes me feel alive.

We kiss for a long time. He is in no hurry. His hands do not leave my waist. He makes no attempts to fiddle with my shirt buttons or slide his hands underneath, which is what almost all (numbering to a grand total of three, including one drunken kiss) the boys I have kissed before have done. But Arush is different.

We break away and look at each other.

Then we kiss again.

All the words of the past few weeks have dried up now. We don't need to say anything.

Our actions have said it all.

I draw in a deep breath.

'We,' I plant a kiss on his lips.

'Should,' another kiss.

'Stop,' I say.

'I can stand here and kiss you forever,' he whispers.

I look into his eyes and melt into them. They are the sincerest and most beautiful eyes I have ever seen.

'We should go,' I say, even though very single cell in my body protests. My body, my lips, all of me craves for his kisses.

He holds my hand and says, 'Yes, we should. We can't... you know...'

He glances at the trekking path.

'I know. We can't possibly do it here,' I tell him.

And I watch him blush furiously.

A large smile forms on my face and I cannot stop smiling for the rest of the trek.

Arush

Through the rest of the trek, all I am aware of is her presence. Sujit has vanished from sight (bless him!) and it is just the two of us. We hold hands till we reach the ticket counter. It feels warm and wonderful, her hand in mine. How I love holding them. As we approach the ticket counter in the distance, we spot Sujit waving to us. It is only then that she pulls her hand away from mine.

'Ah, there you are! I was wondering if you got lost,' Sujit grins as we approach. Leah and Oshan are waiting too. 'We got the tickets, let's go,' he says. All of us follow him.

We ascend the numerous steps slowly. At certain places we have to climb down. After a few arduous ups and downs, we reach the etchings. The six thousand-year-old etchings in the caves are awe-inspiring. This feels like a dream now. As though I have split into two. The real part is hovering around Puja, while the other soaks in the surroundings, the splendour of the caves and the engravings. It takes us about an hour and a half to see all the caves.

Leah and Oshan are wonderstruck, but Sujit doesn't look too impressed. Puja and I stick close, stealing glances at each other. When her eyes meet mine, she smiles and looks away. The others don't notice.

After we finish the caves, we head to the Wayanad Heritage Museum, one of the largest and best archaeological museums in

Kerala. Housed in a traditional-looking old building, the museum is nothing like I have seen before. The architecture is fascinating. The objects on display date back to the Neolithic Age, as well as the 12th and 16th centuries.

I notice that Puja isn't very interested in these. She barely glances through the displays. The pictorial rock edicts, 'Hero stones', that have been erected on the tombs of warriors to commemorate their gallant deeds interest me a great deal. I study them even though I cannot make out the script. The other displays that catch my attention include tribal artefacts, farming implements, clay sculptures and stone idols, exhibited neatly in glass cases, with information about them. I click a lot of photographs to make sketches from.

I can't help musing on how rich Indian history is, and how the British altered India. Having studied it extensively from the British viewpoint, these displays now make me think from the Indian perspective. The British claim they did a lot for India. They built railways, constructed buildings and gave governance to the otherwise disorganised princely states which fought among themselves. According to the British, India was its 'colony'. But how can you colonise an entire culture?

If the British hadn't conquered India, would Puja and I have been able to even communicate? Would we have fallen in love then? What a strange thing, that something which happened so many years ago impacts who we form connections with today.

I am deeply contemplating this, when I feel Puja's arm on my back. She gently rubs my back in soft circular motions. I turn back and see that we are alone in an empty room. I can't resist quickly kissing her. Just a brief peck on the lips. I can't believe I have done that impulsively.

Her reaction is delightful. Her eyes widen in surprise. She inhales sharply and looks around. When she sees that we are alone, she kisses me back – an urgent frantic kiss. Then she admonishes me.

'Enough! We must stop this! This is madness. Anyone could have walked in,' she hisses. I smile and follow her, grinning like a Cheshire cat.

When we finish the museum, Leah, Oshan and Sujit are nowhere to be seen. We wait in the car.

'Where do you think they vanished?' Puja asks.

I shrug.

The driver tells us that there is a multimedia theatre in the adjacent building where they offer a show for tourists.

'A live show? Are there performers?' I ask.

He doesn't understand my question and Puja translates it into Malayalam. I learn that it is not actually a live show the way I imagined it would be. A CD would be played taking us through the history of the museum.

We have no choice but to wait.

'This is annoying,' says Puja. 'How can they just vanish like that?' The shape of her lips changes when she is angry and they form a rigid straight line.

When she sees me studying her, she smiles and that transforms her face instantly. Puja is an animation motion picture come alive, an absolute delight to watch.

'It's okay!' I tell her. I ask her if she wants to look around to see whether there are any shops in the vicinity, in case she is hungry. But she says it is too hot and that she prefers to wait in the car.

Leah, Oshan and Sujit emerge after forty minutes.

'Sorry guys, we got a little held up,' says Sujit.

Leah and Oshan look very content and happy. 'Boy, was it worth it,' Oshan remarks.

'Did you watch the movie?' Puja asks.

'What movie?' Sujit replies.

'The multimedia show?'

'Yes – yes, of course,' he says. 'It was good.'

When we get back to the centre, Mrs Omana greets us with some hot vadas and coffee.

'How was it?' she asks.

'It was magnificent. We also went to the museum,' Leah tells her.

'Oh, I see. I think only people from other countries go there. None of the locals visit the museum. I had even forgotten about it,' Mrs Omana remarks.

'It is a rich history. It is well preserved. In the UK, tickets would have been a lot more expensive. Here, they hardly charge anything,' I tell her.

'It has to be cheap to make it affordable to the common people,' she replies.

'Who don't go,' Sujit quips and everyone laughs.

'You all must be tired. Go and freshen up and we will meet for dinner. Tomorrow is a working day,' Mrs Omana reminds us.

Sujit groans. Leah and Oshan simply nod.

Suddenly something clicks in my head. My senses are on a visual overload from the day's happenings. The visit to the museum has sparked off a splendid idea. I know what to design for the mural on the wall. It is the perfect thing. I can't wait to go to the room and start sketching!

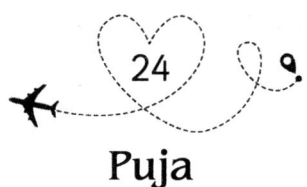

Puja

Arush… Arush… Arush. All I can think of is him. His anxious deep eyes, his tall frame, his hands around my waist. I lie on the bed dreamily, lost in thoughts of him. I thought I had been in love before, but whatever I felt back then pales in comparison with the intensity of this one. The pull I feel towards him is the combined force of a thousand hurricanes. I am swept away.

One part of me wants to rush into his room, hug him and hold him. But the other part of me is a little worried about the intensity of this – this thing between us. Also, I am sweaty, dirty and tired from the trek. I need a bath. I take my time having a bath, brushing my damp hair and then choosing what to wear. I now wish I had brought some nicer clothes rather than throwing in whatever just came to hand. I put on some light make up and then step out to meet everyone for dinner.

Arush, with his back turned to me, is talking to Leah and Oshan. I stand there staring at his back, listening to him speak in his British accent, telling them about how impressed he was with the museum collection. I can listen to him forever. He has made an extra effort with his clothes too. I glance approvingly at his fitted, half-sleeved denim shirt (sleeves rolled up), black pants and casual canvas shoes.

When he turns around and spots me, his eyes shine like beacons. He excuses himself to join me. During dinner, our eyes feast on each other rather than the food. Sujit is nowhere to be seen. Mrs Omana informs us that his dinner has been served in his room as he is unwell.

Since Leah and Oshan eat by themselves, I consider it a stroke of luck that it is just me and Arush now, sitting across from each other.

'So...' says Arush, as he smiles at me.

'So...' I echo, smiling back, gazing into his eyes.

'This feels surreal. All we need is a candle to complete this romantic, cheesy scene, right out of a movie,' I find myself saying. I have never been self-conscious before, but the way Arush looks at me churns up my insides, setting me ablaze.

His aftershave which I can get a whiff of, the same one from the morning, is driving me crazy.

'Nah, we don't need any candles. This is romantic enough,' he says.

I desperately try to think of topics to talk about. My mind blanks out. Words vanish from my head.

'Which is your favourite romantic movie?' Arush asks, breaking the silence that has crept up between us.

'I don't have any. All romantic movies suck,' I say.

'Then you haven't seen the right ones,' he replies.

'Which is yours?' I ask him.

'Hard to choose one. *Eternal Sunshine of the Spotless Mind, Before Sunset* which is actually a sequel to *Before Sunrise,* and *Brokeback Mountain* immediately come to mind.'

'I haven't watched any of those,' I confess.

'Told you, you haven't watched the right ones,' he smirks.

I furiously make mental notes but he catches on immediately.

'Memorising them?' he raises his eyebrows and grins.

'Yeah, I have to keep up with you,' I grin back.

He knows me so well by now, I am surprised. It is only a few days since we met, but it feels like I have known him for a long time.

'Coming to my room later tonight?' he whispers.

'I always do, don't I? What's special today?' I ask innocently.

'You know what's special,' he says in a low voice and immediately blushes.

If there's an award for blushing, Arush should win it. But it would have to be combined with an award for cuteness.

Later, when I knock on his door, I shiver in excitement. He opens the door for me. Every nerve in my body is charged with the anticipation of what is to come. I am giddy. I am nervous. I am delirious. The whole room glows softly from the light from his desk lamp. The music he is playing today is bewitching – gentle, comforting, sensual.

'What music is that?' I ask, as I enter the room. He shuts the door.

'Oh, this is Miles Davis. He plays some beautiful jazz,' he says.

I expect him to draw me into his arms and start kissing me. I am so prepared for that. But Arush doesn't do anything of the sort. Instead he says, 'You know what, there's something I want to show you. Our visit to the museum today gave me a brilliant idea for the wall mural. I made some sketches. I want you to tell me what you think of them.'

He takes out his sketchbook and shows me about ten pages of detailed sketches he has made. The last one is fully in colour.

'*Wow!*' I almost scream in delight. The sketches he has made are exemplary. This is easily some of his best work. I am somewhat of an expert on his art now as I have seen a lot of his work. This one is outstanding. He has sketched a long Indian train with compartments, painted in striped blue. From each window of the train, a child peeps out. They all have different expressions. One has wonder, one has joy, one has surprise, then there's disgust and contentment – the facial expressions hc has captured arc perfect.

'Are any of these kids from the class?' I ask.

'No,' he says. 'It would be unfair to draw some children and leave out the others, they would feel bad.'

This is something that would have never occurred to me. Arush is gentle, kind, sensitive, even towards people he hardly knows. He is the type of person who cares about the tiniest of things like this. It endears him to me all the more.

'Do you like it?' he asks

'It is brilliant. Just perfect. It fits with the brief given. There's travel, exploration and excitement. You have done a great job!'

'It's a lot like life, isn't it? We are all travellers on the train of life. And for a while, we travel together,' he says.

'We have to make the journey worthwhile,' I reply and pull him towards me as I reach out for a kiss. 'Come here,' I say.

'You can't wait, can you?' he grins.

Then he kisses me. The same butterfly kisses that drove me insane earlier during the day. My arms go around him.

Suddenly there's very loud, urgent, frantic knocking on the door. We jump apart, startled.

'What the hell?' Arush exclaims.

The knocks grow louder, more insistent. Like whoever is outside is about to break the door down.

He rushes to the door and opens it.

'Is Puja here?' asks Mrs Omana. She sounds angry. Enraged. Furious. She is yelling. She has been nothing but gentle till now.

I am stunned.

'Yes, what's happening?' Arush sounding worried and nervous, mirrors my confusion.

'Tell her to come out immediately. I knew that we would probably find her here,' Mrs Omana thunders.

Dread rises in me. The tone of voice – the disapproving voice of authority – is a voice I am familiar with. I have been in trouble many times before to know this tone well.

Maybe there are rules against being in a boy's room? But I wasn't told anything. There is nothing wrong in being in another person's room. We're both consenting adults. All these thoughts rush into my head at the same time.

But nothing prepares me for what I see when I go to the door: Mrs Omana, her face black with rage, two policemen and a policewoman dressed in a khaki saree.

'Are you Puja?' the policewoman asks.

'Yes,' I reply.

'You are under arrest. You have to come to the station with us. You are charged with possession of ganja, a punishable offence under the Indian Narcotics Act,' she states.

'What?!' Arush exclaims and looks at me.

I am too shocked to speak.

'I never… I don't…' I say.

She holds out a bag.

'Is this bag yours?' she asks

It is my backpack which Sujit had carried on the trek.

'Yes, but…'

She doesn't let me complete.

'You have to come with us. You can give all explanations at the station,' she says, as she grabs my arm and leads me away.

'Mrs Omana, this bag – it is mine, but I had given it to Sujit to carry. Where did you find it?'

Mrs Omana's face is a fireball. Her eyes blaze in anger. 'This is most disgraceful, Puja! The police conducting a raid on our premises – it has never happened before. Sujit says he has nothing to do with it and he doesn't know anything. The bag was hidden in the bushes. Who is lying here?' she asks.

'That's for us to decide, madam. Make way,' says the policewoman, tightly gripping my hand.

Her rough hands squeeze my arm and it hurts. Tears cloud my eyes.

'I am innocent…' I protest. I want to call my parents.

But no one is listening to me.

'We need to search your room too,' one of the policemen tells Arush.

Arush steps aside. They enter the room, opening every drawer, handling his art materials and worst, his sketchbook, with absolutely no care. They fling it aside carelessly. Arush stands there, not saying a word. I think he is as distressed as I am. I wince. The policewoman's grip is too tight.

'Nothing here. Let's go,' says one of the policemen.

The last thing I see from the police jeep is Arush's pale face, drained of colour, as they drive me to the police station in the middle of the night.

Chaitra

It is when I am rushing to the hospital for a cardiac emergency that the call comes. I frown at the unknown landline number, nevertheless I answer it.

'Dr Chaitra Krishnan, I am sorry to call at this time. Your daughter has been arrested. The police have taken her to the Vythiri police station. She was in a boy's room,' a woman says.

For a few seconds, nothing registers and I wonder if the caller is drunk. From what the Emergency doctor had described earlier, it appears that my patient could have pulmonary embolism and I don't know if he will make it. I have to get to the hospital as fast as I can and Anthony who is driving me there, knows this. It's not the first time I have been on a call for an emergency. In times like this, I completely switch off from my family. I forget about my husband, my daughters. Nothing exists but my patient. Therefore, it is particularly hard for me to even comprehend what is being said.

'Who is speaking? And why has Divya been arrested? She is travelling on work and is in Mumbai. Is this a joke?' I ask after a couple of seconds.

'Dr Chaitra, it is no joke. I am Mrs Omana. Your daughter Puja is in the police station.'

'What? Puja? What boy? Why should the police arrest her?' I ask.

'I have done my duty and informed you, madam. Her behaviour is disgusting and unacceptable. When I took her in on the high recommendation of her college, I did not know she had this dirty habit. The media is here and are asking me questions. It will be all over the papers tomorrow,' Mrs Omana says, all in one breath.

My head spins. But I have to focus. My patient needs me. I make a phone call to Krishnan. From his voice I can make out that he has just about fallen asleep.

'Mrs Omana called. Apparently, Puja has been arrested. Something about her being with a boy. I don't know the details. Find out. I am just entering the hospital,' I issue crisp instructions just as Anthony pulls into the porch of the Emergency section.

'Oh! What? How?' asks Krishnan.

'I don't know,' I say as I rush in. I have to save my patient.

Whatever Puja has done this time, can wait.

She will still be alive at the end of this ordeal. My patient, however, may not make it and it is all up to me.

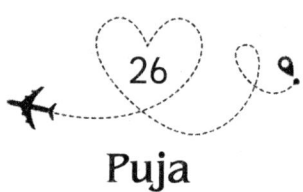

Puja

On the way I throw up all over. The travel sickness, the fear, anxiety, shock, all line up and attack me at the same time. The policewoman asks me how much I have drunk.

'I have travel sickness,' I say. She tells me not to lie. Some of the puke is on my t-shirt and shorts, and some of it is in my hair too. The policewoman darts a look of disgust at me, like I am a worm. I am too distraught to feel ashamed.

At the station, they pat me down and make me blow into a breathalyser. The ride here has been a nightmare. Though it is a warm night, I shiver. The police station is dingy, airless, with files and stacks of papers piled high against the walls and in corners. I cannot believe this is happening

'Am I not allowed a phone call?' I ask. I have seen that in the movies.

'Eh? Phone call? She wants to make a phone call,' says the policewoman who brought me here. The others laugh. 'Your parents have been informed,' she says.

She doesn't let go of my hand and marches me to a cell, the female lock-up, where a few women are squatting, leaning against the wall. It smells of urine and desperation. It is a metal cage, the only source of light being a small, dim, naked bulb that glows outside the cell. She pushes me inside roughly. I stumble and nearly fall, my eyes adjusting to the darkness.

I jump up in fright. I have just tripped over a woman who is lying on her side fast asleep, using her arm as a pillow. She screams an obscenity.

My hands shake.

My mouth is dry.

My breath is shallow.

I tremble. Everything is a haze.

My teeth chatter as I sit on the cold hard floor of the police lock-up room. I cannot believe I have been locked up with prostitutes. They call out to me and ask me what I have done. One of them welcomes me and asks if I am scared. The other one says that I seem to be from a good family, and I will be lucky if my parents reach me fast. Else she says, I have to pray for my safety. 'Hope the heavens don't desert you,' she laughs.

I have never been this petrified in my life.

I clench my hands into fists and shut my eyes. I have never prayed before, but I pray now. I don't even know how to pray. Please god, please god, please universe, get me out of here, get me out of here. I repeat over and over in my head.

I don't know how many hours pass.

There's no way to tell.

Then I hear a voice. A voice I have grown so used to in the last few days that I can recognise it even in my sleep. For a few seconds, I wonder if my mind is playing tricks on me.

I listen. I am not imagining it. It *is* Arush.

I hear him talking to the policeman. I can't see him, but his voice carries over clearly.

'I don't know English,' the policeman says in Malayalam.

Arush repeats himself slowly. 'My friend Puja is inside. I want to meet her.'

'No visitors,' he says.

I don't want Arush to see me like this. I am a mess. I want him to go away. But he doesn't give up. I hear him arguing with the policeman, telling him I am innocent. He speaks fast when he is upset, and the policeman doesn't understand a word. Even I don't get what he is saying; his accent is thick and strong. I catch only a few words: release, unfair, innocent.

Mostly, what I hear is panic, frustration and anger in his voice.

Then I hear another person. Another very familiar voice.

My father. *My father is here.*

That is when I start crying.

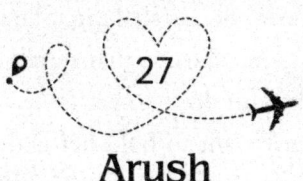

Arush

As soon as I see him, I know he is Puja's dad. Tall and confident, he walks in with an air of authority like he owns the place. He sports the air of a man who knows how to get things done. With him is another person, a well-dressed gentleman with grey hair. His neatly tucked-in white shirt, black trousers and polished black shoes indicate someone who is meticulous, thorough.

'Sir, hello. I am Arush, Puja's friend. I have been trying to ask them to let Puja out,' I say to Puja's father. He barely looks at me, cursorily nods. When he walks up to the policeman and introduces himself, the policeman stands up, his entire demeanour changing to that of respect.

'Oh, sir, I did not know she was your daughter! She didn't tell us. I had no idea.'

Puja's father is in complete control. But from where I stand, I see a nerve throbbing on the side of his head. His hands are clenched too, but the policeman doesn't know this. The person accompanying him, he introduces as his lawyer. The lawyer asks them what evidence they have against Puja, and asks to see the paperwork and the charges.

Puja's father asks if it has leaked to the press.

'Yes, it's too late to stop them. It was a big haul,' says the policeman, his tone apologetic.

In less than ten minutes, Puja is out. Her hair is a tangled mess. I can see the puke on her t-shirt and her shoes. There are dark smudges around her eyes. She is shaking. She is crying too. Of all the things that occur to me, the one that stands out in that moment is that she still looks beautiful.

I want to hug her. I want to hold her and tell her that things will be fine. Mostly, I am just relieved to see her. But Puja doesn't acknowledge my presence or meet my eye. Her head hangs down.

We haven't done anything wrong, I want to scream. I am here for you, I want to tell her. But I just stand there dumb, my hands hanging by my side.

Her father doesn't hug her.

'Get in the car. Let's go to the centre. I want this sorted out,' he says.

Then he remembers me. 'Do you want a ride? How did you come here?' he asks me.

'I... I took a cab,' I tell him. 'It's waiting.'

'Alright,' he says and marches out along with the lawyer. Puja follows them like a little puppy. My heart goes out to her.

I rush back to the cab. It had been difficult for me to get the driver John to come, after having got his number from Mrs Omana. I had called him at least twenty times – till he picked up.

As I get into the car, he asks me, 'Her father?'

'Yes, thank goodness.'

'Where to now?' he asks.

'Of course, back to Ashwaty Bhawan,' I say.

John follows Puja's father's car. I see Puja in the backseat with her father. The lawyer is seated in front. It is already daylight and the bright orange skies rush past us as we speed along. There is so much I want to tell Puja, but there is nothing I can do to reach her, even though she is so close.

As soon as we reach Ashwaty Bhawan, Mrs Omana comes out and greets us.

'Hello Mr Krishnan. I am glad you are here,' she says.

'How could you let this happen? My daughter is innocent,' Puja's father says. He is in no mood for small talk and doesn't return her greeting. He hasn't raised his voice, but the controlled manner in which he speaks and the way he looks at Mrs Omana shows that he is not a man who will let this go easily.

'Come, let's have coffee. We can talk about it,' Mrs Omana says. 'Meanwhile, Puja, you can go and get washed and changed.'

Then she spots me.

'Arush, have you had your coffee?' she asks.

Coffee is the last thing on my mind. I see Puja walking off towards the building where our rooms are located.

'No, thank you!' I rush after Puja.

'Puja, wait…' I call out as I near her.

'Please Arush, give me some time,' she says as she hurries to her room and shuts the door.

There's nothing for me to do but wait for her. I go to my room and lie on the bed. I start thinking about the crazy, bizarre events that have just occurred.

After a few minutes, I head towards the bathroom and brush my teeth.

I hang around outside, in the corridors, waiting. When Puja emerges from the bathrooms, her wet hair is combed and her face looks clean-scrubbed, but pale.

I rush towards her.

'Oh, Puja! You have no idea how worried I was,' I say.

'Me too. Sorry I couldn't speak to you earlier. I… I just wanted to clean up and…'

'No, it's fine. I understand. I can't tell you how helpless I felt,' I confess.

'It meant a lot to me that you came.' Her voice is soft, almost a whisper, full of pain.

'How could I not? How can they take you away like that? The Indian system is so fucked up,' I say. 'I was so angry with those policemen, but showing my anger wouldn't have helped.'

'I know, they won't listen to you. I could hear you from inside the lock-up... I... I just couldn't talk. You have no idea.' Puja is barely able to speak; her voice is breaking as she says the words.

'I was so scared they would hurt you,' I say.

'I was scared too, Arush... I was terrified. It was terrible. Just terrible...' She starts crying softly.

I can't bear to see her like this. I have no words. I step closer to her and then I hug her. I feel her body stiffen, but she makes no attempt to break away. I continue holding her. Then she slowly relaxes.

I feel each breath of hers.

I feel her heartbeats.

I feel her fear.

I feel her tiredness.

I feel her confusion.

I feel her relief.

Above all, I also *feel* her love.

At that moment, all I want to do is protect this girl. Forever. I want to tell her that I love her. But a little voice chimes in my head, 'How can you love someone knowing them for just a few days?' I am also not sure if this is the time or place for this.

So, I just kiss her forehead and tell her, 'Listen, it's going to be fine. Be strong.'

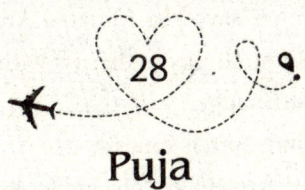

Puja

'Thank you,' I murmur as we hug. Something big has transpired between us just now. Something that was never there before. Like we have crossed a line and there is no going back. I can *feel* his love for me. He doesn't have to say anything. There's a new level of intimacy between us. I am certain of his feelings and mine towards him.

I pull away from him. The last thing I want is someone walking in on us hugging. As it is, Mrs Omana seems to think that me being in his room is a big crime.

'Shhh… no thanks needed.'

He looks at me with such tenderness, I feel a fresh wave of tears coming up.

I am crying now. Again.

'It's okay, it's over,' he gently pats my head.

He walks with me to the reception area where my father and our lawyer, Unni uncle, are seated. I have known Unni uncle since childhood. He is my father's classmate and one of his closest friends. He is also one of the sharpest lawyers in Kerala. With both of them and Arush by my side, I feel protected, safe. Since I have bathed and changed into fresh clothes, I am not as frightened as I was before. It is funny how small things like being clean and wearing good clothes help in boosting your morale.

'Come Puja, join us,' says Mrs Omana. 'Arush, you can go to the dining area. I have some things to discuss with Mr Krishnan.'

But Arush doesn't budge.

'I have some things to tell you, sir.'

I have never seen Arush like this. He looks determined. His jaw is set, his fists are clenched. Gone is the shy, blushing Arush. The person I see before me is a person who wants to be heard. A person ready to fight.

For me.

My heart goes out to him.

'Look Arush, whatever you have to tell, you can tell him later,' Mrs Omana is dismissive. But Arush is having none of it.

'No. I want to say this and after I am done, I will leave you guys to your meeting,' he says. He doesn't wait for Mrs Omana to respond. 'Puja was with me for the entire duration of the trek. She gave her backpack to Sujit. He was the one who carried it and it is obvious that he put the substance in it. There's no way Puja could have done it. I am witness to this and I am willing to testify in court or whatever legal system India has,' Arush declares.

A stunned silence envelops the room. Mrs Omana opens her mouth and closes it without saying anything.

After what feels like a few minutes (in reality probably a few seconds), my father takes charge of the situation. 'Thank you for telling me this. Also thank you for coming to the station.'

I look at Arush and mouth, 'I will see you outside.'

Arush is still reluctant to leave.

But I nod and convey with my eyes that it is okay. I am okay. Only then does he go.

It's like he is afraid to let me out of his sight.

Mrs Omana asks me to sit down. She says that she is sorry about the police taking me, but they do have a zero-tolerance policy towards drugs at Ashwaty Bhawan. She takes out the newspaper that has just arrived.

'Can you read Malayalam?' she asks. I nod.

She thrusts the paper at me. It's the local edition of a newspaper whose name I have never heard before, mostly covering the district regional news.

My heart sinks when I read the headlines: that there has been a drug raid in Wayanad. The story goes on to say that police have arrested three people who are running a ganja racket and have seized roughly twenty kilograms of cannabis. Preliminary investigation suggests a network of peddlers who then sell it to students from well-known colleges, some of who are doing 'voluntary work' at Ashwaty Bhawan. The way it is worded implies that Ashwaty Bhawan is a front for such illegal activities. The story mentions that there are foreign students here and among the ones arrested, is Puja Krishnan, who is the daughter of a reputed businessman from Ernakulam, H.K. Krishnan. It states that my mother is a surgeon in a leading hospital in Kochi. There is a huge picture of the three people arrested who have been made to pose with the haul that they have seized. Thankfully there is no photo of me or my parents.

I freeze as I read this cheap, tabloid-style news. I know they write this way to sensationalise, yet I am shocked. I can clearly see the damage this has done to the reputations of everyone named.

'My daughter would never do such a thing. How could you have not verified with us? Why didn't you call me before handing her over to the police?' my father asks Mrs Omana.

'The police were in no mood to listen. They said with certainty that they have information that cannabis is on the premises and if

I shielded the volunteers or the staff, it would imply that I was in cahoots with them. I had no choice, Mr Krishnan. And to be honest, I was shocked that Puja was in Arush's room. I did not expect her to *not* be in her room. That boy – he is not from India. It must be okay in the country where he is coming from. But Puja – she knows our culture, doesn't she? What business did she have to go to his room, that too so late at night?' Mrs Omana asks.

'That is no crime to be arrested for,' I say softly.

I am angry now. The anger has kicked in at last. I am angry at the accusations, angry at the unfairness of it all.

I had explained all of it to my father and reiterated my innocence on the car ride back from the police station. While he was not happy about my being discovered in Arush's room, he is bristling with rage.

'Look Puja, it may not be a crime, but you should know how these things are perceived here,' says Mrs Omana.

'Where is that boy Sujit? Please call him, I want to talk to him,' says my father. 'Puja says that he carried her backpack, and obviously the substance came into it from somewhere. I want to get to the bottom of this,' my father isn't willing to give up.

Mrs Omana asks the office boy to get Sujit.

'You cannot pass a moral judgement on Puja being in a boy's room. That is between me, my wife and her. It does not imply that her character is questionable as you suggest, or that she is involved in cannabis trade. I expected better judgement from you. Why didn't you question the other boy immediately? And why wasn't he taken to the station instead of my daughter?' My father's eyes are afire. His tone is soft, but deadly. I have never seen my father like this.

I am so proud of my father at that moment. He is defending me, fighting for me.

The office boy returns in a few minutes. 'Madam, he is gone.'

'What do you mean he is gone?' Mrs Omana frowns.

'Gone! He has taken his luggage and vacated,' the boy replies.

'Oh lord!' exclaims Mrs Omana.

'So clearly, he is guilty,' says my father.

'It seems so. I think I have made a terrible mistake. Mr Krishnan, I am sorry. I owe you an apology. When it was discovered in Puja's bag, I presumed she was involved. Nowadays we can never tell,' Mrs Omana mumbles.

'What is the use of apologies, Mrs Omana? You should have acted a bit more calmly. You should have got to the bottom of things before presuming anything. The damage has already been done,' says my father. 'And in future, I do hope you do not implicate innocent students. I am withdrawing my daughter from your programme. Good luck to you.'

Mrs Omana stands there, her jaw hanging open, not knowing what to say.

My father stands up and so does Unni uncle.

My father turns to me and says, 'Pack your bags, Puja. We are leaving.'

Arush

When Puja comes to the dining area and tells me she is leaving, I stop sipping my coffee midway.

'You mean like for good?' I ask her.

'Yes. My dad just informed Mrs Omana that he is withdrawing me from the programme. That jerk Sujit has vanished, can you believe it?' Puja is indignant.

My blood boils when I hear this. How much lower can a person sink?

'Such a bastard. The least he could do is own up. Clearly, he is guilty. How could he implicate someone innocent?' I ask.

Puja raises her eyebrows, grimaces and then sits opposite me. One of the ladies serves her a steaming cup of coffee.

'The scumbag. Deserves to be kicked,' I say.

Puja just shrugs. 'Whatever has happened, has happened.'

'How can you accept it, Puja? How can you be so calm?'

'What can I do, Arush? My name, my parents' names, are all over the local newspapers. It's a mess. Even if I wanted to do something, I cannot change what has happened, right? The damage has been done,' she says sadly.

I do not know how she can be this accepting. Perhaps it is the innate Indianness in her. I have seen this after I came to India. People just accept things – there's so much chaos, and yet amidst all the chaos, there is a strange order. It is as though everyone here knows some kind of a secret that I don't, and it gives them a power to be calm.

'Is it a terrible thing if something negative appears in the newspapers here?' I ask her.

'It is a local newspaper, more like a tabloid. But still, Ashwaty Bhawan and 'foreign students' have been mentioned too,' Puja says.

'Does it really matter? Who reads the papers anyway? Today's paper is tomorrow's fish wrap. My father always says this.'

'Yes, it's just a stupid local paper which sensationalises everything.'

'Isn't there anything we can do? Can't we file a case against him?' I ask her.

I do not want Sujit to get away scot-free. I want justice for Puja. I can't be as accepting as her.

'This is India, Arush. I don't think the judicial system or the police will help,' Puja says.

She knows how the system works more than I do. But that doesn't quell my feelings of infuriation.

'Why do you think he did this? Maybe to escape getting caught himself?' I ask her.

'Who knows! I wish I had never given my backpack to him.' Puja sighs deeply.

'I wish I had taken that backpack from you. I feel responsible,' I tell her.

'Don't be silly,' she says.

She looks at her phone and checks the time.

'I have to leave soon, Arush. Give me your phone number.'

I take her phone from her and key in my India number. I key in my UK number as well. I also add my email id and save it.

The thought of parting from her is so painful that I am trying to dull the pain by giving her as many ways as possible to keep in touch.

She watches me amused.

'Aren't you going to add your social media handles too?' she teases.

'I am not on any social media,' I reply.

'What? You are not on any social media?' Puja is visibly shocked.

'Nope, I don't see the point,' I reply.

'No Facebook, Instagram?' Puja just cannot believe that someone her age isn't on social media. I manage a small smile at her shocked face.

'I do have an Insta account for my art. But I only post my drawings there,' I admit.

'Alright, I will add you there.' She whips out her phone and asks for my Instagram id.

'But I don't talk to my friends on that,' I protest.

'Alright, we will message on WhatsApp then, like old people, okay?' she says in mock exasperation.

'Okay, works me for me,' I smile. 'Or we can email like really, really old people.'

'Email? Really? I don't remember when I last used email,' she says, like I have suggested writing letters by hand.

'The thing with email is, we can take time to think and process things. It is not instant and so we are not immediately reacting to what the other is saying,' I tell her.

'I have to go now, Arush. My father and Unni uncle are waiting.'

She stands up, slightly impatient to leave.

I can't believe she will be gone. I don't want her gone.

I want to see her daily.

But there's nothing I can do to stop her.

'Bye, Arush,' she kisses me on the cheek.

A quick, chaste peck.

With that, she leaves.

I watch her, memorising her walk, her smile, her features. I don't know why I feel this way. I have barely known her for a few weeks.

Yet it feels like my heart is being ripped out from inside me, as I watch her walk away.

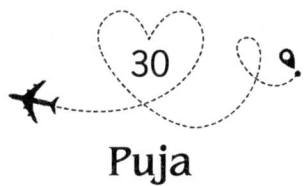

Puja

I dread the journey back. Dread, dread, dread it. I wish there was a way to teleport to places. I take the travel sickness medication which I am carrying. Unni uncle sits in front, and my father and I sit at the back.

My thoughts are all a whirl. I want to stay back at Ashwaty Bhawan. I want to be with Arush; I want to teach the kids. Though I had hated the thought of coming here initially, I had adjusted so well. I had genuinely started enjoying my work. Now it seems so unfair for it to abruptly end, that too, for no fault of mine. But there is no way I am going to let my father down by telling him I want to stay back there, after he has had that showdown with Mrs Omana.

'Molle, are you okay?' asks Unni uncle, turning back and addressing me. His face is full of concern

'Yes uncle, thank you for coming,' I reply automatically.

But am I really okay? I don't know the answer to that.

'How dare they publicise it in the newspaper. I have to find out who is behind all this,' my father says, his face grim.

'Krishnan, to be honest, I don't think this is a business vendetta or anything. It is probably because it was big news – the police having caught all of that – that the local press gave so much importance to it. Do you really think your business rivals would have sent such a young boy to plant the substance in Puja's bag, then make her get caught?' Unni uncle asks.

That angle of this whole thing being a set up by father's business rivals hasn't occurred to me. The calm manner in which my father and Unni uncle are discussing this shocks me.

'Do you remember what happened when I was selling the first company?' my father reminds Unni uncle.

'How can I forget? We gave them back good. Our first victory,' Unni uncle chuckles.

'What happened, accha?' I ask him.

'It's a long story, molle. It was when I was ready to sell my first company many years back. Just as the deal was about to go through, they implicated me in a false case. They said that we were using a mix of kerosene when we topped up the cars that came for servicing. They planted massive kerosene containers in our garages,' my father explains.

'Then what happened?' I ask

'What is to happen? We fought them. We didn't have CCTV cameras those days. Unni here had contacts at the police station. They made some enquiries and took in the labour who were hired to plant the kerosene drums. After two days in the lock-up, they sang like canaries,' my father narrates.

It sends a chill down my spine – the composed, collected manner in which my father narrates the story, with no show of any kind of emotion; Unni uncle chuckles at the memory. I shudder inside. My father has never discussed his business dealings with me and this is the first time I have seen this side of him. He is a ruthless businessman. The thought disturbs me.

'Puja, there are many things like this which happen in the business world,' Unni uncle says, 'You have to be ready to even kill. Else you will be swallowed alive. These are things which you will learn when you enter the real world.' Unni uncle turns back to look at me like he is reading my mind.

For the first time in my life, I think about my father's businesses and what it would have taken for him to be this successful. I don't like what I discover. I don't want to be a part of this kind of a world.

Unni uncle and my father, oblivious to my thoughts, continue chatting.

Exhausted by the events of the day, I lean back in my seat and fall asleep.

I am awakened by my phone buzzing. I have slept for a couple of hours now. I smile at the message.

'What are you up to?' Arush asks.

'In the car, listening to my father and his best friends talking business deals,' I type back.

'Interesting conversation?'

'I am learning stuff,' I tell him.

I ask him what he is doing. He replies he is in the classroom, with his eyes burning due to lack of sleep and that the classroom feels empty without me. All the kids are asking for me and Rukmini teacher has told them that I have gone on vacation. The kids ask which place I have gone to.

'Ha ha! What is she telling them?' I ask him.

'America! Of all places. I wish she had said UK.'

'Why UK?' I type and add a wink.

'Because I would have shown you where I live and the world I know. Not this chaotic crazy world where I have no idea how the systems work,' he types.

'How does it work in the UK?'

'You will have to come and visit me and I will show you all the systems,' he types, adding a wink and a laughing emoji.

This is a new side of Arush I am discovering.

The texting Arush is different from the Arush in real life. The texting Arush is spontaneous, flirty and fast! His replies are almost instant. I picture him sitting at the back of the classroom, typing furiously into the phone.

'Is your design for the classroom approved?' I ask him.

'Yes, all of them loved it,' he types back. 'Now I am to execute it.'

'When are you starting?'

'As soon as we finish chatting. I am making the drawing first. Wish you were here,' he says.

'I wish too.' I type back.

Arush giving me live updates, intensifies what I miss. I want to be there to see Arush making the giant size drawing of the magnificent train sketch that he made in his notebooks. I want to watch it come to life and see the delight and joy on the faces of the kids, Rukmini teacher and Asha.

My phone chimes. It is a message from the bank saying that my account is opened and they have posted the welcome kit. They will also be sending the pin number which would be needed to activate the card, separately, by post. I convey this to my father.

'Oh, good. That's sorted then,' my father says.

Then my travel sickness comes back and Anthony pulls up by the side of the road.

My father and Unni uncle wait while I throw up, wanting this travel to end.

My mother isn't at home when we get there. As soon as I see Shanti chechi, I hug her.

'How was your travel? Was it bad? Did you throw up too many times?' she asks as she pats my head.

I blink back my tears.

'They took me to the police lock-up, Shanti chechi. It was terrible,' I tell her.

'Oh, molle!' she says as she rubs my back. 'It's okay. It's over now. See, I made your favourite aloo bondas for you.'

Tears that I have been trying to fight fall freely now. I wipe them away and sniff.

Shanti chechi hands me a tissue and says, 'It's okay. Don't think about it. It's over. It was just a bad dream. Hot chocolate? Yes?'

'Yes,' I smile through my tears.

I sit on the kitchen platform and swing my legs as Shanti chechi bustles about in the kitchen.

My phone buzzes (again!).

'I have sent you mail. Probably your first. Check. I want a mail back,' Arush has written.

I smile.

Shanti chechi catches it. 'Who is it? Definitely a boy,' she says. She knows me too well.

'Yes,' I admit, 'I met someone there.'

'Really? What is his name?'.

'Arush,' I say.

Even speaking his name aloud gives me a strange secret thrill.

'What does he do? Tell me about him,' Shanti chechi whisks the hot chocolate. It smells divine.

I tell her all about Arush. His British accent and anxious eyes. I tell her about his odd pet – Vincent. I narrate in detail how I first met him, with a chameleon. I am in awe of his art. I tell her how much it meant to me that he came to the police station. Talking about Arush makes me so happy!

'He sounds like a good, smart boy,' says Shanti chechi.

'Yes, he is,' I say.

Later, I switch on my Mac and lean back against the plush, soft pillows on my bed. It feels wonderful to be back in my room. For the first time in my life, I appreciate how luxurious my bed is, how nice it is to sink into the mattress and how fortunate I am to have all of this: my father who turned up immediately to get me out, my wonderful home that overlooks the sea and Shanti chechi who takes care of me. I think of what might have happened to the women I spent the night with at the lock-up and I shudder.

I log into my account and scan my inbox. 'Your first unofficial email,' reads the subject line.

He is so right. All the other emails in my inbox have to do with promotions or some college-related stuff. His is indeed the first mail from a friend.

I smile as I begin to read.

Dear dear Puja,

While messages are great fun, mail has its own charm. I hope you are able to see the benefits of it at the end of this one. If you aren't, I have to upgrade my letter writing skills and try again!

I had fallen into a routine when you were here. I would quickly finish my sketches and wait for you. Since you aren't coming to my room anymore, I find myself at a loss with this block of time that we used to spend together talking about every single thing under the sun. What better way to utilise this time than writing to you?

My drawing is more or less done. I am attaching photos so you can see how it looks.

I have been thinking about our time here. All our lives we do things alone. Then we suddenly get along with someone like a house on fire. When they are gone, it feels like they have taken a part of you with them.

I can type 'I miss you' and throw in a few emojis on instant messenger on the phone.

But I think you would agree, it is not quite the same as declaring it over a carefully composed mail, isn't it?

Let me know your thoughts.

I await.

Arush

Arush

Being without Puja feels like being without arms. With no Puja and no Sujit, I expect lunchtime to be a lonely affair. But I am wrong. Oshan and Leah are sensitive to my plight. They ask if they can join me.

'Please do,' I say.

They pull up chairs and sit on either side of me.

'It is awful what happened,' Leah says.

Oshan nods. 'Did you hear, apparently everything is in the local newspapers. Asha read it out and translated it for us. It makes us and Ashwaty Bhawan look really bad,'

'Yes, I heard. But it is nothing compared to what happened to Puja,' I shake my head.

'I feel like shit. It's our fault too man. I never knew Puja was taken to the station by the cops until the next morning,' Oshan looks crestfallen.

'How is it your fault?' I ask.

'We smoked those joints with Sujit. He sold them to us. But we had no idea he was carrying it or that Puja would be implicated,' Oshan admits.

'Wait, what? You guys *knew* he had weed?' I am not able to keep the shock out of my voice.

'That day at the museum, we smoked up. We never watched that film show. He said he had scored some good quality stuff in the mountains,' Oshan is not able to meet my eye.

They knew all along. I am stunned.

'Why in the world didn't you speak up when the cops came? You could have spoken up for Puja.' My voice is cold.

'We didn't know they had taken her. They knocked on our doors and searched our rooms. They told us we cannot come out of our rooms. I think they locked us in for a brief while. I am guessing they didn't want us to warn Sujit. Well, at that time I presumed they had come for Sujit. I was frightened man. So was Leah,' Oshan explains.

I take a few seconds to digest this information. 'Yeah, I guess there is nothing you could have done. But what I find crazy is that the real culprit Sujit has got away scot-free,' I reply.

'Isn't there something we can do?' Anything at all?' asks Oshan.

'Like what?'

'I don't know – maybe track him down? Where does he live? I am thinking out loud here,' Oshan says.

Leah whips out her phone.

'Wait, let me find him on social media,' Leah says, and does a quick search. She finds him on Instagram.

'Look, here he is. It looks like he is in Trivandrum and Kochi regularly,' Leah says.

'What? Let me see,' says Oshan.

'It is possible that he is in Kochi often,' Oshan says.

'Yes, that's a possibility,' Leah admits.

We scroll through all his photos. Several photos which Sujit has posted show the location as Kochi. One picture has the caption: *It isn't what you have, who you are, where you are or what you are doing that makes you happy. It is what you think about it.* He is posing next to a car with one hand in the pocket of his jeans. He has used the hashtags: smoking, cannabis, weed, vappresso, vapecommunity, cannabis community, bong, marijuana, and instaweed.

'What the fuck? I would like to see if he is happy inside police lock-up,' I exclaim through gritted teeth.

'Look, even if we do track him down, it is not like he will confess to the police and clear Puja's name. The guy has run away. And from his Instagram profile, it seems like he sells this stuff regularly,' Leah says. She voices out aloud what I am thinking too.

'It's a lost cause then,' Oshan agrees.

The anger that has been simmering inside me till now, suddenly rises to the surface. I can't keep quiet anymore.

'If I see him, I will beat him up,' I say quietly.

And I mean it. I want to break every bone in his body. I want to kick him in his face till his nose bleeds. I want to smash his skull with a cricket bat.

I am that angry. I am also shocked at the violent images that are flooding my brain cells.

'I feel like a worm, man. Maybe we can go to the police station and give a statement?' Oshan suggests.

'It won't work, Oshan. I have been there. I kept telling them that Puja is innocent. They didn't bother to listen to me. Things work very differently in India. I don't think they will give you time or take down your statements. And even if they do, the harm has already been done. The news has already appeared and Puja has left.'

Leah considers all that I have said and nods slowly. 'That's true,' she says.

'I am so sorry, man. I feel so bad,' Oshan says.

'Me too,' I admit.

When I get back to the class after lunch to resume my painting, I miss Puja so much I hurt all over.

That evening, though, my heart lights up like a giant Christmas tree when I see a reply from Puja.

Dear dear dear Arush,

You are right. It is indeed the first 'unofficial' mail I am writing.

And yes, you have convinced me. Mails have a depth that Instant Messages lack. You write really well and I am sure I can't match up.

But I am going to try.

You phrased it so well – I feel the same way.

And now I don't know what to say!

Except I miss you. A lot.

There – I have replied!

I know this sounds so disjointed, but hey – it's my first.

Shall we video call? Please? I find it easier!

Puja

I smile at her reply. So her. Direct. Honest.

As soon as I finish reading her mail, I pick up my phone and video call her. She answers as soon as I call. She is in her bed wearing a spaghetti top and shorts, leaning back against the pillows. She wears no make-up and her loose hair framing her face makes her look like a little girl – innocent, sweet and adorable.

'Hey!' she grins into the camera.

'Hey you,' I smile back,

Then we say nothing and stare at each other.

'Say something. This is funny. We're not speaking and we're just looking at each other,' she chuckles.

'I don't know what to say. I write better than I speak.'

'That you do! You write well,' she nods.

'Thank you,' I grin and bow. 'Do you want me to show you my sketches for today?'

'Of course! Show them. Like *now*,' she commands.

I am relieved to have something to do. It is definitely easier for me to text her or mail her than video call her.

I turn my phone camera and show her the daily sketches. Today I have sketched the ladies serving us. I have also sketched the vessels – a close up.

'Ooooh, so good,' she squeals. 'Love them! Arush, you are so good at this!'

I love her reactions, her expression of pure joy.

'You are such a delight,' I tell her. 'You know, I hate video calls. I only call my family. But with you it is different.'

'It better be! You better not hate video calls with me,' she warns in a mock-stern voice. I laugh.

Puja has an effect of calming me down.

She asks if I want to see her room. I do.

Her room is so luxurious that I can only imagine a setting like this in high-end lifestyle magazines. It resembles a hotel room with wall-to-wall carpeting, everything in the room, sophisticated and elegant. I can scarcely believe my eyes when she presses a button and the long ceiling-to-floor drapes open up to the most breathtaking view of the ocean. She walks on to her balcony and shows me the vast expanse of the ocean stretching from one end to the other. In the darkness of the night, the waters appear black. The few ships sailing glimmer like diamonds. The moon is a sliver of white. The dark waves reflect the moonlight in little snatches that bob up and down. The gentle sound of the ocean is a soothing hum.

'Oh, Puja! This is incredible. It is stunning,' I tell her.

'You should see it during the day – it's a dazzling blue. You can't see so well right now,' she says, very matter-of-fact.

I can't get over her room and the ocean view. I think of my cramped room back in Norwich, which faces the brick wall of the next house. Even my room back at home in Derby (which my parents have converted to a guest room, after I left for college), cannot come close to the magnificence of Puja's home.

'Don't you feel so lucky to have all of this?' I ask.

'You know, it is funny that you ask that. I never felt so before. But after Ashwaty Bhawan and what happened there, now I do. I am relieved to be home,' she says, as she steps back into her room, turning the camera towards herself. She sinks into the plush mattress, propping up some pillows against the enormous cream upholstered headboard. Puja looks like a tiny doll.

'What are you thinking? You have gone quiet,' Puja interrupts my thoughts.

'See, this is why I like mails better. They give you time to think and there's no pressure to respond instantly. But you force me to do video calls. I am just a shy boy, I don't know what to say, I really don't. Since you insisted, the onus of coming up with topics is on you,' I tell her.

Puja throws her head back and laughs.

When she laughs like this, all is well with the world.

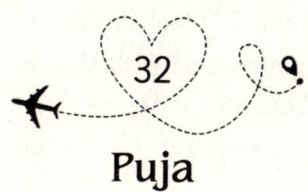

Puja

The next day when all of us are together, I get the third degree. Ma has traded her off day, as 'this is important'. The court martial from all three family members is the last thing I want, but I have no choice.

'Puja, I hope you know the enormity of the problem you have created,' says my mother as she pours tea into her cup.

'Look Ma, it really wasn't my fault. That idiot Sujit – he planted stuff in my bag.'

'Sujit? Sujit Nair? Wasn't he your classmate?' Divya pounces on this information. I instantly regret giving out his name.

I nod.

'Why do you mingle with such idiots? He was a troublemaker even in school, wasn't he?' my mother says, stirring the tea.

'Ma, I didn't know he would do something like this.'

'Who was that other boy who came to the station and who vouched for your innocence?' asks my mother.

It is evident my father and she have had a talk.

'Arush. My friend. Accha already knows.'

'Well, all I want to know is what is going on between you two.'

'He is my friend. That's all,' I don't volunteer any more information.

'What kind of friend? Boyfriend?' My mother refuses to give up, not breaking her gaze as she sips her tea.

'No. Just a good friend,' I look down.

We aren't going anywhere with this line of questioning, but my mother is hell bent on continuing it. 'Look Puja, if he is just a good friend, why were you in his room at midnight when the police came?'

The way my mother phrases it makes what Arush and I have between us sound like something dirty. Something inconsequential. All three give me the condemning look.

'Why? Is that a crime? I like him, I like his art and I was spending some time with him. That's all,' I say, not liking at all that I have to explain this to my family.

'He had an odd accent. Where is he from? Is he not from India?' asks my father.

'He is from the UK.'

'What does he do? What does his family do?'

'I don't know. He is an Arts student and I think he is really decent. He even came to the police station for me. Who does that?' I defend Arush.

Divya sniggers. I want to kill her. My mother shakes her head.

'I don't know what is going on with this boy. But spending the night in his room was not right. That was not what we sent you there for,' my father says.

I say nothing. I have perfected the art of staring at my plate.

'Look, Puja. Focus on your CAT entrance exams. Work hard in the coaching classes and clear it. Get serious about your future. I can't ask Mrs Omana to give you a voluntary work certificate since you didn't officially complete the programme. What a waste,' my mother shakes her head.

'I too would have really liked to continue had Accha not taken me away. There were only two weeks left.'

'Oho! So now that is a mistake, is it?' my father is glaring at me.

'No, that's not what I meant,' I say.

'Well, what did you mean, Puja? You are the one who mixes with all kinds of people and gets caught, that too in the worst possible way. Ganja of all things. *Thoo*! Even saying it makes me feel ashamed. You have ruined the reputation of this family. I have worked so hard to reach this position today. Your father has worked so hard. Not only do you put zero effort in your studies, but you also cause trouble. We could excuse you, Puja, if it was just once. But this is how you have been from class 11. What is wrong with you? Why can't you just take things seriously?' my mother explodes.

I can't help thinking that if this was a fantasy-animation movie, she would probably have morphed into a fire-breathing dragon.

I detest this version of her. I use the only weapon I have. An apology.

'Look Ma, I didn't mean to. I am very sorry.' My voice is contrite. I know from years of practice that this is how I can diffuse the tension.

'You are always sorry. But you don't change your behaviour. When will you grow up?' she is exasperated.

I have lost my appetite now. But I force myself to eat the last bit of the appam. My mother will be angry if I waste food.

'Fortunately, I have managed to erase the arrest from the police records. No FIR was filed. There's no record of detention. We had to pay a few lakhs, but it got done,' my father declares.

My mother shakes her head in disgust.

I feel terrible to have put my father and mother through this. How I wish I had been careful with my backpack! I curse Sujit in my head.

Divya doesn't lose the opportunity to taunt me. 'A few lakhs! Maybe we can recover it from her after she does her MBA and gets a job. If she manages to clear the CAT,' she chuckles.

But my father and mother are not laughing. They look at me in disappointment.

I want to vanish. I finish the rest of the meal in silence.

Once I am in my room, I shut the door and bolt it. Then I reach for my phone and video call Arush, the only person in the world who gets me.

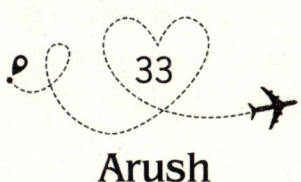

Arush

A distraught Puja describes the whole interaction with her family. She explains how she has been a constant disappointment to her parents, always unable to achieve the desired grades. Being constantly compared to Divya only makes it worse.

'You know, I was so sick and tired of this that I decided I will be nothing like her. I bunked classes, never turned in assignments and always got into trouble. I was such an idiot, wasn't I?' she asks.

'No, Puja. Lots of kids act out like that. I know scores of kids in my class who did such stuff. In the UK, we have a counsellor attached to each school. Generally, kids who behave this way are sent to the counsellor and the issue is dealt with sensitively. I think the Indian system is just too hard. The academic pressure here, from what I see, is a lot and leaves you gutted. Don't be harsh on yourself.'

She carefully considers what I have said. I think she is comforted.

'When do we meet next?' she asks.

'I have just two weeks here. My next one is closer to Kochi,' I tell her.

'Really? Where? Why didn't you tell me what you were going to do after Ashwaty Bhawan?' She is all excited now.

'Mattancherry. I guess we were so busy chatting about other things that we didn't speak about it. This was scheduled way before I left for India. I didn't think much about it,' I tell her.

But secretly, I *have* been thinking about it. I have even looked up the distance between Kochi and Mattancherry, which is where I will be the next four weeks, studying Kerala mural painting at a fine arts school in Jew Town.

'Do you know what it means?' she asks, dancing around her room, breathless with joy.

'What?' I ask, amused.

'It means that we can meet every single day! Hooray!'

'I don't think we would be able to meet daily. I have to put in long hours. And hey, doesn't your college reopen as well?' I ask her.

'Yes, it does. But I will figure something out. Know what? There's a ferry service from right next to my house to Mattancherry. Oh, it's so beautiful, Arush! I can't wait to see you, show you everything.'

'Me too,' I reply.

The next two weeks go by in a whirl. There is a lot of work to be done on the wall painting of the train. The details have to be perfect. The colours have to be right. Even the smallest change of proportion will distort the painting. My neck has a crick from constantly looking up. I have to move to the front of the classroom from time to time and click photos to study the proportion. The kids comment and admire. I think of Michelangelo painting the Sistine Chapel and wonder if he would have done as good a job had there been a barrage of sixty kids constantly admiring and commenting on his work. But the good thing is, I am completely engrossed in painting this wall and am I enjoying it so much that when I am working, I do not have time to miss Puja. I forget everything, but this painting. I love the way it is slowly coming together. Time flies when I work on it and many a time, I skip lunch just because I don't want to break the flow.

When I take breaks, I show Puja the progress of my painting. I love watching her reaction. She insists on video calls. We constantly rib each other about video calls versus mails. I have got her to write me two more (both in response to mine). She reads every book I recommend and we discuss each in depth.

At last, the painting is finished a full day ahead of my deadline. I click countless pictures and my professor, pleased with my work, asks me to mail him high-resolution pictures for the exhibition that is coming up at my college. Jenna hears about it from the professor. I am happy to get praise not only from my professor, but from Jenna as well. She calls me up congratulating me.

'How is Vincent doing?' I ask.

In response, she sends five pictures of Vincent looking happy and content.

'You know what? He has forgotten you. He is now ours. You can adopt a new one in India,' she says.

I grin. 'I have Zelan here, but I can't find him,' I reply.

Mrs Omana, Asha, Rukmini teacher, the kids – all of them are elated with my work. A part of me is now sad to leave this place. Leah and Oshan are leaving and we exchange email ids.

For our farewell day, they arrange a dance show by the kids who dance to Bollywood songs. They are surprisingly good.

'Puja should have been here for this,' I tell Oshan.

'Yeah, man. It is so unfair what happened,' he says.

I describe it all to Puja and send her lots of pictures and video clips.

'Glad you got to see it,' she says. Her smile is sad. But she cheers up the next instant. 'Anyway, you arrive tomorrow. Welcome to Kochi, the queen of the Arabian sea,' she says. We smile, looking into each other's eyes – through the phone.

Heart

Wherever you go, go with all your heart.
– Confucious

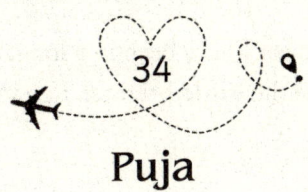

Puja

Just knowing that Arush will be close by soon, makes me nervous, excited, restless. My parents and Divya are attending the wedding of a friend's son in a neighbouring town. Since I told my mother that I have extra coaching for the CAT exams, I have been excused. My mother is pleased that I am taking my academics seriously.

When their car is out of sight, I go to the kitchen.

'It's only a ferry ride, can you imagine? He is only a ferry ride away,' I tell Shanti chechi excitedly, perching on my usual spot on the kitchen counter as she bustles around.

'How exactly do you plan to meet him? What about your college and coaching classes? What will you tell your parents?' Shanti chechi asks, as she cuts a pomegranate.

'Please, Shanti chechi. You have to cover for me. Please? Tell them I have extra coaching?' I beg as I walk to my bedroom. She follows me with some freshly-made pomegranate juice.

'Here, have this. It's good for you. Then we will see,' she says.

I hate pomegranate juice and Shanti chechi knows it. But my mother has impressed upon her the health benefits and she religiously makes it for me. I drink it in a single gulp.

'Happy?' I ask.

'Oh! I can't believe it. You really love this boy, don't you?' she asks.

'Yes, I do,' I say.

This is the happiest I have been in a long, long time.

Love does make the world brighter. I go to my room, switch on some music and dance.

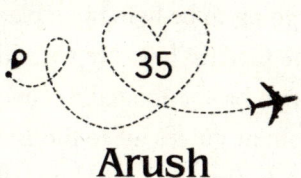

Arush

Kochi is a stark contrast to the greenery of rural Wayanad. I stare out of the window in fascination at the shops whizzing by, surprised to see clothing stores of all the international brands here. Kochi is a bustling, busy city.

When my cab driver drops me off near the Dutch Palace at Jew Town opposite the boat jetty, I am struck by how different it is from the rest of Kochi. The quaint cobbled streets where no automobiles are allowed, a few signboards in Hebrew – all of this makes me feel like I have stepped into a little street in Israel. The path leading to the boat jetty is lined with merchants selling various beautiful handmade items. A few foreigners explore the items while the sellers themselves look disinterested, either reading newspapers or chatting among themselves. Overhung by a canopy of shady trees, the path looks strikingly picturesque and compels me to click a lot of photos. I know my sketchbook will be pretty today.

The main street has shops on both sides. The wares for sale include antiques, jute bags, items made of hemp, beautiful lamps, jewellery, coconut fibre mats, silver pieces, Jewish ceremonial objects, Menorahs, Shabbat candle holders and much more. The range is mindboggling. I have never seen so much beauty in one place. The things sold to tourists in the UK, while pretty, are nothing compared to this.

I love that I am going to be living in a place rich in history and culturally unique. The Cochin Jews are the oldest group of Jews in India, but most of them have migrated to Israel.

The map on my phone guides me to the art school right opposite the Jewish synagogue. I stare at a large shop selling art and artefacts, housed in an old building with a narrow entrance. The shop is long like a passage, and from this end I can see an opening at the other. Where is the art school?

I roll my suitcase inside, and to my surprise, the shop opens out into a café inside a library that faces a flight of wooden steps leading upstairs. A youngish lady is at the cash counter of the café. I walk up to her and ask her about the art school.

'Are you from UK? Arush?' she asks.

'Yes, I am.' I smile. But she doesn't smile back.

'Wait,' she says and makes a call.

In a couple of minutes, a stout, clean-shaven man with long hair tied in a bun, rushes down the wooden stairs. The stairs thud as he takes them two at a time. He is dressed in loose brown linen pants and a white kurta with the 'Om' symbol printed all over.

'Arush? I am Sashi. Sashi Koning. Welcome,' he says. He speaks perfect English with no trace of any accent.

'Hi Sashi.'

'Come, let me show you to your room,' he says. He insists on carrying my suitcase, but I refuse to let him. What is with Indians wanting to carry others' bags!

'You are our guest and we can't let you carry this. If you carry it yourself, you are insulting my hospitality,' he says as he grabs my suitcase.

'Oh, I am so sorry. I don't mean to insult anyone,' I apologise and Sashi laughs.

'I was just teasing you, man. I am not even from here,' he chuckles. I heave a sigh of relief as Sashi carries my suitcase up the stairs.

'Where are you from?' I ask, as we climb up the stairs.

'Netherlands. My parents adopted me from Kerala and this is a kind of pilgrimage for me, to get in touch with my roots.'

'Oh, wow. Did you track your biological parents?'

'Yes, but they have both passed away. And yet, here I am, still holding on. The connection is too strong,' he says, without any show of emotion.

In a strange way, I can relate to what Sashi has said. I have never been to India my whole life. This is my first time here, but there is this indescribable 'pull' I feel. I feel like I belong here. Is that what it means to return to your roots, I wonder.

The stairs lead to a large hall. At the far end covering the whole wall is the most beautiful mural I have ever seen, painted in Kerala style with red saffron and yellow. It depicts a goddess along with demons, elephants, a crocodile, trees and many more things. I stand rooted to the spot, staring at it.

'Lovely, isn't it?' asks Sashi and I nod.

The red oxide floor and the extra low ceiling lend a calm aura to the place. There are no windows, yet it is well ventilated. Natural light streams in through the gaps between the intricately carved wooden panels forming a 'balustrade wall' facing the street.

'This is our classroom. This is where we paint,' Sashi tells me, pointing to a very low table at one end of the room. Instead of chairs, there are cushions on the floor.

'Wow! This place is serene.'

'It indeed is. The energy here is so good, so peaceful. Mukundan is a great teacher too, you will learn a lot,' Sashi informs me.

'Does he have a lot of students?'

'He teaches in a few fine arts colleges where he has many. He is a busy man, also involved in the local politics. Here, it is just you and me. He teaches us the basics and after that, we're pretty much on our own. A lot depends on us – how much we want to learn. He is hardly around during the day. But once he comes back, you can consult him any time. He is always available. That's his room,' Sashi says, pointing to a door at the far end of the hall.

'And this is your room. My room is the next one,' he says. The shop and café downstairs, both are owned by Mukundan. You can have your food there. And if you want a change, there are a lot of cafés around Jew Town.'

'Thank you,' I reply. I am curious now about how settled Sashi seems.

'So how long have you been here?' I ask, as he hands me the key to my room.

'It's been three months now. I have been deputed here under an exchange programme from my art school there. I will most likely stay here for a year because I love this,' he says.

It strikes me then, that I have just four weeks left with Puja. I enter my room with a heavy sense of time ticking.

My room is basic, with a thick mattress on a low bed. It has the same red oxide floors as the hall. The window overlooks a large empty plot. On one side of the room is an old wooden desk and next to it, a large antique wardrobe. It also has an attached bath and toilet which is a huge change from my accommodation in Wayanad.

I unpack my suitcase carefully, arranging all my art supplies in the drawers of my desk. Then I pick up the phone and call Puja.

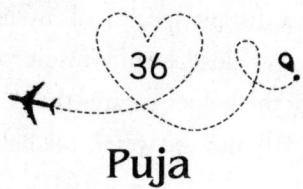

Puja

Though I am expecting his call, my heart somersaults when I hear Arush's voice. I can't wait to meet him. I change into jeans and a t-shirt. Is this what love is? If so, it is delightful.

I apply a light eyeliner and some lipstick as I get ready to leave. Shanti chechi observes me curiously and teases me.

'Ooooh, someone is getting ready to meet her lover,' she says. She mispronounces the word making it sound like 'lavvar'.

'Eeeks,' I say. 'Don't say that!'

'Okay, go. Who am I to stand in between two people who 'luv' each other?' Shanti chechi continues to tease me.

'Thank you!' I say as I leave, happy that the Ernakulam boat jetty is close enough for me to walk down there. I am in such a hurry that I almost sprint. At the jetty, I buy a ticket to Mattancherry. After I board, I will the boat to go faster. I text Arush, asking him to meet me at the Mattancherry boat jetty.

The boat is full with office-goers, fish-sellers and various other people who take it daily to get to Ernakulam. The seagulls fly above me, looking for fish. I stand right in front and crane my neck to see if I can see the Mattancherry boat jetty, gazing at the disturbed, angry trail of water as it speeds. We cut through miles of ocean, and when the shore appears in sight, I am as elated as a sailor who has been away from land for months.

I spot Arush as a distant speck and my heart tumbles around in my ribcage. As we get close, I cannot wait for the boat to moor. I jump out even before the helper secures the boat properly.

'*Ayyyyy*, you will fall into the water,' the helper yells, but I laugh. I don't care.

Arush laughs too as he lifts me off the ground and swirls me around.

'Am I allowed to kiss you here?' he asks.

'As much as I want you to. I think we have already made a spectacle of ourselves to all these people,' I say pointing to the boat.

People stare disapprovingly at us as they disembark.

'Right then, come on. Let's go. Let me show you Jew Town,' Arush says, as he grabs my hand.

'Hey! This is supposed to be my city and I am supposed to show you around. When did you become the local guide?' I protest.

'Jew Town is mine. You can take Kochi, Ernakulam or Wellington Island,' Arush says with a look of pride on his face. I am surprised that he is talking like a native.

'Someone has done his homework, I can see.'

'Newfound knowledge that I am showing off,' Arush says as we walk towards Jew Town. 'Have you been here before?'

'Oh, plenty of times. Anytime a relative visited from outside, this is one of the places we would bring them to. Most of us who live here do that,' I say. 'There's a tiny museum here which not many people know of. Want to see?'

I know that Arush has a thing for museums.

'Of course! You know I do,' he says, perking up.

'This way,' I say, as I lead him towards the museum. The entrance to the museum is through a shop.

'This is the smallest and the strangest museum I have ever seen,' says Arush. 'How in the world do people even find it?'

'They don't, unless they have a Puja to show them,' I reply, and Arush laughs.

God! How I love this guy. It takes supreme self-control to resist grabbing his face and kissing him right there.

The museum itself has some remarkable displays. We stop and gaze at the iron cannon balls used by Tipu Sultan in the 18th century during his invasion of Kerala.

'Imagine getting shot by one of these,' says Arush. His attention wanders to the Bushman stones. 'These are 8,000 years old! Can you believe it!' he exclaims. He is like a kid at a candy store.

Though I have come to this museum a few times before, I have only taken a cursory glance at all these artefacts. Mostly, I have just breezed through without even bothering to think about the objects displayed. No one I have ever been with has shown this kind of interest in ancient objects. Arush, I can see, genuinely loves this. He asks if photography is allowed (it is) and he clicks many pictures.

The burial urns 3,000 years old, which held the remains of the dead along with their dearest possessions (as they believed in life after death) catch his fancy. He pauses in front of the head of a sorrowful Virgin Mary, which is 200 years old. He is also fascinated by a fan which is run on kerosene, not electricity. A handwritten board says that the exhibit is 110 years old. Then there are Torah scrolls which are about 450 years old.

The museum itself is barely more than 600 square feet. You enter it, take a U-turn and then, before you know it, you are back at the shop through which you entered. Yet, Arush spends over an hour inside. A noisy group of students enters the museum and they are out in less than two minutes.

'They aren't interested in the displays,' he tells me.

'Yeah, this is the typical Indian college crowd for you.'

'Why do they come to the museum then?' he asks puzzled.

'It must be a part of what they call the 'study tour' which all these colleges have,' I tell him. I explain how colleges in rural Kerala name these trips 'study tours', as only then would parents consider it worthwhile to pay for them. If the college or the school called it an 'excursion', most parents wouldn't send their children, I explain.

'What an academics-oriented culture!' Arush shakes his head.

'Thank my lucky stars for that, else I wouldn't have been able to meet you,' I reply. I explain how I am using the excuse of CAT coaching and how Shanti chechi is covering for my little escapade today.

'Oh, Puja! You shouldn't have done that. What if you get caught?' he asks.

'It will still be worthwhile,' I say softly.

He kisses me on the forehead. Then he pulls away almost instantly.

'Sorry, I couldn't resist,' he says.

The girls in the shop are grinning at us now. I am embarrassed and so is Arush.

'Sir, do you want to buy anything? These are pure handmade soaps made by local ladies. 100 percent pure coconut oil is the base. Very nice soaps,' one says, as she thrusts a soap at him. It has a beautiful wrapper made of the wider part of the stem of a palm frond. Packaged like an oyster shell, tied up with a little piece of satin ribbon, it is attractive and unique.

'100 percent organic. Once you try this, you won't use any other soap. So many fragrances to choose from too – jasmine, lavender, rose, lemon…' the girl continues.

Arush examines the soap carefully. 'Look at this! I have never seen anything like this before. It is all bio-degradable. Look at the packaging, using palm stem,' he comments.

'I too have never seen this, though I have been here many times,' I tell him.

'This was started recently. It provides livelihood to more than two hundred local women who make them by hand,' the girl says.

'In that case, I will take them all. One of each fragrance,' Arush replies.

The girl is delighted. She packs them in a brown handmade paper bag and hands them over to Arush, who pays for them.

'What are you going to do with so many soaps?' I ask as we walk out of the store.

'These are for you. My gift for you,' he says, as he kisses my hand.

I am so surprised that I don't know what to say. Most guys would buy flowers or jewellery as gifts for a girl they are interested in. Arush is probably the only one who has gifted soaps! That too, bought since it would provide livelihood to local women. My heart fills with so much love for him, I don't know what to do. I squeeze his hand really tight. He squeezes it right back, as we look into each other's eyes and smile.

I could be like this forever. I don't know how this thing called love works, but this is pure magic. I am so happy when I am with him. I don't want this to ever end.

I know at that moment that I am hopelessly in love with this guy and will do anything for him.

Just anything.

Arush

Puja's hand in mine, tiny and soft, makes me fiercely protective of her. We walk back to the art school in silence, her head resting on my shoulder.

'Holding hands okay in public in India?' I ask her softly.

'I don't care. Let people look,' she says, as she moves closer to me.

'Come in! Come in! No charges for looking,' a vendor calls out, as we walk towards the art school. He stands at the narrow entrance to his shop. A small window at the side displays earrings, semi-precious stones and silver menorahs.

'You look every bit the foreigner you are. That's why they are calling out to you,' smiles Puja.

'No way. I am 100 percent Indian. I look Indian,' I say.

'You only have black hair and dark eyes, but you are very British. Show me your passport. Hands up,' she says, making a gun with her fingers and sticking it at me. I throw my hands in the air and mock surrender. We giggle like children.

'You know, this art school doesn't even have a signboard. It is above a café. It also has a library. It is beautiful,' I tell her. I also tell her about Sashi and his interesting story. She says she is eager to see my new home.

'For a few weeks only,' I say ruefully.

'Let's not talk about it. For now, we are with each other and that's all that matters,' Puja replies.

As we get closer to the school, we are greeted by a man with closely-cropped, jet-black hair and a large black handlebar moustache. Dressed in a white shirt and white mundu with arms folded across his chest, he looks intimidating. Puja lets go of my hand.

'Arush?' he asks.

'Yes?' I reply, slightly wary. The man exudes a no-nonsense vibe.

His face breaks into a large smile, instantly transforming his persona into a friendlier one.

'I am Mukundan,' he says.

'Oh, hello Mr Mukundan. This is Puja, my friend.'

'Are you from the UK too?' he asks Puja.

'Oh no! No, I am a local,' Puja replies.

'Oh, nice that you already have made local friends,' Mukundan laughs. 'Have you settled down? Has Sashi shown you around? I couldn't meet you earlier as I had classes at some colleges where I teach.'

'Yes, he has. I am ready to start anytime. I absolutely love this place.'

'Well, what about her? Is she going to join you too?' Mukundan points to Puja.

'No, I don't intend attending classes with him. I just came to meet him,' Puja is quick to clarify.

'That's alright then,' Mukundan says. 'The classroom is open twenty-four hours. You decide your timings and self-govern. I will assist you till 9 am, after which I leave for my classes. Therefore, the earlier you wake up, the better it is. I will be in the main hall from 6.30 am onwards.'

'I'll start at 6.30 am too,' I reply, determined to make full use of the time that Mukundan is available. 'I wanted to show Puja the art school and my room. I hope that's fine?'

I don't want Puja getting into trouble for 'being in a boy's room', like it happened at Ashwaty Bhawan. In India, it is best to take permission and clarify these unwritten rules. It is not viewed lightly here, that much I have gathered.

'Yes, you can have visitors, but please respect the *shala*. She cannot stay over. No hanky-panky. Also, no smoking, no alcohol, no drugs. It is a sacred art and unless you respect it, you cannot learn it,' Mukundan says.

'Of course,' I tell him, secretly amused with the phrase 'hanky-panky'. I know what he is referring to.

As Puja and I walk to my room upstairs I tell her, 'You heard what he said. We can't 'hanky-panky'.'

'I wasn't intending to anyway, I don't know about you,' Puja says and we both smile.

I was going to kiss her in my room, but Mukundan has not clarified if 'hanky-panky' includes kissing or excludes it. But I don't want to take any risks breaking a rule and get Puja (or myself) into trouble.

At the hall, Puja spots the mural and is as overwhelmed as I was when I first saw it. But she is a lot more expressive than me. 'Oh my! Just look at that!' she exclaims. 'I can't believe you will be learning to make this!'

'Me too,' I reply.

Sashi, on hearing us, emerges from his room and I introduce Puja to him.

'Lovely to meet you,' he says.

'Nice to meet you too,' Puja replies.

Sashi asks if she is joining the classes and Puja laughs, saying she is just a friend who is visiting me.

'Have you met Mukundan?' Sashi asks me.

'Yes, we just did. He seems like a guy used to being in charge,' I remark.

'He contested as an independent candidate for the elections and he lost by a small margin. He is pretty well known in this locality,' Sashi says.

'Oh, yes! I remember seeing him in the election campaigns. He had come to my college and had given a speech. Many from my college had voted for him,' Puja recalls.

'Alright, I will leave you guys to talk. I have something to do,' says Sashi and disappears. It is obvious he doesn't want to be a third wheel.

When we enter my room, Puja pulls me towards her and kisses me. On the lips.

My whole body explodes in response. I cannot think straight. Puja is an elixir that drives me insane. Her lips are so, so soft, yet so demanding. I am dying to kiss her back, but I muster all my willpower to push her away.

'No, Puja! Stop,' I say, pulling away.

'No Puja, stop,' she imitates my accent.

'You, so-and-so,' I shake my finger at her and she giggles.

She walks to my desk and opens it without asking me. I am relieved that she has walked away from me. If she had continued kissing me, I know I couldn't have resisted.

'Oh, you have already arranged all your stuff so neatly here!' she exclaims.

Her phone suddenly buzzes.

She looks at it and frowns. 'Oh fuck. It's a friend of mine. Naman. He has seen me here and asks if we want to meet for coffee. I forgot that his father owns properties here.'

'Oh, I see. Don't you want to meet him?'

'I want to spend time with you, Arush,' says Puja as she types furiously into the phone.

'What did you tell him?' I ask.

'That I am with a friend and we can meet another time,' Puja says.

Her phone buzzes again

She reads it and says, 'Idiot!' She then shows it to me.

'Boyfriend?' Naman has typed.

'What are you going to reply?' I smile.

'This,' says Puja as she types again and when she shows me her phone I chuckle.

'None of your fucking business,' she has typed.

'Isn't that rude?'

'Nah, we've known each other since we were kids. We all grew up together. My parents and his are great friends. We even went to the same kindergarten, also attended the same school.'

'Does Naman know Sujit?' I ask her. This Naman popping up suddenly has rekindled my anger at the unfairness of Sujit's actions. I know I am a being irrational, but I am angry with Naman though he hasn't done a thing.

'Yes, we were all together,' she replies and her tone is slightly guarded now.

'Do you think he is in touch with Sujit?' I ask her.

'Why Arush? I have put it behind me. Let's forget about Sujit and move on.'

'I can't get over what he did to you, Puja. What a scumbag. A rat. I want to confront him. I want to punch that bastard.'

'Leave it. It's a closed chapter.' There's a finality in her tone. Her earlier ebullient mood is gone. I wish now I hadn't asked about Sujit.

She glances at the time and says she has to hurry back. Her parents would get very suspicious if she stayed out too late. Shanti chechi won't be able to hold the fort for too long, she tells me.

I walk her to the jetty. In silence. The air is heavy between us now. I want to hug her, but I refrain.

'I wish you could stay, Puja,' I tell her softly.

'I'll meet you tomorrow,' she says and I nod.

'Now go,' I tell her and watch as she gets on the boat.

As I walk back to the art school, a plan forms in my head. The more I think about it, the surer I am it will work.

I have found a way to track down Sujit and I am going to act on it.

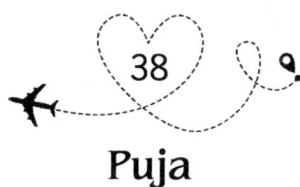

Puja

When I get back home, my parents and Divya are already home, in the living room, watching Discovery, the only channel which all three agree on. *Shit shit shit.* I better say something. Quickly.

'How was the function? Did you have fun?' I ask brightly.

'The function was okay, but the drive was exhausting and I have Emergency duty tomorrow,' my mother yawns. 'How is your coaching going?'

'Verbal ability is good. I am on top of it. But I need to work on numerical data.' The lies come easily. I know what my mother wants to hear.

As soon as I enter my room, I throw my tote bag on my bed and dreamily replay the day's happenings. I remember the soaps that Arush has bought for me. It is the strangest gift I have received. When I open my bag, their fragrances intermingle, making my room smell like a beautiful garden of flowers. I inhale deeply with a goofy smile on my face.

Divya's voice brings me crashing down. 'What's with all the soaps? Where did you get them from?'

I sit up with a jolt.

'It's none of your business,' I say.

'Are they selling soaps at your coaching centre now?' Divya is no fool. She knows there is something that I am hiding. Since I can't think of any clever explanations for six soaps on my bed, I duck her question.

'Just go away, Divya. Don't you have anything better to do?'

'Well, just keeping an eye on you, little sister. I can see that you have decided to stay *clean,*' she taunts, pointing to the soaps, chuckling at her own joke.

'I don't get *dirty* like you and Kar-dick,' I retort, pleased with my clever distortion of his name. When she marches off in a huff, I arrange all the soaps neatly on my desk.

Then I text Arush.

Arush

As soon as I reach my room, I dash off a mail to Oshan and Leah, telling them I have a plan to track down Sujit. I ask them to call me. In the interim, I settle down at my desk, sketching all the artefacts that I have photographed. In a couple of hours, I am done. I adjust the table lamp so my sketchbook is lit up and the colours shine vibrant. Pleased with the results, I click a few photos and I send them to Jenna.

Jenna's reply comes instantly, telling me they are good. She also sends me a few photos of a contented Vincent, along with sketches of him she has made.

'Thanks! For taking care of Vincent as well as your sketches. You're the best!' I text back.

When I check my mail, I see Oshan's reply. He and Leah have reached just a couple of hours back. He asks if I want to do a video call.

I call them.

'Hey man! How is it going?' they both grin into the camera.

'Good, good. This place is really good,' I tell them.

'How was your trip back?' I ask.

They tell me about an Indian family travelling with a lot of snacks, and how they kept offering the eatables to both of them throughout the flight journey.

'That's Indian hospitality for you,' I chuckle.

'Yes, they ensured we don't miss India at least on the plane. Strangely, now that we are back home, we are craving for India!' Leah says.

'I know, India has that effect on you,' Oshan agrees with her.

'Listen, you said you guys had bought the joints from Sujit, right?'

'Yeah man,' Oshan says. He looks ashamed.

'I have thought of a perfect way to flush him out.'

'What is it?' asks Leah.

'Does he know that you have left India?' I ask them.

'No, we never discussed our plans with him. For all he knows, we could still be in Kerala,' Oshan says.

'Then ask him to meet you,' I say.

I have thought this through in detail.

'What?' they both ask together.

'Tell him you want to buy some good quality stuff and ask him to meet you at some place at Kochi. Preferably some area in Jew Town,' I say.

My plan now becomes clear to them.

'Why do you want to do this?' Oshan asks.

'Bro, it feels like I have unfinished business with him. I can't just let him get away. I can't let this go. I have to speak to him. Once. He will get suspicious if I message him. But coming from you – it would seem credible,' I explain.

'What he did was wrong. I wish we were in India with you. We should have thought of this before we left,' Leah says.

'Well, I'll message him and I will keep you informed,' Oshan has a determined look on his face.

'Thanks bro. I owe you for this one.'

'You don't owe us anything. This is the least we can do for Puja, who got arrested for no fault of hers.'

I don't know what I am going to do on meeting Sujit, but I want to confront him. I simply can't rest till I do.

Almost as soon as I hang up, Puja calls me. 'I texted you and you didn't reply, so I called. You know, I want to jump out of my terrace and swim across the backwaters to you.'

I laugh. 'Don't! You will freeze to death.'

'Or drowning is a possibility too, considering I am not a good swimmer.'

'No ferries at night?'

'I can bribe a local person to take me across,' she says. Puja is so impulsive, she might actually do it.

'No, Puja! We have got into enough trouble. Please don't do anything of that sort.'

'I badly-badly-badly want to see you, Arush. You know what, I am coming over tomorrow.'

'What about your college? Are you sure you want to do this?'

'Leave it to me. I've never been surer of anything more in my life. See you tomorrow. I will see you around 10 am. Till then, dream of me,' she says, before she hangs up.

I smile at how certain she is of what she wants. I decide that I will work extra hours to make up for the time I am spending with her. Since there is hardly any time left for me in India, this desperation to spend every minute with her has gone up several notches.

I set my alarm for 5.30 am the next day and jump out of bed as soon as the alarm goes. I brush my teeth and shower. In less than an hour, I am in the classroom when Mukundan appears. Sashi is already there, working on a piece.

Mukundan hands me the canvas and the colours, giving me a history of Kerala murals before I begin. He talks about how Kerala murals are frescos, traditionally drawn on walls of temples.

'Mural artisans were under the patronage of various rulers in Kerala. It was a fine art back then. There were many stages. First, they prepared the wall. Then they applied a mixture of lime and clean sand. After that they added cotton to give a gleaming white texture to the wall. At least 25-30 washes of a mixture made up of tender coconut and quick lime followed. Only after that did they begin painting,' he says.

I am fully engrossed in his introduction to the art.

'After the wall was prepared in this manner, the outline was sketched. Symmetry is very important while sketching faces. So are proportions. There is a meaning behind each figure, each colour. The figures depicted have to be coloured according to their specified characteristics. We cannot use any colour we please,' Mukundan continues. He talks about the colour preparation and how traditionally, only colours from vegetable and mineral pigments were used.

He says that we will begin in the traditional style. I am allowed to use only five colours – red, yellow, green, black and white. He wants to revive the ancient mural style. The colours he has prepared are all natural, vegetable pigments, which he hands to me.

He asks me to start by painting a few traditional patterns. Once I am familiar with the motifs, we can begin work on a bigger project, he says.

I start my work and I love the motifs. I am so engrossed in painting that I don't notice how time flies. It is only when Mukundan says he is leaving and that I have done a good job, that I next look up from my work. I have a severe cramp in my legs from sitting still on the floor for so long, and my neck hurts. But this is a great kind of pain! I don't mind any kind of pain as long as I get to learn something new.

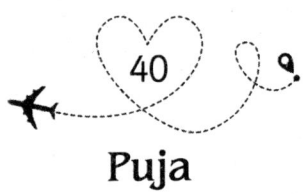

Puja

Two months ago, if someone had told me that I would be so madly in love with a guy that I can't imagine being without him, I would have laughed at them. But now? Arush is a drug I can't have enough of. If only one of us felt this way, the intensity wouldn't be a raging fire consuming us. I know Arush feels the same. We fuel each other.

It's close to two weeks now, that we have been spending almost the whole day together and it still is not enough. We have perfected the routine. I leave – supposedly for college – at the usual time, take a ferry and go straight to Mattancherry.

Arush works till noon. I don't mind waiting. I love watching him work. After that, the day is ours till I leave for home by the last ferry. No one at home is suspicious. Only Shanti chechi knows the truth.

'Puja! If you get caught you know how furious your mother will be,' Shanti chechi warns.

'Don't worry, I won't. I am very careful,' I assure her confidently.

The next morning, Arush tells me that Mukundan has suggested that he can sell his artwork in the shop downstairs. He would take a small commission and Arush can keep the sale proceeds.

'Wow! Are you keeping any of your paintings there?' I ask him.

'No, no way, Puja. I don't want to.'

'Why not?'

'Who'd want to buy my art?'

'Arush, unless you take a risk, how will you know?'

'I am passionate about my art. I would hate to put it out there and have someone treat it like a commodity. I can't put a value on what I create. It's a piece of my soul.'

'You artists are crazy. Sure, it is a piece of your soul. But can't you make copies of it? Keep the original. Sell the copies. That way you make money too,' I come up with the perfect solution.

'Spoken like a true businessman's daughter. You know, I haven't considered that,' Arush says.

'You must, Arush, you must. You are so good. I tell you what, leave the selling to me.'

'Yes ma'am,' Arush smiles.

We go to our usual haunt – a charming café with wooden benches as seating. Housed in a long passage, it opens out to a beautiful courtyard with grape vines. This café sells art as well, and both sides of the passage are lined with paintings.

Determined to sell Arush's work, today, I march up to the owner and introduce Arush as an artist from the UK. I proudly show off pictures of his work, especially the large train that he drew at Ashwaty Bhawan. Arush looks like he wants to disappear.

The café owner is full of admiration though and tells me he'd like a few high-resolution photos. My heart swells with pride, as though I have created the paintings.

'Why did you do that?' Arush hisses when the café owner goes away.

'Duh! Because I want to sell your paintings?'

Arush's phone rings.

'Oh, it's Jenna,' Arush says. I know that she is nothing but a friend to Arush and she is Josh's girlfriend. Yet a bolt of crazy jealousy darts through me. I don't like it that Arush lives in the same house as her.

How irrational! She knew Arush before you knew him. My head chides my heart. But the heart has no logic. I try to push the jealousy away and I greet Jenna, as Arush answers the call. We're on video. Jenna is so pretty!

'Hiya!' calls out Jenna, then she spots me. 'Oh, I didn't know you had company!'

'Meet my friend Puja. Puja, this is Jenna,' Arush says.

Arush hasn't used the word girlfriend.

I micro-analyse it. I wish he had said that. Isn't that what we are? Or is it too early? I don't know if I should read anything into it. It rankles inside me like a creaky door.

'I have some news for you. But don't worry, we have the situation under control,' Jenna says.

'What is it?' asks Arush.

'We had a… err… little incident. Tom forgot to put the lid back on and Vincent got out. He decided to explore the backyard and he climbed up a tree,' Jenna says.

'Oh no!' Arush exclaims. 'Is he okay?'

'Josh rescued him and look, he is doing fine now.' Jenna turns her phone camera to the tank.

Sitting there is a grotesque-looking creature. I can't bear to look. He is so ugly.

But Arush and Jenna coo and fuss over him. I try to keep a straight face.

'Are you switching the lamps on and off?' asks Arush.

'Yes, of course. We'd know the drill even if you hadn't left instructions. All is good,' Jenna says.

She turns to me and says, 'You are so pretty, Puja. What is your Instagram handle?'

Now I feel silly for getting jealous. Jenna seems like a genuinely nice person.

Within seconds we're Instagram friends.

Arush

As the day of departure from India gets closer, I find myself wanting to spend all my time with Puja.

'What will we do after you leave?' Puja voices my thoughts, her shoulders pressing against mine. Her hair smells of vanilla and oranges, making me want to run my fingers through it. I want to take her face into my hands and kiss her, but I resist. I consider floating the idea of getting a hotel room, but I don't want Puja to think I am a creep. After what happened, I am terrified of a police raid. I have read about such things on an India travel forum. I can't expose Puja to such dangers just because one part of me badly wants her. This girl makes me go crazy with desire. But I love her too much to take even a small risk and I drop the idea.

When I get to my room after seeing Puja off at the jetty, Oshan's message is in my inbox.

'Strike! We exchanged a few messages back and forth. He has agreed to meet only because I told him I want a big quantity. Tomorrow at 9.30 am at Jew Town, in the alley behind Nirvana café. Keep me posted,' Oshan has written.

'Thank you! I definitely will,' I reply.

I wanted a chance to confront him and now I have it.

The next morning, I leave as soon as Mukundan does. When I tell Sashi that I am meeting someone, he teases me.

'You got a new girlfriend? You cheating on Puja?'

'Ha ha. Very funny,' I reply.

On the way to Nirvana café, the same vendor who had called out to me when I was with Puja, calls out again.

'Come in, come in! No charges for looking,' he parrots his usual line.

'Another time,' I reply, hurrying towards the café.

Nirvana café is located off the main road. A long and narrow path between the café and the adjacent building leads to the back of the café. The 'alley', which is supposed to be our meeting place, is not really an alley. It is a dead end – an empty strip of land with the surrounding buildings forming gigantic walls. It is deserted with debris strewn around. I don't like the look of this place at all. But I guess that this is the precise reason why Sujit has chosen this place. To be away from prying eyes when he is selling.

A figure appears in the alley with a backpack, the hood of his t-shirt covering his head. Sujit. My anger rises at the sight of him.

He is not alone. Behind him are two more figures. They don't approach me though. They just wait behind him, blocking the entrance to this space. The dark silhouettes they form, quicken my pulse.

Meeting him here doesn't seem to be such a good idea anymore.

'Sujit,' I call out.

His eyes widen in surprise.

'Where's Oshan?' he asks. His tone is guarded. He looks around warily.

'Sorry, I had to trick you into meeting me,' I say.

'What the fuck! Why? What is wrong with you?' he asks.

'What is your explanation?' I ask him, keeping an eye on the figures behind him.

Sujit is agitated now.

'Do you or do you not want to buy? Look, I owe him money. He owes the other chap. They are ruthless. I need this sale, bro. That's why they are here. To oversee the sale and to collect. So, don't mess with me. Please,' Sujit half warns and half pleads.

Something in me snaps when I hear this. Rage churns inside me like a volcano, hungry for destruction. It swallows me completely. I want to hurt him.

'Do you fucking know Puja spent a night in lock-up? Now all of you are going to pay for that. Get ready to spend some time in jail. I have informed the police,' I shout. I have no control over what I am saying anymore. I have no idea where any of this is coming from. I am stark raving mad.

At the mention of the word police, Sujit goes pale. He hesitates for a second.

Then he screams. 'It's a trap. *Run!*' He bolts towards the narrow entrance, dashing past the two figures.

Things happen in the flash of a second. Even before I can react, one of the figures charges towards me menacingly.

'You asshole. How dare you fucking set us up,' he screams.

The next thing I feel is a massive punch right in my eye. I see stars and then I double up in agony. I taste blood at the back of my mouth. I try to stand up straight. I am blinded by blood. Even before I can recover, the next blow comes. One of the guys is holding a broken beer bottle. I hold my arm over my face to defend myself. I hear a thwack and something snaps. Pain explodes. Then there's another blow – this time on my forehead and I can't see anymore. This is unbearable. I stagger backwards as blood gushes out. I crumple to the ground, unable to move. I curl into a ball, shield my face with my hands, and peer out with one eye.

'Fucking bastard. That will teach you,' says one of the guys to me as the other one bolts. The one with the beer bottle chases him. Sujit is nowhere to be seen. I am unable to keep my eyes open.

An ear-shattering scream in the distance pierces my brain. I hear footsteps of people running. Commotion. An ambulance in the distance. Am I imagining things? My brain is foggy. Am I bleeding to death?

Everything goes blank.

When I recover consciousness, I try to open my eyes, but one of them is tightly shut. I struggle to make sense of my unfamiliar surroundings. It takes me a few minutes to see that I am in hospital. Through one eye, I spot Sashi's worried face peering at me. Everything else is foggy.

'Are you okay?' he asks.

I nod.

'How did I get here?' My voice is hoarse and I can barely talk.

'From what I gather, someone told a shopkeeper to get an ambulance and go behind Nirvana café. Then he ran for his life. Another guy was stabbed brutally with a beer bottle. The guy who stabbed him ran away.'

It falls in place like a jigsaw puzzle then. Sujit was the first to run. He alerted the shopkeeper as soon as the two guys walked towards me. He knew what was coming.

'Ah, you are awake now. The police are here. They want a statement from you, can you speak?' a hospital staff asks me

'Yes,' I say.

A policeman in plainclothes comes in. He asks if I can describe what happened.

I tell him I was attacked.

'Can you specify where?' he asks.

'The alley behind Nirvana café.'

'What were you doing there?' he asks.

Despite my condition, I am able to think fast. If I mention Sujit then it means that Puja will get involved in this again. That's the last thing I want.

So, I tell the policeman that they pushed me into the empty space and tried to rob me. But since I didn't have my wallet, they attacked me in anger. The policeman writes it all down. Then he makes me sign it.

I don't want Puja's name to be dragged into this. I want to protect her, come what may.

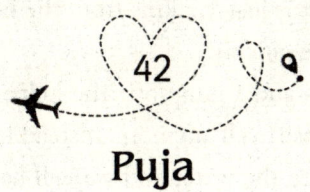

Puja

I am on the ferry, almost pulling into Mattancherry jetty, when I get a call from Sashi.

Why is he calling me? How did he get my number?

'I am afraid there's some bad news,' he says, his tone grim.

'What happened?' My stomach knots up.

'Arush – he is in the hospital. He had an accident.'

'Oh no! Which hospital?' My fingernails dig into my palm as I clench my fist tightly.

The winds lash mercilessly, making it hard to hear over the din of the ferry. I am almost screaming to be heard.

'Ashraya Hospital on TD Road. I am with him.'

'How is he?' I yell.

'He is okay. Don't worry. He gave me your number and wanted me to tell you.'

'Can I speak to him?'

'No, they don't allow phones in the Emergency section.'

'Was it a vehicle accident? Can you tell me what exactly happened?' I yell.

'Puja, come over. He is fine,' is all Sashi says.

There's a lump in my throat and my hands have gone cold. Why isn't Sashi giving me details? I don't know what to do so I open my maps. My hands are shaking so badly, I can barely type. I look up

Ashraya Hospital. It is just 1.7 kms from the boat jetty. Not too far at all. I can get there quickly.

The boat moors and I jump off. The helper is now used to me jumping off. He doesn't yell anymore. Instead he says, 'One of these days you will fall into the water and we will have to fish you out.' I don't reply.

There's a tightness in my chest as I break into a run towards the auto stand. In less than five minutes, I am at the hospital.

I rush to the Emergency section. At the reception counter outside, I tell the guy that my friend is inside.

To my surprise, he doesn't ask me any details or even what my friend's name is.

'You can go inside,' he says. I didn't expect it to be this easy.

The smell of sterile antiseptic assaults my nostrils as soon as I enter. I abhor this hospital smell. It's the first time in my life I am inside an Emergency section. I see a long row of beds cordoned off by curtains all around. Curtains are drawn around some beds. Machines whirring, beeping, distressed breathing sounds from one of the beds – all of it makes its way into my brain and settles down in the pit of my stomach with the heaviness of concrete.

Sashi, his face grave, is at the foot of one of the beds which I walk towards. When I see Arush, I stare in utter shock. I can barely recognise him. A part of his hair is shaved and in its place is a bandage with an angry red clot. His right eye is so swollen it is barely a slit. Red bruises dot his cheek. One arm is in a sling and there's congealed blood on the other.

I wince.

Arush's one good eye looks glazed. I don't know if he has recognised me. He doesn't say anything.

'I am here,' I tell him. I gently hold his hand and he shudders in pain. I draw back my hand quickly.

This is unbearable.

'How are you, Arush?' I ask gently.

'I will live,' he whispers, smiling feebly.

I blink back my tears.

'What happened? Are you okay?' I ask

'Sujit,' he whispers, 'I confronted him.'

'Oh, fucking hell, Arush… Sujit. How? Why did Sujit do this?' I ask. My blood boils in outrage.

I want to find Sujit and kill him.

Arush slowly shakes his head.

'No, he didn't. But he is involved with a dangerous gang. He owes money to his dealer, who owes the gang. They thought I had set up a trap. I lost my head and yelled that the cops are coming. Then they did this…,' Arush's voice is so low that I have to strain to hear him.

'This is terrible, Arush. It has gone too far. We have to expose him now. We can't let him get away with… with this.'

My anger at Sujit has been simmering for a while now. I had pushed it to the back of my mind. When I was with Arush, nothing seemed to matter. But now, seeing Arush in this state is more than I can handle. Arush doesn't deserve this. That worm Sujit shouldn't have involved us in the first place.

'Puja see, that was my intention too. To confront him. But that gang – they are dangerous folks, Puja. Stay away. Stay away from all of it. You were right. I should not have got involved at all. But I couldn't bear what he had done to you. I told the police it was an attack for robbery because I want to keep you out of it.'

My heart goes out to Arush. Even in this extreme pain he is looking out for me. I am shaking now; partly in rage, partly because I feel Arush's pain.

'Can you wait outside please? The senior doctor is here,' says a nurse.

Sashi and I move outside as the nurse draws the curtains.

As we step outside, we see Mukundan marching into the hospital. Following him is a small crowd of journalists and television crew. The television reporter positions herself as the crew begins to film her. She starts speaking in rapid Malayalam.

The receptionist gets up and says, 'Excuse me, please go outside. No TV cameras or press allowed. This is the Emergency section.'

The reporter is unfazed. She coolly takes a few steps away and continues. A retinue of newspaper reporters, photographers and those in the waiting area of the hospital surround her.

The reporter mentions the name of the channel, emphasising it is a live report. She says that in a gang war, Shaju alias Arjun Kumar, a native of Kalady, was stabbed with a broken beer bottle in a bylane in Jew Town, in a scuffle which the authorities suspect involved ganja trade. She mentions that she is at Ashraya Hospital where a British citizen who was beaten up by the gang is fighting for his life. She reports that it is likely that he went to buy ganja from the gang and they had an altercation over money. She says the British citizen is a student of the art school which Mukundan, a well-known figure in the state runs, and then she thrusts the mike at Mukundan.

It takes a few seconds for it to sink in that the 'British citizen' they are referring to is Arush. He is injured very badly, yes. But to blatantly say he is 'fighting for his life' is wrong. Then fear grips me. What if he is? The television drama unfolding is disturbing. A person from the crowd of reporters keeps looking at me, catching my eye. I wonder what he wants but I am distracted by the TV anchor who speaks loudly.

'What do you have to say about this incident?' she asks, thrusting the mike at Mukundan.

Mukundan says that he has been working closely with the tourism police to contain the menace of cannabis in the Fort Kochi area. He blames the present government for their inefficiency. He asserts that he has been campaigning actively for many months now and he calls for stricter laws and more regulations. There's a strange look in his eyes. He seems triumphant. Like he knew this was coming.

'Do you think the presence of foreigners in this area has led to increase of nefarious activities?' asks the reporter, clearly trying to strum up the drama and fear.

'I don't think it is right to blame foreigners. Tourism is after all an important way for currency to come in. I think we need stricter laws. That's the only way to contain this.' He says that his art school has a strict policy on drugs and alcohol, and both are not permitted in the premises. He adds that whatever happens outside, he has no control over.

I am enraged with what the reporter is saying. She is implying that Arush went to buy cannabis. This is not true at all. How can they blatantly vomit rubbish?

One of the reporters, the one who kept stealing glances at me, suddenly approaches and asks, 'Are you Mr Krishnan's daughter? Puja?'

'Yes,' I answer. I study his face carefully. I have no idea who he is. 'Do you know my father?'

'I am from Wayanad,' he says. 'I was home when the ganja haul there was reported. Weren't you arrested for that? What do you have to say about this?'

I am so taken aback I don't know what to say. This is the last thing I expected. To be recognised. Two other reporters have overheard the man. They gather around me now, like hungry vultures.

Suddenly the spotlight is on me. Someone whispers something to the television reporter and I am caught on camera.

'Puja Krishnan, why are you here and what is your involvement in this? Would you care to explain?' the TV reporter asks me.

One part of me wants to die right there. I thought that the worst was behind me. But I am back in the spotlight now. They are all waiting for answers. I blink like a deer caught in a headlight.

'I was framed. I am innocent. The real culprit has got away.' I stammer, not knowing what to say, a familiar dread creeping up coldly into my throat.

'Do you know the real culprit? Is it a coincidence that you are here, if you are claiming to be innocent?' the reporter does not let go.

I am trapped.

I have no choice.

I can't take this anymore. They are staring at me now. Accusatory eyes.

I have to speak up.

'I am here to see my friend Arush. He wasn't there to buy the substance. I was framed by someone I know. And he is involved in some illicit business which my friend Arush or I have no idea about.'

The reporter from Wayanad says, 'Can you name the person who framed you? Why did they do that? Do they have any enmity with you?'

'Sujit. He is the culprit. The police can investigate. I am innocent. My friend is innocent. Please leave us alone,' I say.

And with that, I flee into the Emergency.

A small voice in my head screams that I have made a mistake. A big mistake. My thoughts are scattered. I know I have played right into their hands. It's too late now. The live telecast is on air, all over Kerala state.

Oh, fuck. What a terrible mess.

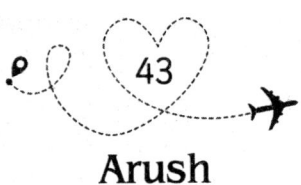

Arush

The doctors do what they do: run scans, take x-rays and look for any possible internal head injury. They want to keep me in the hospital for twenty-four hours, till tomorrow, as they have to administer a particular medication through an IV drip.

I take stock of my physical injuries. My right arm in a cast. The pain is dull, muted, reduced in intensity. The swollen blood vessels in my eyes throb rhythmically. My head feels like there's someone inside pounding on my skull, trying to get out. The stitches above the temple pinch my skin. With my partly shaved head, I probably look like Frankenstein.

Fortunately, my overseas medical insurance covers the hospital bills. It is also a lot cheaper and much more efficient than NHS back home. After checking with me, I am moved to a private room which is surprisingly luxurious, almost like a hotel room, except for the medical bed. I never knew hospital rooms could be this way.

Though the room is nice, I detest the IV drip that they have hooked me up to. With nothing to do, I keep looking at the medication dripping. Drip. Drip. Drip. I doze off looking at the drip.

When I wake up, I see Puja sitting quietly on the couch. She has been crying. Her eyes give her away. Sashi is sitting beside her.

'What happened?' I ask her.

'Arush…the reporters. It's terrible. They are all over. They… they interviewed me. One of them recognised me. I am on regional television,' she says.

'Ha ha, we will be famous now.' I try to joke, but it falls flat.

'That's the problem,' she sniffles. 'They brought up that old case and they are implying that you got beaten up because you went to buy cannabis. I had to defend you. I couldn't bear it.'

'It's okay.' I try to console her. 'And the good news is, the injuries aren't so bad. I can be out of here tomorrow.'

'Do your parents know?' Sashi asks.

'Not yet,' I tell them.

'Dude, I think you should call them,' Sashi says.

'I don't think I should inform them. They will just get worried. I know Ma will go crazy with worry.'

Mukundan comes in then.

'Ah, Arush. How are you feeling?'

'Better,' I say, even though I don't feel better at all.

'The reporters wanted to talk to you, but I have kept them out,' he says. 'For the longest time, I have been asking for a special unit to be posted here to combat all this. They just have the tourism police here, stationed at the police museum compound. But they don't have the power to book anyone. They have to take the help of the local police for that. Now, if it was under my administration…' he trails off. 'I am going to make a strong case to the Kerala government about this,' he finishes.

I see Puja's face turn red. Her mouth is a straight line. Her jaw is clenched. I can see she is making a big effort to remain quiet.

Sashi just nods.

'And Arush, I have already informed your college,' he says.

'Oh, why did you do that? I will be fine,' I say.

'This is a serious incident and you are under my care. The media has picked up this event. I will be failing in my duty and will be accused of negligence if I don't.'

I nod.

He asks if there's anything I need.

'I don't need anything, I am good,' I reply.

'Alright, I shall take your leave then. I have missed some classes. I shall come tomorrow for all the hospital paperwork when they discharge you. Sashi, you can call me if there's anything,' Mukundan says as he leaves.

'He will win this time. He is doing all the right things,' Sashi says as soon as he is out of earshot.

'Win what?' I ask.

'Elections. He handled the media very well. He made a good speech and they were lapping it all up,' Sashi says.

Puja says, 'What a fucking asshole...'

'Whoa, whoa. It's okay. Calm down,' I tell her.

But Puja gets even more angry.

'Don't you get it? That bastard. He is the one who brought the media. He gets political mileage out of this,' she says. I can now see why Puja is so enraged.

My phone rings and it is my parents. I am not able to hold the phone as the needle is in my left arm. I gesture to Puja and ask her to put it on speaker. She places the phone on my chest.

'Hello Ma.'

I have never heard my mother sounding this worried. 'Switch on the video, Arush. I want to see you.'

'Don't worry, Ma. I am okay. I have my friends here,' I say cheerfully.

But my mother isn't having any of it. She insists on seeing me.

I nod to Puja who switches on the video and holds up the phone. I see my mother's worried face and then I get a big jolt when I see my own face in the phone camera. I don't recognise myself. I look like a character from *Breaking Bad* who has been badly beaten up by the drug mafia.

My mother lets out a gasp when she sees me.

'Hey *bhagwan!*' she exclaims, as she covers her mouth.

Then my father comes online

'*Kya haalat bana rakhi hai apni,*' he says. It is very rarely that he speaks in Hindi and when he does, it is because he is extremely upset.

'It is nothing. I am being discharged tomorrow. It just looks worse than it is,' I try to assure them.

My mother starts to cry.

'Ma, say hi to Puja and Sashi,' I say. This is the best way to distract her. Puja and Sashi both come into the frame.

Sure enough, that makes my mother stop crying.

'Aunty, don't worry. We are taking care of him. He will be okay. The injuries are only external,' Puja says. I am surprised how confident she sounds.

My father says, 'Your college authorities told me it was an assault. They want you to discontinue the rest of your programme and return home immediately.'

'Immediately? But how?' I ask.

'They are in touch with the hospital doctors who have cleared your travel. They have decided that India is not safe, especially as the media has implied that drug mafia is involved. They want you out of there. The British High Commission is arranging for your travel even as we speak. You will have your tickets in a few hours and they will assist you. You can leave tomorrow,' he says.

'But... but this is all too sudden,' I protest.

'Look son, your safety is paramount here. This is why I wasn't happy when you wanted to go to India. India is really a terrible country. See what has happened. I don't want you staying in that bloody place a minute more than is necessary. If the authorities have decided to bring you back, they must have good reason for it,' my father is very firm. He doesn't want to hear anything I have to say. He hangs up.

There are so many emotions running through my head now. I don't know what to say. I am so weary. My thoughts are all a scramble. To leave? Tomorrow? What about the rest of the course? Then I look at my fractured right hand.

What about Puja? How can I just leave? I don't know what to say.

Puja is just as stunned as I am.

Her phone rings. She looks at the glowing screen and sits down on the couch, head in her hands.

'What happened? Who is it?' asks Sashi.

'My father,' says Puja so softly that I strain to hear her.

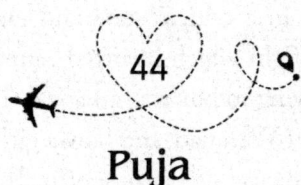

44

Puja

'Puja, come home,' is all my father says. He hangs up without another word. A chill runs down my spine. I sit there for a few seconds, not knowing what to do. This is worse than him yelling at me, demanding an explanation asking me why I spoke to the TV channels.

'I have to leave,' I tell Arush and Sashi.

'Are you okay?' asks Arush. How ironical, I think, considering he is the one on the hospital bed with the IV drip to his arm.

I walk up to him and kiss him on the forehead.

The sinking sensation in the pit of my stomach drowns me.

'Take care,' I tell him.

Then I leave for home.

My father and mother are waiting for me in the drawing room when I enter. The television is on and it's bizarre to see myself on our 72" screen. I hate the way I look. I hate the way I sound. I sound defensive. Like I have done something wrong. The way I am stammering makes it seem like I am guilty. They have edited the clip and removed the part where I named Sujit, and where I have clearly said I am not guilty. So now it seems like when the reporter is asking me to name the person, I am walking away.

My father quietly changes the channels. Multiple channels are playing the same clip. They all report the same thing. The guy who was stabbed is in a critical state and may not survive. They report that it was a fight which involved cannabis trade. A British national who was trying to buy was attacked. They talk about ganja being seized earlier at Wayanad, and how a girl student from Kochi was taken into police custody because of it. They have dragged my parents into this, mentioning that I am the daughter of a prominent businessman and that my mother is a reputed surgeon.

This is worse than my worst nightmare.

'What do you have to say Puja?' asks my father quietly.

'What have we done to deserve this? What is that boy's involvement? Tell us the truth,' my mother says. She isn't yelling. Her face is pale.

I feel miserable to have inflicted this on them.

Shanti chechi hovers nervously in the background.

'Ma, accha, trust me. Arush doesn't do drugs. These television channels – they are lying,' I plead.

But neither my father nor my mother believe me. Their gaze is stern. Denunciatory. They have already judged me. Condemned me.

It is the worst feeling in the world.

'I pulled you out of this once. I told you to stay away from all this. Why did you go to the hospital? When did that boy come here? Why have you been lying to us?' asks my father.

'I am sorry. I never meant to...' I mumble.

'What is the use of your sorry? What is the point, Puja?' asks my mother. 'How can we even show our faces to anyone now? Our reputation, our standing in society is destroyed.'

'The DIG of Police called me after he saw the news. He asked me why you spoke and why you didn't lie low, especially after the Wayanad incident. He said the police have to investigate now and file a report.'

My shoulders slump when I hear that. I am unable to speak. A police investigation. My palms go cold. The knot in the pit of my stomach tightens.

I say nothing and stand there like a statue. Frozen.

But the worst isn't over.

'You have been lying to us all this while,' my mother says. 'You haven't attended a single class in college since it reopened. The principal of your college called me after seeing the news on TV. They are suspending you from college. Neither have you been attending coaching classes. I checked with the centre. Which means that *all* this while, you have been meeting that boy, pulling wool over our eyes. Isn't it? Don't lie. Just tell me the truth.'

'I am sorry... Yes, I have been meeting him,' I confess. I am barely able to speak now.

'You deserve to be whipped,' my mother says. 'Just tell them to take her to the lock-up again. Maybe then she will learn a lesson. Maybe she will learn not to lie.'

My mother's words cut like a sword. I hang my head in shame.

'How is the boy now? Is he fighting for his life?' my father asks.

'No. The TV channels are sensationalising it. He is going back to UK,' I say.

'Good riddance. I want you to have no contact with him whatsoever. Do you hear me? *No* contact. I don't want you involved with *any* of these idiots. They are all riff-raff. Scum of the society. Do you understand?' my mother says.

Arush isn't scum. Arush isn't riff-raff. He went to confront Sujit because he couldn't bear what Sujit did. To me. Your daughter.

I want to say this, but I stand there silently, unable to speak, feeling the noose around my neck tightening. I slowly nod.

'After what you have done, I don't trust you. Give me your phone,' my mother says.

'Eh?' I ask. It takes me a few seconds to understand.

'Your phone, please,' my mother extends her hand.

'Please Ma... Please, do not take away my phone,' I plead hating my whiny voice, but I can't help it. I can't imagine not communicating with Arush.

'Look at her. She is pleading for her phone even after all this. Give it to me,' my mother says. She is standing next to me, her eyes boring into mine. I lower my gaze. I have no choice. I hand over my phone to her.

'Go and get your laptop as well,' says my mother.

'Please... please, don't do this,' I say. I don't budge. I continue standing there, pleading.

'You should have thought of it before you decided to make your parents famous.' My mother's voice is ice-cold.

With quick steps, she walks into my room, goes to my desk and takes my laptop.

Then she marches away with both: my laptop and my phone.

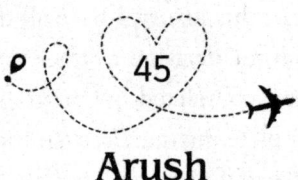

Arush

On the British Airways flight back to the UK, I am treated like royalty. The airline has upgraded me to business class, a first. The flat beds, the individual aisle access, the menu and the service make me forget my injuries for a brief while. Thanks to the British High Commission sending a representative who escorts me right up to the flight, I have been whisked through some special entrances, avoiding all queues and going straight to immigration, where my passport was stamped within seconds.

Mukundan's words come back to me. 'Look, it's best if you go back at the earliest. It is a tricky situation. If the local police press some charges against you, it will become messy,' he had emphasised. He also warned me that he wouldn't be able to help if that happened. With pressure from my father, the college authorities as well as Mukundan, I had no choice but to leave immediately. Things have been happening at breakneck speed since last evening, throwing everything in a whirl.

What pains the most about this hasty departure is that I haven't got a chance to say goodbye to Puja, who has been incommunicado. I have sent her messages on Instagram too, and she hasn't seen them either.

At 35,000 feet up in the air, as I snuggle cosily into my blanket, I feel far removed from the realities on the ground, safe in this cocoon.

Suspended here amidst this luxury, I have all the time in the world to think. I think about my decision to track down Sujit. Had I not done that, I could have completed my programme. I am sad about not being able to complete my murals, even though Mukundan has carefully packed my half-finished work and the colours. He has instructed me to complete it back at home, once my arm heals. He has graciously agreed to guide me through video calls which Sashi has promised to set up.

My eye is much better now – not as scary as it looked earlier. I have worn a cap to hide the bizarre bald patch. The large bandage has been replaced with a medical tape to cover the dissolvable stitches. But for my arm in the sling, I look almost normal.

My mind is in turmoil. All this happened because of my stubbornness to confront Sujit. Though one part of me regrets it, in a strange way, I also feel sorry for him. His fate is far worse than mine. I am going back to my usual life in Britain where I can put this behind me. I can't imagine what he must be going through – owing money to these gangs and being forced to do the dirty job of a street peddler. Another part of me is angry that he involved Puja and me.

I am landing in a couple of hours. My father will be waiting.

I don't want to face him. But I have no choice.

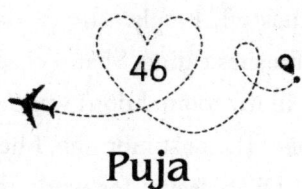

46

Puja

I run into my room, shut the door and bury my face in my pillow. I sob and sob, unable to stop. I don't want anyone to hear me crying. All the disappointments, the regrets, the wrong decisions, the injustices, form an army marching together, invading my brain. Thoughts swirl around overwhelming me, submerging me. They come in relentless waves. I cry, thinking of the unfairness of it all. I cry thinking about how my mother has always taken Divya's side since childhood. I cry because I haven't ever done well academically, and have never succeeded like Divya has. I cry because it was so not my fault that I got arrested. And it wasn't my fault that those reporters pounced on me. I cry thinking of Arush – his swollen eye, the IV needle in his arm.

After a while, when I am exhausted, I stop. I wash my face and sit at my desk. My eyes are swollen from all the crying. Without my phone and laptop, I feel lost. From my past experience I know my mother has locked it in the vault in her room, where she keeps her jewellery, and it is impossible to try and sneakily take it. It feels like I have lost a limb. I don't know what to do. I pick up a paper and a pen and I start doodling idly. The doodles turn into angry scribbles and I end up tearing the paper, because I press the pen too hard.

There's a gentle knock on my door. Shanti chechi says my mother is calling me, asking me to join the family at the dinner table.

'Just tell her to fuck off,' I reply.

After everyone finishes eating, Shanti chechi quietly brings me my meal. I eat alone in my room. I don't want to talk to anyone. My family leaves me alone. The next morning, I hear them going about their daily business. Divya leaves for work, my mother leaves for hospital, my father goes to his study. Life hasn't stopped for anyone but me.

I wonder how Arush is. I am desperate to make contact with him. Has he reached? Does his arm hurt? Is he okay?

In the evening, my father comes to my room and knocks.

I don't answer.

'May I come in, molle?' he asks.

I don't reply.

'I am coming in now,' he says, opens the door and walks in.

I am lying on my stomach, reading a book. It is another of the books that Arush had recommended.

'Molle, I know you are angry. But this is for the best. The reporters are waiting for more, but Unni uncle and I have somehow managed to keep them away,' he says. His tone is gentle. He doesn't sound angry.

I don't say anything.

'You have to come out now. Plainclothes policemen have come home. But don't worry. This is just a formality. The DIG has assured me it's all good.'

I continue pretending to read the book. The thought of policemen in the house makes me anxious, bringing back memories of my time in the lock-up. Thin beads of perspiration form on my forehead.

My father doesn't miss it.

'It's okay, molle. I am with you. Come, let's get through it together,' he says, placing his hand on my shoulder.

My father being nice to me brings a fresh wave of tears.

'Come, come outside, and give your statement. And that will be the end of that. This is just a formality; don't worry,' he coaxes me.

I brush my hair and go outside.

The policemen seem a little uncomfortable and ill-at-ease in my father's presence.

They ask me why I was at the hospital. I tell them I had gone to meet my friend Arush as I had got a call that he was hurt. They ask me how I know him. I tell them we met at Wayanad. I tell them about Sujit, how he took my backpack and how Arush or I have nothing to do with the substance. I tell them it is very unfair for the TV reporters to pounce on me like that. They should be chasing the real culprits. Surprisingly, I feel slightly better once I am done. Like a weight has been lifted off my shoulders after narrating my side of the story.

'We know all this. Sorry, sir. We are just doing our duty. We have to file the report and we have to show that we have taken a statement from your daughter,' they say apologetically.

Then they thank me as well as my father, and leave.

'Can I have my phone back?' I ask my father as soon as they leave.

'Your mother and I have decided that it's best you don't have it for a few days,' my father answers firmly.

'What about my laptop? At least give that to me,' I tell him.

'Puja, instead of thinking about your laptop and phone, you should worry about your suspension from college!' My father shakes his head, his lips pressed tight.

'Have you thought of your future? What are you going to do?' he continues. He is pacing up and down the drawing room now. 'What is your plan Puja? What is your plan for the future?'

I have been so busy feeling miserable about not having my phone and laptop, and upset about Arush going away all of a sudden, that I haven't thought about my future plans or college. It is only when I see how agitated my father is that I think about it.

What am I going to do now? I have no idea.

All I can think of is whether Arush has reached the UK and how I am going to communicate with him without my phone or laptop.

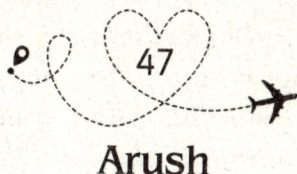

Arush

When my father sees me, the first thing he says is, 'We need to get your head shaved. We can do it before we get home.'

There's no hug or any display of emotion. My father has never been demonstrative and yet I feel comforted by his familiar presence and his practical approach.

The moment we are outside Heathrow, the cold air hits me and it feels wonderful . Compared to India, Britain is so quiet. So peaceful. So clean. So *familiar*. It feels great to be in these surroundings I know so well.

I remember reading somewhere that if you have comforting memories associated with a place, it fires up the neurons in your brain cells which generate serotonin, the feel-good hormone. I wonder if that is what is happening here. After all, I *am* home. This *is* home! There's a happy hum in my heart as we speed along the highway. I gaze at the English countryside with fond eyes as we drive through small towns. The horses, the cows, the sheep – all of it puts a smile on my face. India had engulfed me so much that I had forgotten how serene life here is.

Before I left for India, I was excited, eager and I looked forward to the experience. But now that I am back here, it is mostly a sense of relief and safety I feel. Who would have thought that of all things, feeling safe would even be a point to consider?

'Let's stop at Burton and get your head shaved. We don't want you going home looking like this,' my father says.

We drive into town and head to Supercuts.

'Whoa, what happened?' asks the lady at the counter.

'India happened,' my father says.

'You travelled to India?' the lady asks, making it sound like I went to the other end of the world.

'Yes,' I smile. Her eyes widen and she nods understandingly. Perhaps I have confirmed her worst fears – that people who land in India get beaten up badly as soon as they set foot on the soil.

Once all my hair is removed, it doesn't look so bad. Without my hair and with the small medical tape on my head, I look tough. If I was in high school, this is what my friends would have called a badass look.

When we reach home, Rhea rushes out on her bouncing ball and greets me. My mother is behind her.

'You look cool. Like Caillou!' she exclaims giving me a tight hug, referring to the central character in her favourite cartoon she watches on YouTube. Her hair smells of the strawberry shampoo she loves and she wears denim shorts and a t-shirt that says 'sunshine' with a yellow sun drawn on it. She *is* sunshine.

'Have you been watching too many cartoons?' I ask her as she throws her arms around me.

'Only when mama is busy in the shop,' she replies.

My mother hugs me next.

'Have you eaten?' she asks.

'Yeah, Ma. They pampered me silly. I travelled business class. It was worth getting beaten up for that,' I tell her.

'Shut up,' she says and smacks me lightly on the shoulder.

'Owww, that hurt,' I scream.

'Oh no, I am so sorry. I am sorry!'

'Ha ha! I was just fooling you,' I laugh.

'Silly boy. You really had me there,' says my mother.

Rhea dances around laughing, saying, 'Arush fooled mummy. Arush fooled mummy.'

The smell of fresh hot parathas is in the air and I am certain I can also smell paneer butter masala.

'You made paneer?' I sniff appreciatively.

'Why? Didn't you get paneer in India or on your business class flight?'

'*Touché*, mother.' I smile.

'I didn't make it. Your uncle sent it from the restaurant. They are coming over to see you in the evening,' my mother says.

My uncle and aunt visit me. They ask about my experiences in India and whether I liked it. We all laugh about how Chandru mama is still complaining about me distributing the goodies to the children at Wayanad.

'So, now that you have this fracture, you can't go back to college till it comes off?' asks my aunt.

'Technically, I can. But after my stint in India, I was supposed to be on a break anyway. I guess I will get time off till this heals,' I reply.

'Good. I need help in the shop. This is a busy time. A lot of weddings are happening this month,' says my mother.

I don't particularly like working in the shop, but it doesn't make any sense to sit at home either.

It is only late at night, when everyone has left after dinner, that I think of Puja. I open my phone and check my messages, my emails. I even check my Instagram. I haven't heard from her at all. I don't know what to make of her silence.

She is probably angry with me because I left so suddenly. I feel a little foolish now about having tried to confront Sujit. When I was in India, it seemed very important. But now that I am far removed, it feels distant and irrelevant. I feel like I got my hand broken and stitches on my head for nothing. Puja hasn't bothered to write me a single message.

It makes me feel like a prize idiot.

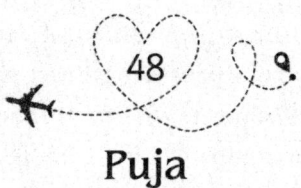

48

Puja

If Shanti chechi owned a smart phone, I could have used it to send an email to Arush. But she only has a basic phone. I can't call any of my college friends either as I haven't memorised anyone's number.

There's a desktop in my father's study, but my father locks it at night. I know this because at night I tried to sneak into his study. Even if I do manage to get to that desktop, knowing my father, it would probably be password protected, yet it's worth a try. I wait for him to leave home so that I can get to it. But for the past five days, my father hasn't left home at all.

Each day that passes feels like a year. I have never felt this lonely, this lost, this helpless, this trapped. I don't know how I am surviving without my phone and laptop. I am a prisoner here.

I keep thinking about Arush. What is he doing? How is he? Is he worried about me? Has the wound on his head healed? Does he miss me? Does he miss India? I long to hear his voice. I wish now that I had given him Shanti chechi's number. Then perhaps he could have called me.

Each day I wake up thinking that my parents might relent and give me the phone. But each night I go to bed disappointed.

'Have you thought of your future? What's your plan?' That's all my parents ask over and over. I have no answers for them.

Shanti chechi brings my meals and I eat alone in my room. I haven't joined my family for a meal ever since they took away my phone. Shanti chechi eats with me on the terrace a few times and I appreciate her company. I am completely cut off from the outside world. All I have are books and television (which I don't watch).

My parents come to my room to talk to me.

'You can sulk all you want; you aren't getting your phone or laptop back. You don't seem to have any goal, any interest in making a career for yourself,' says my mother, making herself comfortable on the sofa opposite my bed.

I sit on the bed, my legs folded, my arms around my knees. I rock back and forth, avoiding meeting their eyes.

'Look, Puja molle, be reasonable. You have to make some kind of a plan for your future, isn't it?' my father says.

'I can write the exams privately,' I tell them.

'Okay, you have to start studying for that, isn't it? I have been observing you these last few days. You haven't touched your books,' my father remarks.

Can't you see how badly I want to talk to Arush?

'I will study.'

'Shall I arrange a home tutor for you? I can get someone to come and help you,' my mother offers.

That's the last thing I want.

'No thanks, I don't need a tutor. I can read the textbooks and understand the subject myself.'

'Alright then, get cracking. Don't waste time,' my mother commands.

'When will you give me my phone?'

'When I see that you are serious about your studies.'

'Do you mean to say that if I sit at my desk and pretend to study, you will give my phone to me?' I ask. I find her answer and her attitude ridiculous.

'Look at her! Even now she can only think of cheating us. *Pretend* to study indeed. What is wrong with you, Puja?' My mother is getting angrier by the minute. Riling her up gives me a sadistic satisfaction.

'Leave it, molle. Don't be stubborn; don't disrespect her. After all, she is your mother,' says Accha.

What is that supposed to mean? Of course, she is my mother. What is the 'after all' that my father is talking about? Do mothers get a special pass to be unreasonable because they have given birth to you? I suppress my anger, say nothing. The more I speak, the longer they will remain in my room. I want them to leave. The best thing to do is sit silently. My strategy works.

My father sighs heavily and gets up.

'Start studying. I will make enquiries about giving the exam privately,' he says.

'If you don't study and you intend to fail, then the best option is to get you married to a rich guy. At least then he will take care of you,' my mother says. I am not the only one who knows how to rile her up. She knows exactly what buttons to push too, to make me furious.

But I don't want to give her the satisfaction of knowing she has irked me.

'Sure, start searching for grooms. Make sure they are very rich,' I tell her coolly.

Yes. That should serve her right.

My mother's jaw clenches. I know I have won this one. She stomps off without saying a word in reply.

The next morning, I overhear my father telling someone on the phone that he will meet them at the Taj in an hour.

Hurrah! I can try to get access to his desktop.

I wait impatiently for him to leave. Every second that passes feels like an hour. When he leaves, I wait for about fifteen minutes, just in case he returns for something. I try his study door. Locked, as expected.

Shanti chechi watches me as she dusts the house.

'Do you know where the key to this room is?' I ask her.

As much as she loves me, I know she doesn't want to betray my parents.

'Come on, Shanti chechi, I am *desperate* to speak to Arush. It's so unfair. It has been six days. Please, if you tell me where the key is, I promise I won't breathe a word,' I beg her.

She doesn't say anything. She walks to my parents' bedroom and I follow her.

She starts dusting the chest of drawers furiously, after which she silently walks away.

I watch her puzzled and then it clicks. She doesn't want to *tell* me where it is, but she has probably *shown* me. I smile at the clever but convoluted logic she has used. I rummage quickly through the drawers and under a pile of towels, I find a single key.

I can't contain my excitement. I rush to my father's study. The key works. I sit at his chair, switch on his desktop, and wait excitedly as the screen comes on. Of course, it is password protected. I try to guess the password. Maybe it is my mother's name and her date of birth? Maybe it is my name? Maybe it is Divya's? It shows me a warning that I have entered the incorrect password too many times. I stop then. I don't want my father to find out I have been trying to break into his computer.

I sit at the desk wondering what to do. I open his drawer and go through the stuff. I see two envelopes, both addressed to me. What in the world are these? I open the first and see that it is the welcome kit from the bank. The first has my account details, my ATM card, my account statement, my net banking instructions and a little information booklet. The second contains the system generated password on a two-layer sealed perforated covered slip. I pause and stare, not believing what I am looking at. This is *my* bank account. *Mine*. I look at the amount and gasp. Have I made a mistake? I can't believe it. I count the zeroes again. There's no mistake, as the figure is written in words at the bottom. It is thirty-five lakhs! I can't believe it. No wonder Accha was in a hurry to get the forms signed. He had sent Anthony all the way to Wayanad for this. This is a bounty! I *have* money! I am rich. I hesitate for a few seconds. Is this stealing? But how can it be stealing when the money is in my name and my grandmother *gave* it to me?

I quietly pocket the envelopes and glance around once to check that nothing in the study has been disturbed. I lock the study and place the key back. I hide the envelopes in my desk.

Once I calm down a little, a plan begins to form in my head. It is a wild plan. My heart beats faster at the thought of it. But now that I have money, *anything* is possible.

I sit on the terrace for a long time, thinking about my plan. I gaze at the ships at sea. The more I think about it, the more certain I am that it can be done. One part of me is paralysed with fear and bad childhood memories of travel. But another part of me so badly wants this, that it goads me on.

I rush to the drawing room and grab the newspaper. I know what I am looking for – a prominent advertisement of a travel agency which offers travel packages. It isn't in today's paper. I pull out the

196 of 288 • *Preeti Shenoy*

newspapers of the last five days and go through them meticulously till I find it.

I run to Shanti chechi and ask her for her phone.

'What happened?' she asks. 'Did you manage to mail him? Is he going to call you? Did you give him my phone number?'

The questions tumble out from Shanti chechi because I am dancing about in excitement.

'No, Shanti chechi, it's password protected,' I tell her airily.

'Then?'

'I am going to do something even better than mailing him.' I smile.

'What?'

'I am going to travel to the UK and see him.'

Arush

I am tired of waiting for a message from Puja. I have sent her four emails and three messages. They all remain unanswered. It is clear she doesn't want to be in touch. It's been a week of silence now. Over a hundred and sixty-eight hours. I can't believe she has ghosted me. A thought creeps in. Is it possible that whatever it was that we had between us was not real? I am desperate for answers.

I recall reading about holiday romances on a psychology website. I search for it and look up the article. It says that even the savviest of us lose our perspective on relationships when we are in a new country. It is the excitement, the charged-up adrenaline, the openness to new experiences, which turn even cynics into hopeless romantics. This makes perfect sense to me now.

Perhaps that is exactly what happened.

The more I think about it, the surer I become. My India trip had put me in a time-warp. Was I attracted to her only because my brain was on an overdrive with new India experiences?

Now that I am back home with a broken arm, all of it seems like an enormous mistake. What an absolute idiot I was to 'trap' Sujit. My brain wasn't working the way it should have. I was in some altered reality perception. Right now, those memories seem like from another lifetime.

Also, with my life being here and her life being there, what future did our so-called relationship (if it was even a relationship) have, anyway?

We hadn't even talked about it.

It hits me like a brick. Deep down, Puja *knew* there was no future and hence she decided to break it off. She has dropped out of my life simply because she doesn't want to be in it anymore.

'Hello, dreaming at the cash counter?' asks my mother as she smacks me lightly on the head. I am perched on the stool at the cash counter and a customer is waiting to be billed.

'I am so sorry,' I say, taking the purchase from her and using the barcode scanner with my left hand.

'No worries, love. I wasn't sure if you could bill with that,' she says, pointing to my cast.

Before I can reply, my mother takes her card, swipes it, packs the purchase neatly and hands it to her.

'Have a lovely day,' she calls out as the lady leaves the shop.

'What are you thinking about? Are you worried about your hand and your course work at college?'

'Yeah, Ma,' I lie.

There's no way I am telling my family about Puja or the real reason my hand is broken. I have beaten myself enough over my foolishness. I don't want to drag my family in. It was a misadventure in India, which I am going to put behind me and move on.

Later that night, I call up Jenna. I tell her all that had happened in India. She is shocked when she hears the story of how I was beaten up. I confess I haven't heard from Puja and I want to know the female perspective.

'Why would a girl do that?' I ask.

'After all you have shared with her, I admit it is puzzling. That is a classic guy dickhead move,' she says.

'Is it possible that she didn't see how this would work out and I was just a fling? A foreign exotic boy she had fun with and got bored of?' I ask.

I want Jenna to deny it. I want Jenna to tell me it is simply not possible. That girls don't do things like that. I hold my breath while Jenna thinks.

After a long silence she says, 'I hate to break it to you, but I think you have been dumped.'

'Alright. Thank you for being honest. I appreciate it,' I tell her. Then I hang up.

I sit for a long time on my bed with my weeping heart for company.

The pain of rejection is excruciating.

Relationships I had before this have ended, but never have I felt this way. I burn in the embers of rejection. Bitterness rises to my mouth like bile.

I drown in pain and shame, raging at the unfairness and the futility of it all.

The pragmatic part of my brain tells me that what has happened has happened. I can't do anything about it.

The only thing I can do now is to move on.

After two more days of unbearable agony, I decide to do just that. I have to put this behind me and move on.

Places

Oh, the places you'll go.
— *Dr. Suess*

Puja

My hands tremble as I call the travel agency from Shanti chechi's phone. It feels safer to call from her phone rather than from the home landline.

'Akbar Travels, how may I help you?' says a girl.

'I... er... I saw your advertisement in the newspaper,' I tell the girl. My voice comes out funny.

'Yes, yes ma'am. Which package are you interested in? Domestic or international?' she asks, bright and chirpy.

'International.'

'Oh, that's very good, ma'am. May I know which place you want to travel to? Europe, USA or the Far East? We have very good offers for all international packages.'

'I actually want to know if you do visas,' I tell her.

'Yes, ma'am. We take care end-to-end: visa, air tickets, Indian meals, hotels – everything. The package rates are inclusive of all this,' she clarifies.

'No. I meant I need a visa to go to UK. I don't need a holiday package. Can your agency help with that?

'Oh, I see,' she says, her enthusiasm dropping immediately. 'Please hold on while I transfer you to the concerned department.'

A hundred butterflies flutter in my tummy as I wait for someone to answer. It feels like my life depends on whether or not they would be able to do the visa for me.

'My name is Fahad. How may I help you?' asks the voice at the other end.

'I would like a travel visa for UK please. And also, tickets,' I say.

'Sure, I can help you with that. May I know what is the purpose of your travel, madam, and what are the dates?' he asks.

'As soon as I get the visa. How long will you take? It is to a see a friend in the UK,' I tell him.

'So, you will need a standard visitor visa,' he says.

'Yes. That's the one I need.' I say, 'How long will it take and how much would it cost?'

'Do you have all the documents ready?' he asks.

'What documents?' I ask him.

'We need a valid passport. It shouldn't expire within six months of your date of travel, two recent colour photographs, matt finish 80 percent face visibility, bank statements for the last six months, Income Tax returns for the last three years and last three months' salary slips, as well as a covering letter stating the purpose of visit.'

This gives me a jolt. I never knew that all of this was needed for a visa.

'What? I am not employed,' I tell him.

'Are you a housewife then? If so, we need a marriage certificate,' he says.

'No, no. I am a student. I can't give a bank statement for the last six months. My bank account is new.'

'But that's mandatory. Also, they need to see a minimum balance of 1,200-1,800 pounds, which is about two lakhs in INR.'

'That won't be an issue,' I confidently tell him. 'Will it do if I submit my parents' bank statements along with mine?'

'Yes, yes that should be fine. We need it with the bank seal,' he says.

'Oh, I see,' I reply, my heart sinking. I don't know how I will get the bank seal. 'And how long will it take after that?' I ask.

'Once we submit all the documents, generally less than fifteen days,' he says. 'It might be even lesser as now UK is really promoting tourism. You will have to go the VFS office at Ravipuram for biometrics.'

'Okay,' I say. 'And how will I get the visa?'

'You can choose the option of having it delivered or you can collect it from VFS.'

Then I ask him what it will cost. Including the agency commission, it comes to around 9,500 rupees.

I am happy that I can easily afford that. I tell him that I will get back in touch with him.

'Is this your number, madam? I can follow up with you and assist you if you need any clarifications,' he says.

Yes, I need you to clarify how to get attested bank statements.

'Oh, yes – yes. I will call you once I organise all this,' I tell him, sounding a lot more confident than I feel. Then I ask him to repeat the list of documents that are required to get the visa, writing it all down.

Shanti chechi is looking at me curiously. 'You are really going to do this, aren't you?'

'Yes, I am,' I tell her. 'Please help me keep a watch on the door. Alert me before anyone comes.'

Shanti chechi nods, staring at me in disbelief.

Now that I have made up my mind, I am determined. I go back to my father's study and rummage through all the files in his cupboard. My father is meticulous with his files – they are neatly labelled and organised. I open the one which says bank statements. He has conscientiously done bank reconciliation. In the joint account with my mother, he has more than 15 crores. (I count the zeroes thrice.) That too, this is just *one* of his bank accounts. There are a couple more accounts with astronomical sums that make my head spin. Till now, I had not even thought about money and banks. Now I furiously gather every bit of information I can.

'Puja molle, here's juice for you, come fast!' Shanti chechi's tone is loud and frantic. Her warning tone. I hurriedly lock the study, slipping the key into my pocket. Dying of nervousness and fright, I hastily sit at the dining table and open the newspaper, acting cool. Seconds later, the key turns in the door and my mother walks in.

'Oh! Good to see that you have come out of your room at last,' my mother says.

'How was your day?' I ask. I am so nervous; I have to say *something*.

'He died at the operating table. We couldn't do anything,' she says. 'Shanti, get my pomegranate juice.'

My mother doesn't say anything else to me. She is in a sombre mood. Whenever she loses a patient, she is like this. I know from experience that my mother will go and sleep now, not waking up till late evening. She always goes into deep sleep after stressful surgeries.

My mother finishes the juice which Shanti chechi gives her and announces that she is going to rest. She doesn't want anyone to disturb her. Shanti chechi and I know the drill only too well. When I was a child, Shanti chechi would play with me for hours, while my mother slept.

I ponder over what the travel agent had said. I need attested bank statements. I know that my parents have a banking Relationship Manager Viji, who comes home every now and then to discuss things with them. There is a way around this problem. It's a daring one, but it will work if executed well. I am in no mood to back out now.

I wait for an hour or so, till my mother is in deep sleep. I sneak into my parents' bedroom. The key to my father's study feels heavy in my pocket. I tiptoe silently and gently open the drawer. It slides out. I place the key exactly where I found it.

My mother snores softly. Her phone is next to her, beside her bed. I grab it and walk to the balcony. My hands shake.

Holy shit. I have done it.

I open my mother's phone. She never keeps it locked because she thinks it is easier and faster if she has to message someone if the phone isn't locked. I am glad she is an Emergency surgeon, and for a moment, I am even glad that the patient died. As soon as the thought comes, I feel terrible, but not terrible enough to stop doing what I am about to do.

I scroll through the contacts. I find Viji and compose a text: 'I need attested bank statements of the last six months. Can you please have it delivered urgently to my home? Please acknowledge. Please hand over to my daughter as I will be at the hospital.'

I send it and wait.

In eight minutes, I get her reply. 'Yes, ma'am. I will send the runner tomorrow with the attested statements. Is that okay?' she asks.

'Please send at 11.30 am,' I reply.

I know for certain that my mother will be at the hospital then.

'Yes, ma'am. Will do,' she replies.

Yes! Yes! Yes! One major hurdle solved.

I delete the messages and tiptoe back to my mother's room. I place the phone carefully back. She is still sleeping.

I have done it. I can't believe it. I am going to have the statements soon.

I comb through my desk for recent photos of me. My father had made me click them saying they would come in handy. I also know the kind of photos needed for a visa as when I had gone to get the photos clicked, the guy had announced that these photos could be used for any visa too. He was proud that he was giving us a 'dual purpose' photo, as he called it.

I can't wait to get my tickets to the UK.

Fifteen days, the agent had said. Perhaps twenty.

If I get to see Arush at the end of all this, it is going to be worth the wait. I switch on some music and all I can think about is Arush kissing me in the English countryside.

Arush

Being at the shop and being at home with Rhea keeps me completely occupied. For most part of the day, I don't have time to think about why Puja disappeared without a trace. My aunt and uncle keep visiting us.

My hair has started growing back. I am happy to be home. My body *needed* this pampering, this care. I feel loved, content and fortunate to have my close-knit family.

My mother keeps fussing over me and cooks all my favourite dishes.

'Ma, stop! You will make me so fat that my arm will burst out of this cast,' I tell her.

'Really?' asks Rhea, her eyes as big as saucers.

Overjoyed to have me all to herself, she plays her version of Scrabble with me, keeping me amused for hours. She snuggles up to me like a kitten, resting her head on my chest as she holds up a book, prodding me to read out loud.

My mother, happy to have me around the shop, chatters about all the people in the neighbourhood. I soon turn into the official resident expert on all the local gossip: whose daughter is going around with whose son, who is going to India, who is going to college in which part of the world, what course they are studying and even the gory details of bad marriages.

My father asks every day, 'How is your arm today?'

Every day my reply is the same, 'It's okay.'

I could have never imagined a single day without being able to draw. But now I am forced to slow down, forced to accept this phase of my life, where I have to do nothing but rest my arm.

I am shocked to discover that Puja's image is fading day by day from my mind. What remains is the sharp sting of Jenna's words that keep playing in my head.

'I hate to break it to you, but you have been dumped.'

I can't understand why in the world people do this. She could have dumped me if she so wished, but I deserved to know the reason. Disappearing like this leaves the other wondering what happened. It is worse than a break-up as there is no closure. You are just left hanging, hanging, hanging. It simply isn't right.

The next morning when I wake up, there is still no mail from Puja, no messages. I want to stop obsessively checking my mail. So, as painful as it is, there is only one thing left to do. I uninstall all the apps where she can reach me.

Then I steel myself and with a heavy heart, block her on mail.

If she has moved on, I have to move on too.

Goodbye, Puja. It was nice knowing you.

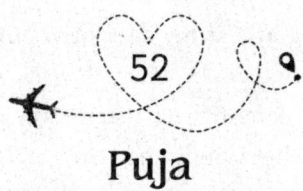

Puja

It is eighteen minutes past 11.30. The runner ought to have come with the bank documents by now. I sit nervously in my room. If my father finds out about the runner, it is 'game over'.

Around noon, when the doorbell rings, I rush to the door. Shanti chechi hurries out of the kitchen at the same time, getting to the door before me, her saree pallu wrapped around her. She blocks the door with her frame when she opens it.

'Who is it, Shanti?' my father calls out and my heart nearly pops into my mouth.

'I had ordered some vegetables, sir,' she says, and she opens the door. A few seconds later, she shuts it. When she turns, she has a bag of vegetables in her hand. So that was what she was hiding under her saree pallu! God bless Shanti chechi.

She gestures furiously with her eyes. I casually follow her to the kitchen. Right on top of the bag of vegetables lies the envelope from the bank. A large envelope.

I open it gleefully. Yes! The statement of accounts for the last six months has been attested. I slip it under my t-shirt, rush to my room and hide it in my cupboard.

Now all I have to do is wait for my father to leave the house, so I can make a call to the travel agency.

It takes him four whole days to leave the house again. Whenever my parents are around, I pretend to study at my desk, so they leave me alone. But sitting idle at my desk drives me nuts. Out of sheer boredom, I start a notebook, where I write every day to Arush, telling him how my parents have taken away my phone; I tell him how I got into my father's study and how I stole my mother's phone. I write about how obnoxious Divya is when she daily checks upon me, offering to help with my academics. She is doing it to taunt me. I make it a 'daily update', a book of letters to Arush and pour my heart out. I discover how therapeutic writing is.

My mother sees me 'studying' and says, 'I am really happy to see this, Puja.' I squirm, but only for a second. Their making me a prisoner has left me with no other option, but this.

As soon as my father is out of the house, I borrow Shanti chechi's phone. I have already taken my passport from the cupboard where my father stores it, and have put it along with the necessary documents in an envelope. When I call up the travel agency, they tell me that half the money has to be paid in advance and the other half, when I get the visa. Oh, hell! This is a new complication I had not anticipated.

'Look, I am trusting you with my passports and documents. Can't you make an exception? I will pay you in full after the visa is done,' I plead.

'Really sorry, madam. This is the policy,' he says.

'Alright, please send your person in an hour. I will hand over the cash,' I say.

There is an ATM machine on the other side of the road, across my apartment complex. It will take me less than five minutes to get to it. I would have to make this very quick, before my father gets back. I tell Shanti chechi that I will be back soon.

'Look, Puja molle. I can go and get you the money. There's less suspicion that way,' Shanti chechi offers.

But I want to do it myself. I have never used an ATM machine in my life and it is high time I learnt this. After all, I plan to travel on my own. I memorise the pin which came in the second envelope from the bank. To be doubly sure, I write it on my palm. I don't want to make any mistakes.

'No, Shanti chechi. I will be back,' I tell her. I grab my bag and dash out of the house, down the elevator. I almost break into a run to reach the ATM machine. There's no one there at this time, except for the security guard, who looks bored. He doesn't give me a second glance. I enter the cubicle and insert the card. Sweat drips from my forehead and I wipe it with my sleeve. The screen guides me. It's just a few clicks. And oh, the satisfaction to hear the 'whirrrr' as the machine doles out the money! Whoever knew it was this easy!

The maximum amount allowed per transaction is 5,000 rupees. I repeat the procedure four more times. I now have twenty-five thousand rupees. I have never had this much cash before. Giddy with excitement, I rush back, expecting to get caught anytime. But nothing happens.

In less than an hour, the person from the travel agency has collected everything.

Fahad calls on Shanti chechi's phone to confirm receipt. He is confident of getting the visa in two weeks. He asks me if I have any preferred time for appointment for biometric scan at the VFS office. He says the earliest appointment is at 8 am for which I will have to report at 7.45 am.

I quickly process that information.

'Yes, please take the 8.00 am appointment,' I tell him.

'Alright. I will text you the appointment confirmation on the same number,' he says.

When I hang up, I squeeze Shanti chechi's hand in excitement.

'Puja molle, how do you know this isn't a scam?' Shanti chechi asks.

'This is a reputed international agency with offices all around the world. They aren't some fly-by-night operators.'

'That's okay then. But are you 100 percent sure you want to do this?'

'200 percent sure. What is the use of living if you can't follow your heart?' I tell her, sounding like a new age spiritual guru.

Maybe this is what love does. Pushes all your boundaries.

'What happens when your parents find out?' Shanti chechi is ever the voice of caution. But I have an answer for her.

'You will have to see that they find out only after about six hours after I leave home. By then, I will be on the flight to UK,' I say, dancing around her.

Shanti chechi has a worried look on her face. But when she sees my unbridled joy, her expression softens.

'Go, molle. Go meet him. But just take care,' she says.

I plant a kiss on her cheek. She is surprised. Then she chuckles.

I dance all the way to my room and continue dancing.

I am going to meet Arush! No one can stop me now.

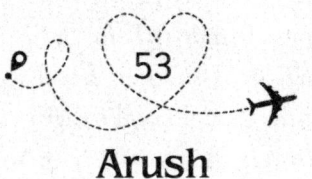

Arush

I am at the shop, helping my mother when Jenna's name flashes on my phone screen.

'Hiya! What's up?' I greet her.

'I am afraid I have some terrible, really terrible news,' she says.

'What? What happened?' I ask. By her tone, I know it is something grave. But nothing prepares me for what she says.

'We lost Vincent. He is no more. We're all shocked,' she says.

For a few seconds, I am unable to speak.

'Are you very sure? Could it be that he is sleeping?' I ask softly.

'We're all in shock, Arush. Josh feels terrible. The basking light malfunctioned and overheated the cage. Since he had escaped the other day, Josh had put the lid very securely. Oh, Arush! I can't bear it. His whole body is swollen and his eyes are bulging. There's blood dripping from one of his eyes. It is a terrible sight,' Jenna is unable to speak. She hands the phone to Tom.

'So sorry, mate. We're in shock too. We're going to bury him now. Do you want me to send you a picture before we bury him?' Tom asks.

'No, no!' I say. I don't want to see him dead.

'Yes, I understand. It's heart-wrenching. I don't even know what to say. Josh is beating himself up. Says it was his fault and thinks he left the light on too long. We called the vet's office. They say it is hard, almost impossible to prove negligence.'

'Vincent didn't deserve this,' I say quietly.

'No, definitely not. He didn't,' Tom says.

When Tom hangs up, I shudder. I feel so sick that I want to throw up. I can't bear the thought of the cage getting overheated, like an oven. Oh, good lord – what would have Vincent gone through before he died? I go to the restroom and sob.

Later that evening, Jenna calls.

'I am so upset, Arush. I think it was Josh's fault, though I haven't told him so. He left the bloody light on and vanished without a trace. He knew I would be away visiting my mom. He could have been more careful.'

When Jenna visits her mother, a single mom who works as a psychiatric nurse in a hospital in London, she gets back on the same day, as she detests her mother's cramped one-room apartment. This means that she must have been gone for over six hours.

'It's okay. It's happened now. And look at the timing. He died just when the vacation started. He didn't want to inconvenience anyone during the hols,' I comment wryly.

'Tom was staying back for vacation, just for Vincent. But now he can visit his family,' Jenna says.

'What are you going to do for the vacation?' I ask her.

'My mom wants me to visit my gran. It's been a while. Since my gran lives alone, I guess I will do that.'

'Where does she live?'

'Kirby. She has the most beautiful cottage surrounded with all kinds of flowering plants. Her garden – it's almost magical. I think I need that. I am miserable about Vincent.'

I don't want to talk about Vincent. I can't bear to think of what happened. It's too painful. I change the topic.

'So is your gran a fan of Liverpool then?' I ask.

'Uh?'

'Isn't Kirkby close to Liverpool?'

'Oh... no. Sorry I meant Kirkby in Ashfield,' Jenna says.

'Ashfield?'

'Yeah.'

'You do know it is my neighbouring county, don't you? If your gran lives there, you have no excuses. You have to visit me,' I tell her.

'Oh, yes, I will. I had forgotten you are in Derby. It is a short drive. I think it is less than thirty minutes away. I will borrow my granny's Mini Cooper and drive down to see you.'

'When are you going to be in your granny's place?' I ask her.

'Next week. I will be there for a month.'

'Come by. I would love to see you,' I tell her.

My mother notices that I am terribly upset. This grief is unbearable.

She asks me what happened and I tell her that Vincent has died. My mother has never understood how I could be attached to a reptile, but she knows how important Vincent was to me.

'It's okay, his time had come,' she says.

But her words do not placate me.

I feel empty inside. Life – so fragile. There's no telling how long we have with someone. It is best to spend time together when you can. I now regret leaving Vincent and going to India. Perhaps if I had not made that trip, Vincent would still be alive. The emptiness inside me gnaws at my insides.

One should not get attached to anyone.

Love someone, and sooner or later, you will get hurt.

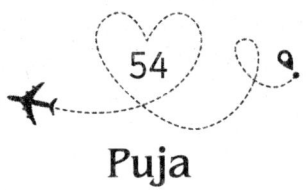

Puja

The visit to the VFS office is completed in less than two hours. By 11.00 am, I am on my way home in an auto. Shanti chechi has lent me her phone.

I had left home at 4.30 am this morning, before anyone woke up (so it was easy to get away without anyone noticing). I walked to the Taj, a five-minute walk away. With my hoodie down, I waited at the hotel lobby, (genius me!) till it was bright outside. Getting an autorickshaw outside the hotel was easy-peasy and I came straight to the visa office where someone from the agency met me with the papers. He was also in charge of a large group of senior citizens applying for Schengen visas. But he pushed mine first as it was an individual application.

I am impressed by the efficiency in the ease of application and the speed of the process.

When we pass a phone showroom on MG Road, an idea strikes me. Now that I have money, I can get my own phone and sim card. This is an empowering thought. I ask the auto-driver to wait for a few minutes.

'Waiting charges extra,' he says. I don't care!

In less than twelve minutes, I am the owner of a brand-new smart phone. All I have to do now is to figure out how to activate the sim card. I can't wait to get back home now.

Shanti chechi and I have made an elaborate plan for me to get back home unnoticed.

I am to call the home number from Shanti chechi's phone. If my father answers, I simply hang up. Shanti chechi's name will show up on the caller id and she can tell him she dialled our home by mistake. This way I know if my father is home or not. (My mother is at the hospital.)

Lady luck is smiling at me today. When I call, it is Shanti chechi herself who picks up.

'Puja molle. Your father has gone out for the whole day! Is your work done?' she asks, speaking softly.

'Yes!'

Shanti chechi greets me with a hug.

'Now what?' she asks.

'Now can you get a new sim card for me. Please?' I ask her. I don't want to risk going out again. I have been really lucky this far.

'Use mine, molle. Use it as much as you want; it is not like I have anyone to call anyway,' she says.

She states it without any emotion and she says it casually. But that statement hits me hard. Shanti chechi is always so cheerful and calm, that it is easy to forget what a gruesome past she had. She has been with us for thirty years now. As a child I would always ask her about her parents, but she would say she knew nothing about them. When I was about 14, it was Divya who told me her story.

Shanti chechi was raised in an orphanage. At 16, with stars in her eyes and hopes of a brighter future, she had gone to Abu Dhabi as a domestic house-help through an agent. She was physically abused, mentally tormented and kept as a prisoner for years. She escaped with great difficulty and with the help of the Indian embassy, she returned to India.

My mother was involved with a social service agency back then. They had placed her with us. It had taken my mother many years to convince Shanti chechi that they were nothing like her previous employers. My mother had insisted that Shanti chechi complete her education, and enrolled her in an online university. With my mother's help, she completed her graduation. After this, my mother got her a job in one of my dad's companies, but Shanti chechi refused to go. She said our home was her home now.

When Divya told me all this, I had rushed to Shanti chechi to ask if it was true. In response, Shanti chechi had showed me the scars on her back. I had cried then. I couldn't imagine anyone going through such a life. 'It's okay. We don't have to think about the past at all. If we do, we simply ruin a good present,' Shanti chechi had said.

I look at her smiling face now and give her a hug.

'But Shanti chechi – you have to get me a new sim. If I take yours, how will I call you from the UK?'

That convinces her. She tells me that she will get the sim card that very afternoon.

We call up the phone company and find out the requirements. They are fairly simple – all we need is a proof of identification, and a proof of address along with a photo. Shanti chechi already has all of this. She comes back from the phone showroom in an hour. After about four hours, my sim card is active! My brand-new number. Hooray! I can scarcely contain my excitement. I am like a drowning man who has suddenly found land beneath his feet.

I rush into my room, quickly setting up my new phone. When I check my mail, I see lesser number of emails and messages from Arush than I had expected. He asks why I haven't replied. I check his Instagram. There are no stories and no new posts; I am disappointed by his emails. I expected he would be writing to me every single day. That's what I have been doing, the only difference being I have been writing by hand in a book.

I dash off a mail to him, explaining my plan, telling him everything that has been happening since he left and how much I miss him. That evening I join my family at the table for dinner.

'What happened? How come you are joining us now? Done sulking?' Divya asks.

'Divya, no. Please do not talk to her that way,' my father corrects her.

My mother wants to know if I am confident enough to take the final exams by preparing on my own.

'Yes, I can,' I lie convincingly. 'It's not that hard, I have been studying.'

'Good, I am happy to see that,' she says.

'So, can I have my phone back?' I ask. I pat myself inwardly for this clever tactic. If I didn't have my secret phone, this is what I would have done. I want to stay in character here.

'Well, continue like this and we will see,' says my mother.

'Please, Ma. I have been studying and preparing hard. Can you at least give me my laptop back?' I plead. I should get an Oscar for the best actress.

'Puja, don't push it. I have seen you reading books these last few days. I think it is a good thing that we have taken away your laptop and phone. Else you would never read,' my father says.

I want to tell them that they are wrong. That I have started reading solely because of Arush. Of course, I say nothing.

'She is asking only because she wants to text her boyfriend who got beaten up and who she defended on television, making us all famous,' Divya remarks, stirring up a very sensitive issue.

She is being deliberately mean. All the nasty things that she has been doing since childhood come back to me at that instant. She has always been Miss Perfect, smiling happily by my mother's side, while I have been the useless one. She has always got praise, attention – all of it.

The anger that has been simmering for long now and the stress of the last few days shoot up inside me like a rocket. Something snaps.

'If you can be a fucking bitch, I can too,' I say calmly. I pour my dessert, the sweet sticky payasam, on her head. There is a stunned silence around the table as the payasam slowly trickles down her face. She is too shocked to react.

'Be thankful I didn't break the bowl on your head,' I say. Then I coolly walk way.

'*Puja!*' My mother thunders. 'Come here, right now!'

But I am in no mood to listen to her. Let them shout all they want. I can't wait to see if there's a reply from Arush.

My father comes into my room and tells me what I did is not right.

My mother shouts from the dining table, 'Learn to control your emotions. This is unacceptable behaviour. You are not getting your laptop or your phone back. Do you hear me?'

I don't respond.

Later, I check for messages from Arush.

My heart sinks. There are no replies.

Arush

Jenna is to visit. When I tell my parents, my mother says that they will take turns at the shop and come home to meet her. My mother makes samosas and marinates vegetables and paneer for pakodas. My father makes his specialty – badam milk. As much as my father pretends not to care about Indian customs and traditions, as soon as we have guests, he can't help turning on the Indian hospitality. It is something deeply ingrained in him.

'This Jenna, is she special?' my mother asks.

'Ma! Please don't print the wedding invites yet. She is just a friend.'

'Is she white? Or is she black? Or yellow?' my father asks.

'Dad, that is racist! You can't ask things like that.'

'Why? Don't they look at us as brown? I am only asking my son, as I want to know what his choice is.'

'Dad, please. She is just a friend and nothing more.'

'She has golden hair, blue eyes and looks like a doll. I have seen her picture on Arush bhaiya's phone when he wasn't looking,' Rhea says.

Thanks Rhea.

'A friend who will drive from the neighbouring town to visit? Hmm…' my aunt comments.

'Yes, yes. Your father and I were 'only friends' for a long time,' my mother says and they all laugh like it is a big joke.

It seems like my family is going all out to welcome Jenna. This is what happens when you don't bring a single girl home ever, and then you suddenly announce that someone is coming home. I brought it upon myself, I think.

When Jenna arrives, I know she has been crying. I know her well enough to see that she is holding back something. She doesn't tell me what it is immediately though.

'Hiya! So good to be here,' she says, rolling down her car window. 'Where can I park?'

I show her to the common parking lot adjacent to our home. Jenna parks and emerges with a gift for Rhea.

'Thank you, you are very kind,' Rhea says. She is displaying her best manners today. I feel a surge of brotherly pride.

'Hello Jenna. Come on in,' my mother greets her at the door.

'Hello. These are for you,' says Jenna, as she takes out a bouquet of yellow carnations and white roses from a paper bag.

'Thank you! These flowers are so beautiful, Jenna,' my mother says as she takes out a vase, fills it with water and arranges the flowers in them.

'I am so glad you like them,' Jenna says as I show her to the living room. 'I stopped to buy Rhea a present and the florist was right outside.'

'May I open my present now please?" asks Rhea.

'Yes, please,' laughs Jenna.

'Your dress is very pretty,' Rhea says, as she begins to unwrap the present.

It is only then that I notice that Jenna has indeed taken the trouble to dress up nicely. She is wearing a black polka-dotted sleeveless dress with frilly straps. Back at our flat in Norwich, Jenna is always in shorts, or track pants and a t-shirt. She has also done something with her hair and it looks a lot nicer than it usually does.

'You also smell nice,' Rhea says, sniffing appreciatively.

'Pay her any more compliments and your eyes will turn into stars, Rhea,' I say.

Rhea blinks her eyes rapidly and smiles at both of us in a look-at-me-I-know-I-am-cute way and we both laugh.

Jenna has got Rhea a set of beautifully illustrated Roald Dahl books and one of them is *The Minpins*. Rhea looks at the pictures and squeals in delight.

'Aren't you a ray of sunshine!' says Jenna and Rhea bobs her head up and down slowly.

Full marks for cuteness! Rhea has totally won Jenna over.

'Bhaiya will read this to me later tonight. Thank you, Jenna. I really love the book,' she says.

'Bhaiya?' asks Jenna mispronouncing it, making it sound like 'bey-ya'.

'It's an Indian term of respect for older brother,' I explain.

My mother serves all the goodies that she has made for Jenna's arrival. Jenna relishes every single thing. She makes a note of the names of each item. She says she wants to look up the recipes later and thanks my mother for all the trouble she has taken to cook. My mother is elated.

'See you later, Jenna. Come over again, soon. I have to go to the shop now. My husband will drop by to meet you,' she says as she leaves. Rhea goes with my mother to be dropped off for a play date at a friend's.

As soon as we are alone, I ask Jenna, 'Are you going to tell me why you've been crying?'

'How did you know?'

'Come on, Jenna. We have been friends for so long. I knew as soon as I saw you.'

'I broke up with Josh. It's over,' she says.

'Why? I can't believe it. What happened?' I ask.

'He has been cheating on me, the swine,' Jenna says, as she stares at the floor.

'How do you know?' I ask. I can't believe Josh would do such a thing. To Jenna, of all people.

In response, Jenna hands me her phone.

'She texted me. See?' she says.

It's a text from someone named Mollie who says that Josh and she have become very close over the past few months. She writes that she knows that Josh will find it hard to break it off with her. He has been talking about it for the last six months but doesn't have the courage to do it and so she is forced to send this text.

'Oh Jenna! What a horrible way to find out,' I tell her. 'Did you speak to Josh?'

'Yes.'

'And?'

'He didn't deny it. He apologised and said we both knew it was coming. You know what, Arush? That's simply not true. I had no idea. I thought things were fine between us. And the worst thing – he had gone to meet *her* that day when Vincent died.'

Her voice is shaky, but she doesn't cry.

I don't know what to say.

'I am so sorry, Jenna', I say.

Jenna shrugs.

My father walks in right then and greets her. Jenna instantly puts on her happy face and greets him back. She asks about the shop and all that my father does. My father asks about her mother and her life in London. He tells her about the time he was working in London. They chatter away like old friends.

After Jenna leaves, my father says, 'She is a really nice girl.'

That is the 'highest' compliment my father can give.

Silently, I agree with him.

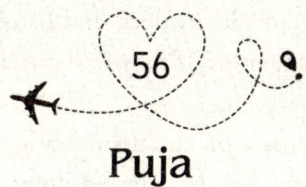

56

Puja

Waiting for Arush to reply is like waiting for rain in the desert. There's nothing new on his Instagram profile other than his brilliant artwork. I remember what I had told him – that I would try and sell his work

After what seems like an eternity when my father leaves the house, I look up the number of the art school online and get Sashi on the phone.

'How have you been? Where did you disappear?' he asks.

'I'm sorry, I haven't been in touch. I am in a not-so-good place, but soon will be better.'

I am honest with him, updating him about all that happened after I left the hospital.

'Have you been in touch with Arush?' I ask him.

'He mailed me to tell me he reached and he is recovering. He says he is happy to be with his family. Other than that, nothing.'

'I was just thinking about Arush's art. Can you please make prints if I send you high-resolution photos? I think Arush's work deserves to be sold. When Arush was here, I had spoken to the gallery owner of the café and he seemed interested. It will be a nice surprise for Arush, don't you think?'

'Sure thing,' Sashi says. He promises to do it immediately.

The next evening, Sashi messages me saying he has made high-resolution prints and the gallery owner is happy to display them.

I hear footsteps outside my door, and I stuff my phone into my pillow. This is too dangerous. If they find out my secret phone, that will be the end of everything.

Then there's a knock on the door. My mother enters without waiting for an answer. She has started doing this of late and my father is right behind her.

Great. They are here to give me another talk about my future.

My mother makes herself comfortable in her usual spot on the sofa opposite my bed.

'Puja, your father and I have decided that your being at home like this indefinitely is not a good thing. You need to go to college. But since your college here, or any of the other colleges here will not take you, I have used my contacts and spoken to the principal at the St Bethesda college in Changanasherry. As a very special case and as a favour to me, she has agreed to take you on probation. You can move to the hostel there. They are a bit strict, of course, but I think you need discipline at this point.'

'Ma... Please,' I try to tell her my views, but she silences me with a raise of her hand.

'Right from class 11, you have been doing as you like – breaking rules, getting suspended, scraping through the exams. Now you have put us in this crazy situation. You were given a good chance in your current college. Also, here you are living in the lap of luxury. You need a taste of the real world. You can complete your final year there. Since the college is under the same university, there is no problem about previous years too. I have already spoken to the present college principal about your Migration Certificate and Transfer Certificate.'

Great. My mother has it all figured out.

I hate my mother at that instant. I have heard of horror stories about this college that my mother speaks about. Their hostels are like jails. They treat their students like school kids. I think they even have a uniform. Prayers are compulsory in the morning at 6.30 am, and if you don't attend, you are punished.

The last thing in the world I want is to go there.

My father tells me, 'Look Puja. You have left us with no choice. We had trusted you, given you all the freedom and you have misused it. Now it is time to get serious.'

I can't stand my family. I want to get out of this place. I can't wait for the visa to arrive. It's about time. But I don't show any emotion.

'Alright, I will go,' I say quietly.

I think my mother expected me to protest. She is taken by surprise when I don't.

'You will see Puja, all this will soon be behind us. You will be glad that I took this decision,' she says.

What am I expected to do? Thank her? I am furious with them. But I swallow my anger and nod again.

My visa arrives three days later. I already know it is coming, as we have received a message on Shanti chechi's phone. I hover around the door. My father is in his study. Shanti chechi has an excuse ready (the ironing guy), if my father asks who it is. But this time, we don't need any explanation. My father is on a call with headphones on, deaf to the world. From his conversations, it looks like his new company is taking off. He goes out for meetings almost every day now.

When I open my passport, I want to scream with joy looking at the six-month visa. I can leave this place for six months if I wish to!

I text Fahad, asking to him to send me the tickets. At the VFS office, when the person met me, I had paid for the tickets using my cheque book. I have opted for a ten-day trip with a flexible fare.

Fahad emails the tickets to me. I am all set to travel in three days. I can't believe that I have done it!

It's only now that the enormity of what I have done sinks in. All my fears, all my panic related to travel, comes back. I hadn't thought of too many things while I was planning it. But now that I have done it, I am a nervous wreck. I pack a little of my stuff every day. UK is cold. I have looked up the temperatures online. But I have an insulated jacket as well as a sweater. I put those in a backpack. I have to be very careful about packing as I don't want my parents to get suspicious. I pack when they are not at home. Shanti chechi helps me and we store the suitcase in my walk-in wardrobe in the usual place. Nothing looks amiss.

I look at all the hotels in Derby and I carefully study the reviews. I book a hotel which is part of one of the big chains. It is not too far from the city centre as well. I have no idea where Arush lives, but I am guessing that wherever it is, it will not be too far from the hotel.

I still haven't heard from Arush, but that doesn't deter me. I reach out to Jenna via Instagram. When she hears about my crazy daring travel plan, she can't believe it.

'Ohmygod! Ohmygod! Arush will go crazy with joy! I kind of feel like an idiot. I told him you had dumped him, going by how you went AWOL. But I am happy that's not the case. Do you want to surprise him?' she asks.

'I think it will be a surprise, as he hasn't read my mails. Or if he has, he has chosen not to reply,' I tell her.

'You know he does miss you. I can tell. And yes, I don't think he has read your emails, else he would have told me for sure,' she says confidently. 'We sure are going to surprise him,' she adds.

She offers to pick me up from my hotel in Derby and drive me to Arush's place. I thank her. She is genuinely a nice person. She thanks me for including her in my grand surprise.

On the day of my journey, my stress skyrockets to a level I've never experienced before. I don't sleep the entire night.

My flight is at 9.30 am and I have an hour's layover in Doha. I am to land at Heathrow at 17.30 local time.

I think Shanti chechi is more nervous than I am.

'Don't let me down. They shouldn't find out. Please don't tell them anything,' I tell her for the hundredth time.

'You be safe. You have to keep in touch with me. Send me text messages,' she instructs for the hundredth time.

I leave home stealthily at 4 am. I have my backpack and a suitcase – that's it. I have packed light. I pull my suitcase behind me and walk all the way to the Taj, where Fahad has arranged for a cab. I don't want the cab anywhere near my building. I huff and puff as I drag the suitcase. The car is waiting as promised and the driver helps me with my luggage.

'Madam, I would have picked you up from home. There was no need to walk with the luggage,' the driver says.

'No, that is fine,' I act nonchalant.

I have triple-checked my passport, forex card, visa, phone charger and my Indian ATM card a hundred times. I have also activated an international roaming pack on my phone. Oh, the things money can do! It is like I have become an adult overnight. This is a huge learning curve for me.

I am so nervous that I throw up thrice on the way to the airport, despite the medication I have taken. The worried driver asks me if I am okay and I nod. Once I reach the airport, I withdraw more cash from the ATM. I convert this into UK pounds at a forex counter.

At immigration, I feel like they will haul me out and tell me to go home. I shift my weight nervously from one foot to the other as I await my turn. The immigration officer asks me, 'Why are you going to UK? What is the purpose of your visit?'

'To see a friend,' I reply.

'Travelling alone?'

What business is it of his, I think. But I keep my thoughts to myself. I don't want to piss him off.

'My friend will meet me at Heathrow,' I reply. I don't know why I say that. I am going to take a bus from Heathrow to Derby. From the bus station to the hotel, I plan to take a cab. He nods and stamps my passport.

Then there's a security check – and that's it! I am through.

I text Shanti chechi. I get a reply almost immediately.

'Good. All ok here,' she has typed.

I explore the shops in the airport while I wait. At an electronic shop which sells international travel adapters, a helpful salesgirl asks me which county I am travelling to.

'UK,' I reply.

She says I would require an adapter pin as the plug points there are different. I end up buying one, mainly because I am still nervous.

Even when I board the flight and settle down in my seat, I can't believe it. I am on my way to UK!

I have done it. I am euphoric with exhilaration, but also exhausted.

The childhood memories of travel come flooding back. It has been so long since I have been on a plane. I had been dreading the travel, but now I discover that it isn't so bad after all.

Just when I think that air travel isn't quite the monster I presumed it to be, I feel the bile rising again. There's an air sickness bag in the seat pouch in front of me and to my horror and embarrassment, I throw up inside the bag. Fortunately, I haven't thrown up anywhere else. The passenger next to me, a middle-aged man who looks as old as my father, gives me a disgusted look and turns away. I look down in shame. I am seven years old again.

The flight attendant hands me water and asks if I am fine. I tell her I have travel sickness and ask her if there's a seat where I can sit by myself, and if so, I would like to shift. She points me to one in the very last row and I gratefully accept.

I sleep for a few hours. The seats are cramped and do not stretch out flat. They are uncomfortable. I have carried books with me to read, but I am not in the mood to. I barely eat anything on the flight, though they keep offering me. By the time we land in Heathrow, I have thrown up a few more times. I am dehydrated and ready to drop down dead.

Heathrow is scarily huge.

And busy.

And alien.

And foreign.

The queues for immigration are long, with shorter, separate queues for citizens of UK and the European Union. Feeling lost in this massive sea of humanity, I follow my fellow passengers. When it is my turn, a Border Force officer asks to see my passport and the card which I have filled up in the flight.

'Are you visiting UK for the first time?' he asks.

'Yes, I am,' I say.

My heartbeats increase as he checks my passport and checks something in his computer. Irrational fear grips me. What if he turns me back?

'Welcome to the United Kingdom. Have a pleasant stay,' he says, as he stamps my passport.

I am so exhausted by the journey that I am not elated or euphoric, as I expected to be – merely relieved. I follow the others and reach the baggage collection point. After I get my suitcase, I don't feel up to finding the bus station for the trip to Derby. I am ready to collapse. I decide to just take a cab. The signboards guide me to a fixed price taxi counter. The fare to Derby costs a small fortune, but I do not care. I just want to get to my hotel now.

As soon as I step outside the airport, I draw in a sharp breath. The cold hits me like a bunch of knives. The wind slaps me hard. It cuts through the insulated jacket I am wearing and I shiver. Apart from the cold, the first thing that strikes me as soon as I come out of the airport is how quiet it is! The silence is deathlike. The air is so clean. I inhale deeply. In less than ten minutes, my cab arrives.

When the driver, a well-built white guy, sees me struggling to lift the suitcase, he helps me put it inside. The car, a kind I've never seen before, is very roomy.

'Hello there. Good evening. Where are you from?' asks the cab driver.

'India,' I say.

He is instantly fascinated. He speaks very fast and his accent is very different from Arush's. I struggle to understand what he is saying. So, I mostly nod.

It is only when we pull up outside my hotel in Derby two-and-a-half hours later, that it strikes me – I have not thrown up even once! It is the first time in my life this has ever happened on a car journey. I am totally surprised. This means that if I am mentally pre-occupied, I don't throw up. The trick is not to think about it. I have been so busy gazing at the picturesque towns we passed, that I have forgotten to think about my travel sickness. Strange, how a problem I have had for a lifetime seems to have vanished in a single journey. It was a matter of changing my mental orientation to travel. Whoever would have thought!

The check-in process at the hotel is smooth. I see foreigners all around me. But then, I smile at the irony as I am the foreigner here. Unlike in India, no one helps me with the luggage to my room.

As soon as I am in my room, I throw myself on the crisp, white, soft, plush bed. Heaven! Then I rush to use the luxurious pristine clean loo. What a change from the awful, cramped airplane toilets. The drapes in the room are automated. I have to use an iPad which is by the bed to open and shut them. Once I explore the room, I make myself a cup of green tea.

I text Shanti chechi, 'All good, I reached.'

'Ok,' I get her reply almost immediately. There's nothing more. Are my parents searching for me? Are they worried? She hasn't said anything.

Serves them right if they are worried, I think.

Then I text Jenna.

'I am here woooo hoooo,' I type.

'Welcome! I can't wait to see you tomorrow at 8 am!' she types back.

There's a basket of fruits in my room. I have a shower, eat an apple and stare out of my hotel window for a few minutes. The city lights shine bright.

I still cannot believe I have done it. I have travelled all by myself. I am five thousand miles away from home. A stranger in a strange land. It feels so bizarre. So surreal. So comforting, and yet a tiny part of me misses home, misses the familiar surroundings, misses my family and Shanti chechi. Here no one knows me – other than Jenna. Who I am yet to meet.

I draw the curtains and fall into bed, sleep washing over me almost instantaneously.

Destination

One's destination is never a place, but a new way of seeing things.

– Henry Miller

Arush

It's a busy day at the shop. I am helping my mother with stock-taking when Jenna calls. Stocks have just arrived from India and dad is busy supervising the unloading. It is going to be a tiring day as each item that has arrived has to be examined for damages, quality, colour variations, etc. It has to be matched against the order placed, the prices agreed upon. All of it has to be repacked using our branding and price tags. I am learning so much about my parents' business during this forced sabbatical from my art. I am full of admiration for my parents and all that they have done to bring us up in this foreign land. My father and I have been having long conversations and now I know a lot more about their lives, their reasons for migrating and the hardships they have gone through.

I have also had ample time to reflect and think about things. If my hand hadn't broken, I wouldn't have spent this much time at the shop and with my family. I wouldn't have appreciated what a family means. My mother always says, 'Whatever happens, happens for a reason.' I am beginning to see the truth in this.

Jenna's phone call out of the blue is a surprise.

'Hiya! What's up? What are you doing?' she asks.

'I am at the shop helping my parents. You sound suspiciously cheerful,' I answer.

'Well, well, well. I have a tiny little surprise for you. I was wondering if I could drop it off as I was passing your town,' she says mysteriously.

'What? Christmas came early? What gifts do you come bearing?' I ask.

'Did the three wise men announce what gifts they brought before they called?' Jenna chuckles. 'Text me your shop address. I will be there soon.'

'Ummm... I won't be able to spend much time with you. Today is a busy day,' I reply.

'Oh, you don't have to spend time with me at all. Trust me, you will love this little surprise. I will just drop it off and be on my way,' Jenna sounds gleeful.

'Alright. The shop is on the parallel street to my home. It is a two-minute walk if you go through the alley. But I will text you the address anyway.'

'Who is it?' asks my mother.

'Jenna. She says she has a surprise for me. But don't worry. I told her it's a busy day.' But my mother disapproves.

'Arey! How can you say that to your friend? Ask her to stay for lunch. Tell her I insist,' she orders me.

'But it is such a hectic day.'

'Yes, but we have to eat, right? We will be taking a lunch break. She can join us,' my father says as he walks in, mops his brow and plonks down into the chair. The men have finished unloading the crates and the truck has left.

My parents are looking at me, waiting for me to say something 'Alright then, I will call her,' I say and dial Jenna's number.

She sounds delighted to be invited. 'That's really kind of you. Are you sure?'

'Yes, but please don't bring any flowers or presents. You impressed them enough the last time.'

Jenna laughs and my parents chuckle as well.

'She is a good girl,' my mother says.

Jenna pulls up as promised, a couple of hours later. But there's someone else with her in the car. I wonder who it is.

Nothing prepares me for the sight that greets me. I stand still and stare, barely believing my eyes. Am I hallucinating? Is this for real? How? How in the world is this possible?

Jenna chuckles as she alights, her laughter cutting into my thoughts.

'Look at your face,' she says.

It sinks in completely only then. Ohmyfuckinglord. This is no hallucination. It *is* Puja.

'You are staring as though I have produced a dinosaur!' laughs Jenna.

Puja is smiling as she walks towards me.

'Hi, Arush,' she greets me softly.

'What the hell…? Puja! How?'

'Is that any way to welcome someone who has travelled thousands of miles to see you? A fine friend you are,' Jenna says.

My mother has come out and so has my father.

'Er… Dad, Ma. This is Puja,' I say dumbly.

My parents don't know what to make of it. They greet both Puja and Jenna and tell them to come in. Once we are inside, my mother invites both girls to stay for lunch.

'So, where do you live?' my mother asks.

'I live in Kochi, aunty,' Puja replies.

I can't believe she is so cool about this.

'Which county is that? I haven't heard of it,' my mother frowns. My mother has no clue. She doesn't remember or recognize Puja from the video call in the hospital. She thinks Puja is from a town in England.

'Ma. She lives in India,' I say.

'Oh! Then are you visiting relatives?' my mother asks.

'Aunty, actually I just came to meet Arush,' she says.

My mother raises her eyebrows and looks at me. My father too is looking at me for explanation.

I have no idea what to tell them. I am reeling under the shock of her sudden appearance as well.

'Well… Puja was in the same camp as me in Wayanad,' I say.

'Ah ha, I see,' says my father.

From his tone, it is obvious that he has caught on that there's something deeper between Puja and me.

Jenna now looks uncomfortable. But Puja? Puja is gazing at me with lovelorn eyes, like I am the greatest guy in the world. I can't believe this. This is a nightmare for me. I want to disappear. Like now.

I have to get away. I need to talk to her. What in the world is she doing, turning up here? What is happening?

'Ma, Dad, Jenna… please excuse us… I need to talk to her, in private,' I say, as I walk away from the shop.

'Excuse me aunty, uncle,' I hear Puja saying. Then she follows me.

How can she do this? Turning up like this. How could Jenna do this to me? Are these girls idiots? What in the world are they thinking?

I walk to the park two streets away. I am walking fast. Am I acting like a jerk? Perhaps I am. But this is too much for me to handle. Puja follows me quietly and I don't know what to do.

I stop and sit on a bench under a large, shady oak tree. Puja follows suit.

'Hi again,' she says. She is smiling at me.

'You look cute with this crew cut. It suits you,' she says.

I am in no mood to smile back at her.

'Could you please explain this?' I ask.

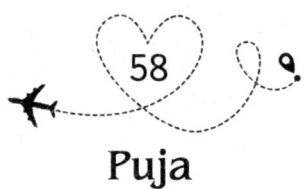

Puja

This is not the reaction I am expecting at all. Arush looks livid. There is no hint of even a small smile. I can't understand.

I thought he would be blown away, delighted to see me. I thought we would hug. I thought he would ask me how I came to the UK. I would explain and he would be awestruck at my boldness. I would tell him all that I have been through and he would comfort me. Instead, he stares at me, his eyes rigid; a narrow, hard stare. He is almost hostile.

His eyes are cold. This is not the Arush I knew. Or thought I knew. This is a stranger. A stranger who I have travelled thousands of miles to meet. I don't know what to say. My blood drains. My heart hammers. My palms go cold.

'Explain? Explain what?' I ask.

'First you dump me. Then you travel all the way to see me? What game are you playing Puja? Are you messing with my head?' he asks.

I take a few second to process what he is saying.

'Arush! No, no,' I say. I hasten to explain, 'My parents – they took away my phone. I... I wrote to you, didn't you get my emails?'

'Took away your phone? What do you mean? Didn't you have your laptop?' Arush frowns.

'No Arush, they took away my laptop as well. I was kept a prisoner. I wrote to you every day,' I say, hating the way I am desperately explaining this.

'I didn't get any emails. I checked.' His voice is frosty. He doesn't believe me.

'I wrote to you in a book, Arush,' I say.

That's when I remember. I have forgotten the book at home. I had meant to bring it along and give it to Arush. I wanted him to see how much I missed him. How I craved for him and how I did all this just to be able to see him.

'You wrote in a book. Why?' he asks.

Doesn't he get it? I have just explained that my parents took away my phone and my laptop.

'Because I didn't have a phone or internet access,' I am a little exasperated now with his line of questioning.

'But you told me you emailed me,' Arush says flatly.

I feel like shaking him.

'I did Arush… I did… I managed to get a phone later,' I am speaking fast in desperation.

Is he deliberately being a dickhead? I don't get him.

'Wait a minute,' he says. 'You tell me that you didn't have your phone. So, you wrote to me in a book and then you tell me you got a phone and then you emailed me?' Arush asks.

'Yes!' I say. 'Now you get it!'

But Arush is shaking his head. 'Umm… something doesn't add up.'

'What? Why would I travel all this way then?'

What is wrong with Arush?

'I don't know. You tell me,' he says.

Is this even the same guy I was crazy about? I can't believe he is so cold. Disbelieving. Unrelenting. What has happened to him?

'Arush, check your emails,' I tell him. 'You will see my mails explaining everything.'

'Ah... well... I blocked you,' he now admits.

'Blocked me? Why?'

'I don't know how to put this, Puja. I think I wasn't in my senses back in India. I was out of my comfort zone. You see, the brain goes into an overdrive with new experiences in a new country. We aren't thinking logically. It is the rush of serotonin and dopamine that makes us act in ways we don't usually do. I think that's what happened there – a holiday romance,' Arush says.

His precise, measured statements feel like someone has poured a bucket of ice-cold water on my head. What is he saying?

That what we had was not real? The kisses were nothing? He feels *nothing* for me? I can't believe this.

'What are you saying, Arush? That you don't love me?' I ask, looking into his eyes.

He looks away. What he says next kills me.

'We never spoke about love, Puja,' he says. 'I don't think either of us said that to each other, if I recall.'

Arush is distant, matter-of-fact, logical. Why? A thought creeps in. Jenna. Is that why he is saying all this? On the way here, Jenna had mentioned how she has visited him and how she loved his family and his sister. I had felt intensely jealous as soon as I heard it, but then pushed my jealousy aside because Jenna was being so nice. But perhaps Arush has something for Jenna?

'Is this because of Jenna?' I ask pathetically. I can't help myself.

'What?' he asks, looking at me like I have lost my mind.

'Is there something going on between you and Jenna?'

'Are you insane, Puja? he asks. 'There's nothing going on between us.'

'Then why are you behaving this way? Like I am a stranger to you?'

Arush pauses for a few seconds. Then he says, 'Look Puja. You have always been impulsive. You do things and then think about them. I admit I got a little carried away in India. Maybe what we had was real in those moments. But was it true love? I don't know.'

His words feel like blows. Slaps on my face. I asked for this, I think. I should have known it was leading to this when my messages to him went unanswered. Oh, how it kills me. I want to disappear right there. I don't think there exists a bigger fool on this planet than me. I feel moronic being there on that bench in that park in Derby, thousands of miles away from home, trying to convince a guy who has just said that what we had wasn't real and he doesn't think he loves me.

I can't bear to sit there any longer.

'Alright. Thanks for letting me know,' I say. I stand up. Someone has ripped out my heart from inside me and tossed it away.

I am hollow. Empty. Bereft.

But I am *not* going to beg.

I gather whatever little shred of self-respect I have and walk away.

Arush hurries behind me. 'Look, I am sorry.... Can we talk?'

What is to talk? I have made the biggest mistake of my life.

I don't know how to set it right.

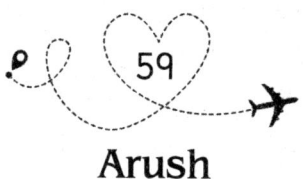

Arush

She is walking away fast.

'Puja, stop,' I call out.

I feel like a total jerk now. I have told her the truth. But I think somehow it has come out all wrong.

'What?' she asks without stopping

'This is too sudden for me,' I explain. Or try to.

'I get it,' she says.

But I don't think she does.

'Look, Puja. How did you travel here? Where did you get the money?' I ask.

'How does it matter, Arush? I came to see you. Isn't that enough?' she speaks without looking at me.

'Well, I appreciate it. But were your parents okay with it?'

I want to know what has happened. How did she manage them?

'They don't know I am here.'

She is still not looking at me.

'What? You just left?' I can't believe this.

'Yes.'

'How did you get the money? The air travel, the visa – they cost a lot.'

'I had some money in my account. A lot of money. That's how. I got the visa, the tickets – all of it myself.'

Do I detect pride in her voice? Or is it regret? I can't tell.

'Secretly?' I ask.

'Yes, secretly. What do you think? My parents would have let me come if I had told them?' She is defiant.

'Puja, you could come because your parents have money. Because you are rich.'

'How is that relevant?' she asks. Her eyes show a mixture of anger and regret.

'It is relevant, Puja. You just decide that the situation at home is uncomfortable. So, you pack your bags and come to see me. Have you thought of how I will explain to my parents?'

That gets her attention. I think I am getting through to her.

Puja pauses and leans against a tree. It is clear she has never considered that.

'I thought... I thought your parents were cool with you having girlfriends,' she says.

'Puja, I haven't even told them the truth of what happened in India. I haven't told them simply because I haven't understood it myself. I was trying to find Sujit to confront him. For what, I don't know. Next thing I know, I am at the hospital and then you vanish. How does this story make sense if I try to tell this to my parents, tell me?'

Puja just stands there.

'You are right. I hadn't thought of it from your perspective. I am sorry I came,' she says. She stares at me, not breaking her gaze.

This makes me feel worse. She is apologising for having come to see me. I have given her a lecture and dumped 'my honest feelings' on her. She is accepting it without a protest, without a murmur.

If there's an award for being a jerk, I should win it.

'Puja all I am saying is, let's give this time. We have been acting impulsively. I don't think it is the right thing you have done – running away from home. How can you subject your parents to this? Do you have any idea how worried they will be?' I am speaking fast, telling her things which are not easy to hear. And I can't seem to stop.

What she did was wrong. I can't *not* say it.

Puja says nothing.

'Look, Puja. They might be the worst parents in the world. But you do owe them something. You can't just get up and leave with the money they trusted you with. That's... that's just not right.'

And what does she expect me to do anyway? She has come to see me – but what now? I don't know.

Puja stands silently for a few minutes. Her arms are crossed.

I say nothing.

When she speaks, there is resolve in her voice. 'Arush, it is for me to decide what is right and what is not. If you don't want to see me and if you think whatever happened back in India was a mistake, that's fine. That's your prerogative. But do not judge.'

I have to try to explain to her. I have to make her see what I am trying to get at.

'Puja, I am not judging you. All I am asking for is to look at things from your parents' perspective. Your father came all the way to Wayanad to pull you out of jail. He is a good man. Your mother sent you to camp because she wants something good for you. They do have your best interests in mind. You have come to see me. What do you expect me to do? It's not like we can check into a hotel, can we?' I say.

Something about the brazen, stubborn attitude that Puja sports ignites a spark inside me, which turns into a flame. I speak my mind.

'We can't just follow our impulses, Puja. We owe something to our parents. You can't run away from your problems. You have to face them. As difficult as things get, you have to sit down and talk it over with them. I have spent the last few weeks here with my parents and it has been an eye-opener for me. I think we all take too much from them, Puja. Please speak to your parents. They must be worried sick.'

Puja stands there and continues staring at me. It is like she cannot believe what I have said.

'They won't get me,' she says.

'Have you ever had a plan for your career for them to get you? Have you even thought about what you are going to do? Are you just going to goof off for the rest of your life? Look, I get that nobody has it all figured out like I have. But you should at least have a plan. Any plan. For your future. One of the reasons your mother is upset with you is that you have no goals, no aims. You just drift from day to day. Have you ever considered that?' I blurt out.

I can't fathom her expression. She is breathing deeply now. I don't know if she is going to cry.

God, what a messy situation.

How could Puja just pack her bags and decide to come and see me? It's something I just don't get.

'Puja, I am sorry. I have spoken the truth. I have been honest,' I say.

Puja's expression changes. She shakes her head and walks towards the shop.

'I understand your concern about not wanting your parents to know about us. Just pretend I am a friend, okay?'

Her voice is steely. Her eyes are pools of darkness.

I think whatever love she had for me, I have managed to kill it.

I follow her quietly. There's nothing else I can do.

Chaitra

Krishnan paces up and down the room.

'How can she just disappear?' he asks.

'I don't know,' I reply. It has been more than nineteen hours since she was last seen. What shocks me is that it took us all this long to find out she is gone. What kind of a family are we?

Krishnan called me up at the hospital and asked me to come back home immediately. He has been pacing around the drawing room since I entered home. His pacing is driving me crazy, but I say nothing. I don't want to start a fight. We have to focus on finding Puja.

'Are you sure you didn't see her after you gave her dinner last night?' Krishnan asks Shanti.

'No, sir. I haven't,' Shanti says.

She avoids looking at us, which makes me think she is hiding something. But I am not sure. Perhaps she is just as worried as us.

'Why didn't you call her for breakfast?' Krishnan asks Shanti.

'She had said not to disturb her. So, I didn't,' Shanti tells us.

'We don't even know if she was home last night,' I reply.

'I have called her college friends to check if she is in their homes. She isn't,' Divya says. Divya rushed back from work as soon as she knew.

Krishnan sits down on the sofa next to me and calls up the DIG of Police. He closes his eyes. His brows are knitted as he speaks.

'I see… Ok. Yes… Alright. Thanks,' I cannot make out much from his side of the conversation. I wait for him to speak.

'We have to wait for three days for them to start looking. She is above eighteen and if she left home of her own accord, they can't really do much,' Krishnan says. His shoulders are slumped and he looks like he is on the verge of collapsing.

Divya says, 'She might have left a note or something? Let me go look.'

In less than ten minutes, Divya is back.

'Ma! Look! She has run away to UK,' she says, waving a book triumphantly.

'UK?' Krishnan and I both say it together.

'United Kingdom? London?' Krishnan clarifies. He cannot believe what he is hearing and neither can I.

'Yes. She has written everything here. I don't think she meant for us to find it. It is addressed to—,' Divya trails off.

'Show it to me.' I take the book from her.

Krishnan sits next to me and we read the book together. This is a book of letters to that boy, Arush.

I cannot believe this.

'Oh, good lord,' says Krishnan.

'I had no idea she felt this way,' I croak, finding it difficult to speak.

Page after page, word after word – they are all assaults on us. She hates me the most. She also hates Divya, but not as much as she hates me. She is even resentful towards Krishnan. She detests our fights, our differences of opinion. She has written everything in great detail and I had no clue what was on her mind.

The lump in my throat grows by the minute. I can't believe she has turned against me. I have done everything for her good.

Everything. I am angry that she has misused the money in her name.

'Your mother should have never given that money,' I tell Krishnan.

He explodes in rage when he hears this. '*You* – you were fine when she gifted it. In fact, you said it was extremely generous of her. She gave a similar amount to Divya too. You had no problems then. And now you say she shouldn't have given it? How dare you?' Krishnan's voice rises with each sentence he utters.

'This is *your* fault. Yours and Divya's. You both can never let her be. She is not good enough for you. Anything she does is wrong. She is *not* like you both – don't you get it? She is her own person!' Krishnan shakes in rage as he speaks.

'You spoilt her rotten. You are okay with anything she does,' I counter his arguments.

'I only did what any father would do. I got her out of lock-up. What did you expect me to do? Leave her there to rot?'

'You were not strict enough,' I tell him. I am angry that he is pushing all the blame on me.

'You were never there for her. That is the problem. Strict or not, at least I was there. For all intents and purposes, Shanti here is her mother. Shanti raised her. Not you. You were always busy with your hospital. You neglected her, Chaitra,' Krishnan roars.

'Oh, I see. And where is the rule book that says mothers have to give up their careers and be there for their kids? Why didn't you wind up all your businesses and stay at home, eh? Was she my responsibility alone?' I ask coldly.

There's stunned silence in the room now. No one speaks for a few minutes.

After a while Krishnan says, 'Anyway, there's no point fighting over whose fault it is. We are all wrong. Very wrong. We've driven her far away from us with our actions. She is to blame, of course, but I think we are to blame too. Have we ever attempted to understand why she did all those things? What was wrong? I don't think we ever sat down and spoke about it.' His tone has changed. He sighs.

'Do you know what is ironic? One of the people in the family had to run away for all of us to take a day off,' Divya observes wryly.

Divya's observation and Krishnan's words hit me hard. I re-read Puja's journal to that boy. Every word pierces my heart like a shard of glass, tearing me up. I look back at her childhood. Sadly, I do not remember her milestones. I think there is truth in what Krishnan has said. No one was ever there for her. It shouldn't come as a surprise that she has been gradually but steadily distancing herself from us, but it does.

How could I have been so blind? So oblivious to her pain, her fears, her hopes? I see myself through new eyes as I read her letters. I am a monster. She views me as one. And for the first time in my life, I see an alternate perception of me, through my own daughter's eyes.

It destroys me, because it is the truth.

I might have succeeded as a cardiac surgeon. I might have made a great success of my life. But I have failed as a mother, failed spectacularly. Her book has decimated me.

'Look Ma, don't feel upset. Teenagers write all this in angst,' Divya comforts me. Her words don't help. Even if it is written in angst, the bitterness is hard to bear.

'I have to accept my part in this. I am at fault. All of us have to re-evaluate how we have been treating her. I have always wanted the best for her. But it was the 'best' from my perspective. I never really paused and thought about what she wanted. I never thought about why she might have been acting out the way she did,' I say, full of remorse for all those lost years.

Krishnan and Divya are silent for a while.

'As parents, we always want the best for our kids. I think you only did what you thought was right,' Krishnan says after a long silence. His words, meant to comfort, feel like a slap.

'Why didn't you point this out to me earlier? Why didn't you tell me I could have been wrong? She has run away, Krishnan. Run away. She has *chosen* to leave. Which means, this home, this atmosphere, all of it was unbearable for her.'

'I don't know why I never pointed it out. I guess I was busy with my own things. It is not your fault alone. I am sorry for the things I said in anger,' Krishnan speaks quietly.

'I think I might have been harsh on her as well,' Divya admits. 'I have always wanted her to do well, but maybe I was a bit too mean to her.'

We don't have anything left to say anymore. We sit in silence, thinking about the way we have been treating Puja. A part of me is angry too. How could she have done this? After all that she put us through! But on the other hand, I feel it is my fault and that is a sinking thought. Deep down, I feel responsible. I pushed her to this. The words she has written keep coming back to me. It is unendurable.

Shanti serves us tea.

'Did she mention anything to you? Were you aware of what she was going through?' I ask Shanti.

'No madam, I did not know anything,' Shanti says.

'If we had not searched her room and found this notebook, we wouldn't have known at all,' Divya sighs.

'How do we reach her?' Krishnan asks. 'I just want her to come back. I can't rest knowing she is out there. Anything can happen. I am worried for her safety. She is *alone* out there – all alone.'

He is getting worked up and guilt courses through my nerves. If only I had done things differently with Puja.

'We can all write her mails,' Divya comes up with the solution.

'What?' I ask.

'Emails – she has bought a smart phone. She said so in her book. It is likely that she will be checking her mails,' Divya says.

For a minute, none of us speak.

'I guess that's the best option,' Krishnan agrees.

'Why couldn't she have brought up all her issues with any one of us?' Divya asks.

There is a pause as each one of reflects on the answer to this question.

Then Krishnan says quietly, 'Maybe we never made her comfortable enough to speak her mind. Mailing her is a good idea, Divya. Let's all write to her and let's hope she comes back. If you deduct the amount she might have spent on this trip, she still has a cool thirty lakhs. She can live comfortably on that by herself for a couple of years.'

The possibility of her never coming back has not occurred to me. Krishnan, the ever-practical businessman, is right. If she can run away, she can also decide to live on her own. I don't want to lose her.

I sit down at the desk in my bedroom to write the mail to Puja. I think back on all those years of her childhood. Have I been unfair to Puja? It strikes me that indeed I have. I did not mean to, though. Divya was an easy child. I had a difficult pregnancy with Puja, and the first few years of her life were hard for me. She was a sickly child – prone to all kinds of infections and allergies. Did I resent her?

Deep down, perhaps I did. I remember how I used to be annoyed when as a child, Puja used to beg me to stay with her when I had to rush off to the hospital. I would hand her over to Shanti and escape.

Every small incident comes back to me and plays itself out like a movie in my head.

At what stage in a child's life can a mother pursue her own dreams, her own career? Does motherhood mean sacrificing everything you aspired for and staying at home to be with your children? Have I been pushing Puja away, simply because she is different from Divya?

Her words about me form a noose around my neck. In her own words, I am an overbearing, autocratic dictator.

I think the reason it is so painful is because it is the stark, naked fact. I face it now. Its nakedness is too harsh for me to bear. I am happy as long as she makes life easy for me. I haven't been accepting enough for her to trust me with her dreams, her confusions, her fears. I've tried to mould her into someone like Divya, making her feel inadequate.

The love she has for that boy has jolted me. How can she become this close to a stranger and turn against her own family? I know the answer to that as well. We have never made the effort to understand her, but he has.

Regret envelops me. Too much has happened. Too much has been said and done.

All I can do is desperately hope and pray she is safe.

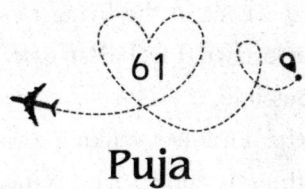

Puja

When we reach the shop, Jenna is chattering away to Arush's parents and they are engrossed in conversation. As we approach, the three of them turn to look at us questioningly. One part of me wants to stomp off and leave. I can call a cab back to the hotel. But that would be unfair to Jenna, who has taken the trouble to pick me up and bring me here. It would be unfair to Arush's parents as well, who don't know what happened in India.

'Sorry about walking off like that aunty,' I tell Arush's mother.

'Don't worry about it. Come, let's go home for lunch. Dal and chicken are already made, I will quickly make rotis,' his mother says.

Arush's father calls out to one of the people in the shop, telling him he will be back very soon. We walk towards Arush's home, his father leading the little procession.

'Did you come all the way from India to see Arush?' his mother asks me.

'Actually aunty, I have cousins in London who I came to visit. Jenna is a good friend, and she thought we would spring a surprise on Arush, as I know Arush from camp,' I lie smoothly.

Jenna gives me a sharp look and then plays along. 'Yeah, that's right. I thought it would be fun. Your face was something,' she tells Arush.

'Ha ha,' Arush says mirthlessly.

At Arush's place, we sit in the living room, while his mother bustles around in the kitchen. I feel ill-at-ease. I want to get back to the hotel as fast as possible.

'Aunty, may I help?' I ask her, walking towards the kitchen.

'No, no – everything is done. I have some biriyani too. Just sit,' she says.

Arush helps her lay the table with one hand. They don't allow me or Jenna to help. I can't wait for this charade to end.

'What do your parents do in India? Which part of London do your cousins live?' Arush's father asks me.

I have no idea what to reply to the question about my non-existent cousins, as I don't know any residential areas in London. To dodge the second question, I answer the first elaborately, going into detail about my father's various companies. I also tell them about my mother and about Divya. As I speak, it occurs to me that I am actually proud of my mother's achievements, and I am happy that Divya has a great job as well.

Arush's father is listening intently and nodding. 'Being a doctor is one of the noblest professions,' he says. 'Nothing like saving human lives.'

As soon as we finish lunch, there's a knock on the door. A little girl charges in like a whirlwind.

'Rhea!' Jenna exclaims

Rhea flies into Jenna's arms.

Arush's sister. Cute as a button.

'Hello! I am Rhea and you are…?' she asks, holding out her hand when she notices me.

'Puja,' I say and shake her hand.

'Do you have any gifts for me?' she asks.

'Rhea, you don't ask things like that,' Arush reprimands her at once.

'I am sorry. I sometimes forget my manners,' Rhea says looking contrite. 'Jenna got me a book. Arush bhaiya finished reading it to me so I was hoping to get another book.'

'Rhea, that's hinting for a gift and that's not cool, you cheeky monkey!' Arush tells her.

'Oh, no. I am sorry Rhea. I forgot to bring you a gift. I will make up for it,' I tell her.

'Really?' her eyes shine. 'When are you coming next?'

Everyone laughs and I manage a small smile. I haven't remembered to buy anything for Arush or his sister, or their parents. And I have had a meal at their house. My parents have always said: never to go empty-handed to someone's home. I have forgotten it in the excitement of seeing Arush. I feel crushed now.

Nobody notices it.

I am thankful when the meal ends. I can't wait to escape.

Jenna thanks Arush's mother for the meal. Arush's mother tells her she should visit again. Then she addresses me as an afterthought. 'You too, beta. When are you going back to London?'

'I came to Derby to see Arush – and Jenna. Now that is done, I will probably leave this afternoon,' I tell them.

I look at Arush as I say it. I don't know what I am trying to prove. Arush looks away.

In the car, on the way back, Jenna comments, 'That didn't go so well, I presume. I feel responsible for this.'

'Oh, no! Don't be silly. It was really nice of you to pick me up and take me there,' I tell her.

Jenna is too nice to ask what happened between Arush and me. She asks me what my plans for the rest of the day are.

I don't want to stay in Derby after this interaction with Arush.

'I will text you, Jenna. I am not sure of my plans. Thank you so much for all the help today,' I tell her, as I get out of the car.

'Don't worry about Arush. He will come around. Perhaps he is in shock,' she tells me. She waves as she drives off.

My eyes cloud with tears as I go up the elevator to my room. I feel defeated. I was stupid, really stupid, to have come all the way. What in the world was I thinking? What did I expect? For Arush to drop everything and spend time with me? Deep down, I'd hoped for that. I thought he would show me his school, the places where he grew up and we'd make happy memories in the English countryside.

What a hopeless, foolish, stupid, romantic idea I had in my head. It has all come crashing down now. He is entrenched deeply in his family life. His life is here. Mine is in India. It is clear to me now.

I stand at the window of my hotel room and look outside at the breathtaking view. Steps lead down from a boulevard to a river. Ducks swim peacefully in the placid waters. A few families with children feed the ducks. I feel alone now.

I miss India terribly. The excitement of seeing Arush is gone. Reality is very different from what I imagined it to be. What is worse is that Arush hasn't even asked where I am staying or when I am going back.

I make myself a cup of tea. When I finish it, I lie on the bed for a long time, thinking about all that has happened. Arush's admonition – there's a grain of truth in all that he said. It only adds to the bitter aftertaste, leaving me with uncertainty and doubt about life itself. It's too depressing to think about.

I check my phone and can't believe what I am looking at. Three emails – one from each of my family members.

Oh, hell.

After this encounter with Arush, I don't know how much more I can take today.

One part of me wants to pretend I haven't seen the mails. The other part of me is curious to know what they have to say. I wrestle with my thoughts for a few minutes, furiously debating in my head whether deleting the mails without reading them would be okay.

Arush's 'voice of reason' plays in a loop in my head. That I can't do this to my parents. Deep down, I know there is so much truth in what he says. It's just that I had refused to see it for so long.

I open my mother's mail first and I begin to read.

Dear Puja molle,

How are you? Hope you are okay.

I am sorry. I am sorry for many of the things I said and the way I behaved with you over all these years.

I was in a state of shock after I read the book which you wrote for Arush. I am also sorry for reading it. We were worried sick about you and we didn't know what had happened till we found the book.

To state that I was deeply affected by it would be an understatement. I am still in shock. I have never once paused to examine my actions or the effect they would have on you. I was hell bent that you achieve academic success at any cost, little thinking about what it is doing to you. Since that was what I wanted all my life, I couldn't comprehend why you would not want that. You are such a bright girl and I felt you were wasting your potential.

Now I see the futility of it all. If it is going to make you hate us so much, if it is going to make life so unbearable for you that you can't even stand seeing me, I don't see the purpose of it.

As a child, you were very difficult. Divya comparatively was an easy child, as she listened to instructions, excelled in academics and never once gave me any trouble. I admit (shamefully, I must add) that I wanted you to be like Divya, without once accepting you for who you are.

It is you who has to decide what you want from your life. I seemed to have not allowed you to do that.

I am upset and angry with you for having taken off like this. But now (unlike earlier), I can see why you did it too.

Forgive me Puja. And come back please.

Let's start over. It's never too late.

Love,

Ma.

I read it and I start crying. The tears that I have held back till now pour down freely. I cannot believe that my mother has apologised. She hasn't scolded me. She wants to make things right. She wants me to come back. She hasn't even mentioned the money I have blown up on this trip.

There's a lump in my throat now.

I read my father's mail. It's a short one.

Dear Puja molle,

Don't do anything foolish. Be safe and please send me your number. If you do not want to talk, I understand.

But please come back safely. I am worried sick.

Take care, molle,

Accha.

I wipe my tears and then read Divya's.

Dear Puja the Hooja,

I smile reading it. It was a nickname we used as kids. She would say I am Puja the Hooja, and I would say she is Divya the Manavya. We would then be brave conquerors sailing in our ships, carrying out attacks on distant kingdoms. Divya would drape our mother's saree over the dining table, and our 'ship' would be under it. We had to enter the ship by lifting the saree and it would serve as a door once we were inside.

It is strange how a single word, a nickname, evokes such strong vivid memories. I blink back my tears and read her mail.

Just come back. Ma and Accha are shattered. You have taught us all a lesson.

I feel guilty too – don't ask me why, but I do (even though you are the one who dumped payasam on my head). I am not going to write you a cloying, sentimental email – because I think Ma and Accha would have done that. But I am going to admit: I admire your guts!

I have always been the 'good child' and sometimes, the pressure of living up to Ma's dreams and expectations is too much. I don't think I will ever get a break from that in this lifetime. I have always done what she wanted. I did not have a choice.

Therefore, I am glad you got to do what you *wanted.*

Come back soon, though. I don't have anyone to nag or trouble.

Love,
Divya the Manavya.

Now I miss home terribly. I have been selfish. I have done what I wanted, without pausing even once to think of them. I realised this after Arush's talk. And yet, my family is there for me. They are being so nice to me.

Even Divya. Who knew that she was under pressure? I had never seen it that way. And I had never in a million years thought my mother was capable of self-reflection. I feel terrible now that my mother is actually apologising to me. I have given her ample grief over academics. Yet she has somehow convinced herself that it is her fault.

Oh, how I miss them now!

I suddenly know what I have to do. I want to go home.

Arush

I have been honest with Puja. Yet why does it feel like I have betrayed her? I don't know. Was it a holiday fling? I am not so sure now. Do I love her? I am confused about that as well. While in India, I was almost certain I did. But now I wonder what love is.

I look at my parents and the hardships they have been through. They have stuck together through thick and thin. Never once have I heard them speak harshly to each other. That is true love, I think.

I go back to the shop with my parents. There is a lot to do. But my thoughts are with Puja.

Have I been a jerk to her? Most certainly. But then, what did she expect me to do? Drop everything and go away with her? How could I do that? Her turning up like this unexpectedly has jolted me.

'What is with the girl, Arush? Why did she turn up here like this?' my mother asks.

'Ma, you heard her. She was with me at camp and she is a friend of Jenna's.' I go with the convenient story that Puja conjured up.

My conscience doesn't let me rest. Puja has travelled all the way to see me. I have all but turned her away. I don't know whether what I have done is right or wrong. My head throbs. Like someone is chiselling away inside with a drill.

My mother sees that there's something troubling me. Mothers always know.

'What is it that you are hiding from us? We are your parents after all. Don't you think I will know if you lie?' my mother asks gently. I am at the cash counter, trying to focus on the invoices on the screen. My parents are on the floor on a mat, merchandise spread out before them, sorting out each item, checking for damages.

I decide to tell them the truth. I think I owe them that, at the very least. There's no point hiding it.

I start with what happened in Wayanad and how I met Puja. I tell them about Sujit. I tell them about Puja getting arrested and how I went to the police station. I speak about my obsession to find him. I tell them about how, acting deranged, I had thought I had trapped him, how I got beaten up, and how Puja appeared on TV, complicating things further.

When I finish, my father says, 'I knew there was something more than he was telling us. That girl is nothing but trouble.'

But my mother contradicts him. 'Don't blame her. She has travelled all the way from there to see him. What does that say about her?'

'That she has money to throw around,' my father answers.

'Come on, Dad. You can't judge her like that,' I find myself defending her.

'Well, it seems to be that way if she has simply travelled all the way just to see you,' my father states.

'Or it could just be that she loves him so much that she will do anything,' my mother says quietly.

When my mother says that, something in my brain clicks. She is right. Why in the world hasn't that thought struck me in the first place? Like a righteous ass I have given her a sermon on right and wrong, and sent her away. I haven't even asked where she is staying.

'I think Ma is right. I think I have acted like an idiot,' I tell them.

'What do you want to do?' my father asks.

'I will go see her. I haven't treated her right. I owe her an apology,' I say.

'If you think you haven't treated someone well, there is nothing wrong in apologising,' my mother says.

'I don't even know where she is staying,' I tell my parents.

'Ask Jenna,' my father says.

I call Jenna, but she doesn't answer her phone. I text her, asking her where Puja is staying.

There is no reply from Jenna. I continue working with my parents at the shop. I am restless now and I keep checking my phone to see if she has texted back.

Then it strikes me that I can mail Puja and ask her where she is staying. I can apologise to her for acting this way. I remember what Puja has said about having sent me mails. They must have straight gone to the trash, as I had blocked her. I go to trash and check. Sure enough, there is mail from her sent days ago where she explains everything. And what is this? She has also sent a mail today. Two hours ago. Which means she has sent it after she has left here.

I open it with my heart thudding and begin to read.

Dear Arush,

You are right. I have been impulsive and not so good to my parents. It has taken me a journey across the ocean to see light. I am glad I have.

I thank you for it.

By the way, before I had come to UK, I had spoken to Sashi about displaying your art work at an exhibition. Congratulations, all your paintings (the ones I had chosen and sent high-res pics of) have been accepted for the exhibition. I've just heard from Sashi, who tells me that they have received offers for a few of them from a high-end art gallery in India which invests heavily in upcoming young artists. They want to sign you up with them. Sashi is mailing you the details. I am glad I could make a difference in your career.

I wish you the very best and I thank you for opening my eyes.

Puja.

I don't know what to think. All I know is that I have to see Puja. Like now. It is urgent.

The phone rings and it is Jenna.

'Sorry, I missed your calls. I had taken my grandma to hospital and my phone was on silent.'

'Where is Puja staying? Which hotel?' I ask her.

When she tells me, I thank her and hang up.

I wish my hand wasn't in a cast. I have never felt this helpless. If my hand was fine, I would have driven down to the hotel immediately. Now I have no choice but to ask my father.

'I need to see her,' I say. 'Could you please drive me there? Please?'

'What happened?' my father asks.

'I don't know dad. I think I have made a mistake,' I say.

'Go on and drive him. If his hand was okay, he wouldn't have asked you, would he?' my mother tells him.

On the way, I tell my father about Puja's mail.

'Maybe I have judged her a bit too early,' my father says. 'Go on and fix it with her. I think your mother has a point.'

I jump out of the car and rush to the reception lobby as soon as my father parks. At the counter, I ask for Puja Krishnan from India.

'I'm sorry, sir. She checked out a few hours ago,' says the man.

I come back to the car, my shoulders slumped.

'What happened?' asks my dad.

I tell him she is gone.

'Want to make a dash to Heathrow airport? Like they do in the movies? This is the scene where the hero chases the heroine. The airport mad-dash scene. Except that here, the hero's hand is broken and his father will be driving him,' he chuckles.

My father does have a sense of humour. I am tempted to say yes. But where in the world will I find her at Heathrow? I don't know if she is flying back home or has gone elsewhere. I don't know her flight number, her airline, her terminal of departure – nothing.

'No dad, let's go home. That works only in the movies,' I say.

My dad smiles as I get in the car

'Don't worry, it will be okay,' he says.

And at that moment, with all my heart, I want it to be.

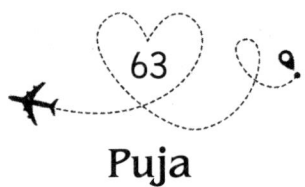

Puja

Travel is a funny thing. It is supposed to change you in some ways, make you a better person. But I can't imagine how this awful seat that I have got on the flight back will make me a better person. I am wedged in the middle seat between a rotund potbellied overweight Indian man who keeps munching goodies which his mother hands over to him over my head. Twice I ask if I could change seats, but she says she wants the window seat. They are a large family and I am caught in their loud chatter. The airline staff apologetically tells me it is a full flight. To add to my woes, there is a wailing baby as well. It is a terrible journey back. I hate the smell of the snacks the family keeps munching on. Non-stop. They offer some to me, but I refuse.

The only good thing in all of this is, I can block out all the noise with my noise cancelling headphones. I begin to think about what I want to do with my life. I think about my family. I had called my father. The relief and unmatched joy in his voice made me want to crawl into a hole and never show my face again. He had so many questions. Where did I stay? Was the hotel good? Was I safe? Was I scared? Do I have enough foreign currency? Should he ask a friend of his in London to take care of me? I answered all his questions patiently. He suggested that since I had anyway gone to London, I could spend a day or two looking around if I wanted. He would ask his friend to show me around.

The idea of going around London had occurred to me too.

But I am not in a mood for sight-seeing. I just want to go home. I am not in a state of mind to explore the beauty of this city.

'Accha, if I managed to come all the way here in secret, I can perfectly manage in London on my own. But I want to come home,' I told him.

'You have no idea how I was waiting to hear that,' he says.

The return flight to India feels longer than the one to UK. The best part? Not once do I throw up! I think about how powerful the human mind is. We all have free will and we have our narratives. When we change our narratives, our life itself changes. We can decide to do anything and we can take small logical steps to make it happen. I had decided to go to UK, and I think about how calmly I went about it, overcoming every single obstacle. Why can't I do the same with my life?

Right now, I am rudderless and lost only because I have no compass. I think about my time in Ashwaty Bhawan. As much as I loved spending time with Arush, I loved the classroom too. I liked making a difference in the lives of those kids. I felt valued there. I mattered there. My life had a meaning back then. I keep thinking about what I want to do with my life, and slowly an answer emerges. Then I fall asleep.

When I land in India and clear immigration, it is a strange happy feeling that I experience. I am home. This is *my* country. I don't expect my family to be waiting outside. I expect Anthony to be there, as my father said he would send the car to pick me up. But now I see the three of them standing there.

I emerge feeling ashamed, embarrassed and very guilty.

'Puja, molle,' says my mother, as she stretches out her arms and envelops me in a hug. She hugs me tightly, refusing to let go. My father hugs me next and then, Divya.

'Happy to see your dirty, grubby face, Puja the Hooja,' Divya says.

'Shut up. Tell that to your Kar-dick,' I retort smiling, and am delighted when she laughs instead of getting annoyed.

When we reach the car, I don't see Anthony anywhere.

'Where's Anthony?' I ask.

'I gave him the day off. Thought it would be nice to spend some time, just the four of us,' my father says.

'You have accomplished the impossible, Puja. Ma has taken two days off from the hospital this week. Two whole days, can you believe it?' Divya says.

'Enough girls, don't rub it in. We still have to decide what Puja is going to do. We need to talk about that,' my mother quips.

'*Noooo*, don't bring it up. She will run away again,' Divya groans.

I am so overwhelmed at that point that I start crying silently.

'She is crying. She is crying. She regrets it,' Divya announces.

She is being a pest, but her droll manner helps diffuse the awkwardness. I am not used to my family behaving this way.

When we get home, I fly into Shanti chechi's arms. I have missed her so much. She serves us tea and her famous onion pakodas.

We sit on the terrace overlooking the ocean.

'Tell us about your journey. How is your Arush?' Divya asks.

'He is....' I say, not knowing how to complete the sentence.

The three of them look at me, waiting for me to speak.

'Let's just say I understood one thing on this journey. That no matter who you choose to love, we must always remember that family comes first. If there are misunderstandings, we need to speak and sort out things, rather than running away. Running away just creates more problems. I wasn't thinking and I am sorry. I apologise for everything I have done.'

'No, Puja. I am sorry. I have never bothered to ask you what you want to do,' my mother says.

'Ma, I have been thinking about it. I definitely do not want to do a management course at an IIM. At Ashwaty Bhawan, I discovered I am good with children. I enjoyed teaching them, correcting their papers, but most of all, making a difference in their lives. I think after I graduate, I would like to do a course related to early child development. Then I will work with an organisation like Ashwaty Bhawan and get some experience. Someday, I will open my own centre for children like them,' I say.

All these years that my mother had asked me what to do, I had no answer. But ever since Arush threw those questions at me, I have been thinking about it. For the first time in my life, I have come up with a plan, a definite thing I want to do.

My father is the first to speak. 'You know, that's an excellent idea. You will definitely succeed since you sound so passionate about it. Puja, look at the courage that you have shown in all that you did with this travel to UK. You are resourceful, brave, smart. Just put all those qualities to good use and I have no doubt in my mind that you will make a success of it.'

'I am happy you have a plan. I am not going to insist on your doing a management degree. Just do what makes you happy. Thank you for being open and honest,' says my mother.

We have dinner together. It is different from the meals we have had together earlier. Gone is the stress, the tension, the burden of expectations. In its place is love, laughter and jovial ribbing.

'This doesn't feel like our family,' Divya quips.

'Maybe it will feel like it if I start nagging you about CAT exams,' my mother says with a serious face, and we all laugh.

Whoever thought my mother was capable of taking a dig at herself! This is the happiest our family has been in a long, long time.

Later that evening when I log into my mail, my eyes widen in surprise. I never expected a mail from him. I can't believe Arush has written to me.

With bated breath, I begin to read.

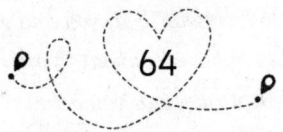

Puja and Arush

Dear dear Puja,

A *million emotions and thoughts run through my head right now. I don't even know where to begin and what to say first. Let me begin with an apology. I am extremely sorry for the way I reacted. I have been a total idiot. I shouldn't have treated you the way I did. For this, I apologise. Unconditionally. I hope you have it in your heart to forgive me.*

Allow me to explain my actions. After I came back to the UK, I wrote you mails, waited to hear from you. Shortly afterwards, I lost Vincent which sent me plummeting into sadness. I am still not over losing him. Then I didn't hear from you for weeks. Put yourself in my place – wasn't it but natural to presume you had moved on? It was painfully hard for me to accept that. I was hurt. Really hurt. This tore away a part of my heart. In order to heal, I had to distance myself. I rationalised it saying it was a holiday fling and nothing more. I was perhaps deluding myself, as a self-defence mechanism. Hence, I blocked you on mail, uninstalled all the apps where you could reach me.

I had no idea how strongly you felt about me or the lengths you would go to reach me. I am not a person who reacts well to surprises. I need time to come to term with things. Just when I thought that my India chapter was closed, you turned up with Jenna. It was a massive shock. I reacted instinctively, speaking whatever was in my mind. I should have been kinder. I was too stunned Puja, too unnerved.

By the time I came to terms with it, you had gone. My father drove me to the hotel (yes, I told my parents about us after you left) and he even offered to drive me to Heathrow – can you believe?

I spoke to Jenna and she told me you have left UK. Oh Puja – how I wish you had stayed for a couple of days in London! I would have come and seen you then. I needed just a day for the shock to sink in. But you didn't even give me a couple of hours. I guess I deserve it for the way I behaved. Please know, it wasn't deliberate.

I can't thank you enough for the exhibition of my paintings. Sashi has connected me to the art gallery and they seem keen on having me. I am yet to think about it. I will discuss it with my college professors and have a lawyer look at the legal aspects of it. (See, I told you I am a careful guy. I cannot take spot decisions like you.)

Now that I have read your mail (the one which went to trash because I had blocked you, and once again I reiterate, I was doing it only to protect myself from pain) I can only say that you are a brave person. You were not afraid to chase what you wanted. I can't even imagine doing something like that.

I hope things are okay at your home.

Please forgive me, Puja.

Love,
Arush.

15 minutes later

Dear Arush.

I am replying immediately. See, I don't need time to 'process things'.

You idiot! You have no idea what I went through to reach you. You didn't even ask. How could you say that I came there only because I was rich? But you know what? Your words struck home because they were true. They made me reflect, think deeply. They gave me a direction to my future. I am so sorry about you losing Vincent. Trust me, I know what it feels like to lose someone you love.

Yes, I have reconciled with my family. For the first time in years, we seem to be having a real connection, and a real closeness. This wouldn't have happened but for your words and but for the journey I made. Sometimes we travel far to discover ourselves.

I am not going to forgive you so easily though. Just a mail won't do.

Puja.

11 minutes later

Puja!
Thank you for writing back! I am replying immediately too. I don't know why that makes me happy, but I am smiling now.

See how you are changing me? Whoever thought that was possible. Please tell me what I have to do to earn your forgiveness.

Love,
Arush.

4 minutes later

There's only one way to earn my forgiveness. Come to India and fall at my feet. Then I will consider it. (Kisses also can be considered, in lieu of falling at my feet.)

1 minute later

I will! Maybe I will surprise you when you least expect it. Let's see how you take it then. Maybe I will set sail in a boat from England, climb up your terrace when you are in the midst of dinner with your family.

30 seconds later

I will keep an eye out for the ships!

10 seconds later

Video call? Emails are too slow!

5 seconds later

Someone once convinced me that they can say a lot in emails that they can't say face to face. They said they are shy and freeze on video calls. I wonder who that is.

3 seconds later

I wonder who that is too. Whoever it is who managed to convince you *to write emails must be one hell of a guy! Calling you. Pick up!*

Acknowledgements

To my daughter Purvi – for everything! She was my first editor for this book, and gave me a lot of insights into the minds of young adults. I also owe her for the beautiful illustrations and the fabulous cover design of this book. Purvi played a big part in this book.

My early readers and to my close friend who made the book better.

My son Atul, for the technical inputs and some details; and for reading the book. My husband Satish, who is a rock.

To my father KVJ Kamath and my mother Priya Kamath, who are my source of strength and inspiration.

To Arup Bose, JK Bose, Stuti and the fabulous team at Srishti for their faith in me.

To Sandhya Sridhar for the numerous detailed discussions about the book.

To Pranav Shah and his team for the ever reliable, super-fast technical support. Thank you, guys!

To Murthy and Pradeep for the author photo.

To my Zumba classmates for the much-needed relief while writing this book.

To the fabulous folks at my gym, who inspire me with their dedication to fitness.

To Lostris for lighting up my life.

Other books by Preeti Shenoy

Life is What You Make It
Tea for Two and a Piece of Cake
The Secret Wish List
The One You Cannot Have
It Happens for a Reason
Why We Love the Way We Do
It's All in the Planets
A Hundred Little Flames
Love A Little Stronger
The Rule Breakers
Wake Up, Life is Calling